the swansong conspiracy

NICK VOSSEN

PART I

Last of the Swansongs

Chapter 1

IF THE BRIGHTEST of minds are the most susceptible to madness and gloom, then let it be known that I, for one, am glad that Quincy Swansong has his off days just like the rest of us, living or dead.

Quincy simply couldn't concentrate in class today. He slumped down at his training table, looked around the lecture hall at the colorful mix of people attending, and sighed. The young man next to him was drawing some kind of horned creature in the corner of his journal, and some girls in front of him giggled through hushed whispers.

The philosophy teacher droned on in the most annoying monotone voice he had ever heard, and the lecture itself consisted of the same grasping-at-straws theories.

"So, in the light of the events from the past three years… the realms of science *and* philosophy have changed dramatically," the teacher continued while standing with his back to the class, endlessly writing gibberish on the whiteboard.

Quincy rolled his eyes. *Same stuff, different day,* he thought.

The student on the other side of Quincy was clicking his pen over and over, the soft ticking of the plastic making a nice distraction from the teacher's buzzing voice, as well as the slow descent into madness Quincy was feeling by attending the lecture.

He stopped taking down notes for a moment and breathed in, slow and steady.

"With the existence, and now absence, of God, the Almighty Creator, proven… the great philosophical conundrum shifted in its wake."

Click, Click, Click, Clack.

Quincy shifted uncomfortably in his seat and glanced down at his lecture notes; a drawing of a small bunny with rows of enormous teeth would certainly not help him during the upcoming midterms. He looked over at the drawing of the student next to him. The huge horned rat now gracing the bottom of the paper looked way scarier than Quincy's scribbles. His drawing was definitely below standard...

Then again, what was even considered standard anymore? Daily life itself wasn't exactly what it used to be a few years ago. He figured the fact that he was still sitting here taking lectures was a miracle all by itself.

"Therefore, the great philosophical questions in life no longer stem from *Why are we here?* We know that now; it was to serve God in all His glory. No, the right existential questions would currently fit more into the lines of answering *What the hell did we do?* and/or *How the hell can we get Him back?* Now, if you turn to page three hundr—"

The loud buzzing of a bell sounded through the hall. Both the student next to him and Quincy himself jerked to attention. It was an obnoxious sound, but it did just the trick to snap them out of trance and back into reality.

"For next time, I want you to study chapters five through eight. Afterwards, we will discuss the philosophical and moral consequences of having to choose a new God in favor of our old one. Perhaps we need to be able to sell ourselves as a good and obedient planet to the best possible candidate."

Quincy yawned and grabbed his bag before straightening the sagging glasses on his nose and leaving a big smudgy fingerprint on them, to his disdain. He made his way towards the door—towards freedom from the dull classroom—and the weekend. It was not like he had many plans, but college had been rough on him these past few days: he had been late a couple of times, and lately he noticed his interests in the subjects at hand started to wane. Thus, he hoped a little relaxation might absolutely do the trick to set his mind at ease.

You see, Quincy was a strapping young lad at twenty-one. He was slightly older than most college students, but it wasn't his fault that the school systems basically shut down for a couple of years before he could finish his studies and graduate.

Anyways, he dressed and spoke like a refined gentleman, most of the time, and his hair was cut neatly into an executive contour with a dash of pomade that really did the trick to get it as slick as possible. He was not bad-looking by any stretch of the imagination, but his smartness often exceeded his social interaction and banter. Often, but not always.

"Hey, Swansong!"

Quincy stopped at the classroom door and turned around to see one of the stereotypical frat house jocks strolling towards him and braced himself, wondering what kind of stupidity was going to flap out of Todd's mouth this time.

"Yeah?" he replied, keeping a bored expression on his face.

"Maybe Great Tharon will be our new God. *Wuuuuu hooooo*, can you imagine?" The meathead nudged his friends to join in on the banter, and one bobbed his head along, giggling like one of those electronic Elmo dolls in the process.

"Look at this nerd. Weirdo!" another one joked.

Quincy took a good look at the tall, ugly jock in front of him. He wanted to go ahead and congratulate the buffoon on remembering one of my—I mean, one of his great-uncle's stories and to remind him that apparently most of what he had written had turned out to be true. But he decided to let it slide, secretly hoping that something would materialize around the guy sooner or later, making him pee his pants… That would be neat. I should make a note.

But for today, Quincy simply struck where it would hurt—the brain.

"Good one, Todd," he replied sarcastically. "Say, maybe you could then ask Tharon why you're failing every class."

Quincy could see Todd's face getting redder by the second and enjoyed every last bit of it. The disapproving look from their professor broke Todd from the spell, and after the knucklehead tried to come up with a fitting reply for about forty-five seconds, he simply gave up.

Quincy grinned before he turned and marched outside. It was not always the case, not even for him, but he liked it when brains got a one-up over brawn and made a mental note to tell his sister about this later; he was sure she'd love to hear it. Ah… Lilly Swansong, I believe I have never laid eyes (quite literally, I should say) on any young woman fiercer than her. The perfect balance to her twin brother; together, they could move mountains.

The view from Lakeshore Drive across Lake Pontchartrain was especially stunning today. Even though taking the bus back to his apartment was usually a lot faster, on days like this Quincy definitely enjoyed walking home. He loved to move along the paved pathways while taking in the nice green stretches of grass to the north of the drive. The ancient oak trees grew tall and wide here, and Quincy appreciated their company.

Today, however, he decided to walk straight home instead of continuing onward and taking his favorite detour along Milneburg Lighthouse.

The slight breeze blowing into town lifted his spirits a little bit, but for most of the walk, Quincy was lost in thought. He couldn't shake the feeling that his life was about to change drastically and wondered again if quitting college was the best idea for him: Do a de-stress from everything and just *live* for a while. He certainly seemed to like the idea of simply living in the moment with no major responsibilities instead to himself and his sister Lilly. We all want things; not being a featureless mass of aether distortion would be nice, but hey, things happen for a reason.

It was at the intersection of Lark and Marigny that he saw someone approaching him just from the corner of his eye.

"Hey, man. Could you perhaps spare some change? Maybe a dollar? I want to get me a sandwich or summing. Please help a guy out."

Quincy sighed, turning to face the battered old man. He was wearing rags, for the most part, and used old dented tin cans as knee protectors. He looked very low on personal hygiene; his beard was long and tangled. He also had the most crooked eyes Quincy had ever seen. On a more peculiar note, his skin was very transparent—literally.

"Look, Old Man Walters..." Quincy shook his head. "We've been over this, man. You are *dead*. A ghost. *Gone*. You don't need any money. You've been dead for as long as I can remember."

The old man looked puzzled, clearly trying to find the right words to reply. Quincy was hopeful that perhaps he had finally gotten through to Walters to leave him alone, when the ghost replied with,

"You wanna buy some porno tapes? C'mon, man, I only need a few dollars."

"Ugh! See, this is what I mean." Quincy rubbed his forehead. "We don't use tapes anymore. We now have DVDs, and with the Internet, I can't even begin to tell you how redundant tapes are and... Wait, why am I even having this conversation?"

"No tapes then?"

"Move into the light or something, Walters. I'm done here," Quincy snapped as he doubled his pace to shake off the somehow still horrible-smelling apparition.

A few years ago, Quincy would've been absolutely mortified to bump into a real-life ghost in the streets of New Orleans or pretty much anywhere else. Strangely enough though, ghosts are some of the least troublesome things you could encounter nowadays.

Let me start at the beginning…

It all started about three years ago, when, in the deserts of Egypt, a giant obelisk, comparable in size to the Empire State Building in New York, erupted from the ground seemingly overnight. Many experts were baffled and couldn't possibly find an explanation for this so-called latest *Wonder of the World*. It was only when the discovery of writing was made upon the face of the obelisk many, many feet up that the world truly went into shock.

The writing upon the obelisk, when translated from such languages as Ancient Sumerian, Latin, Biblical Hebrew, Sanskrit, Old English, and Navajo, revealed that the message on its surface was from God. The message entailed that God, while having enjoyed being our keeper and creator for these past millennia, simply couldn't handle the responsibilities and damage control expected of Him anymore.

The message further stated that He, the Almighty God, ruler and creator of the Earth and all of its creatures and marvels, was disappointed and… He was leaving.

Naturally, skeptics and believers alike raved upon hearing the message, and for the first couple of months, it was generally perceived as a giant prank, however unlikely it was to pull off. However, soon all hell started to break loose on Earth, and the general population started to take the Obelisk's message seriously.

You see, the last thing that God warned humanity about was that in His absence, the amalgamation of absolutely everything terrible in this known universe, and others, would probably be either heading for (or waking up on) Earth. Now, imagine mankind's surprise when not only did they find out God really existed... but had abandoned them on the day He revealed Himself.

Oh! And then there was the small footnote about the entire world going down the toilet faster than humanly possible.

It started slow with people reporting feeling uneasy in places they always perceived as comfortable. Then, slowly but surely, reports came in of strange sightings of unknown creatures: ghosts, zombies, and vampires, but also of angels and demons. The scientific world was turned upside down; experts in pretty much every scientific field were baffled because suddenly, every single supernatural creature or beast imaginable was as real as the morning sunrise—it literally shook the world's foundations.

Exactly one year after the discovery of the Obelisk, a war broke out in Egypt. It was not a war of feuding countries, crazy presidents, or malevolent dictators; rather, it was the first war for mankind's survival. The war to delay events of such magnitude that they would border us on the brink of extinction.

From beneath the Valley of the Kings, an old giant entity rose up named "Alghuurl: *The Old, Tired, and Hungry,*" and crawling from the hot desert sands with him were tens of thousands of crab-like monsters. Alghuurl was a distinctly nasty specimen of Elder Giant, a race of huge stone-like humanoids that presumably went extinct, or at least left the Earth, billions of years before humanity was even considered a thing.

The nations of the world banded together, and a global army was formed to combat the entity. Ultimately it fell, although rumors persist that it was really trapped in a separate reality. You see, there are countless realities swirling around in the void, all of which are created at the exact moment a choice, any choice, is made somewhere along the world. Next to this possibility of limitless versions of our own reality, there are other dimensions entirely. Shadowy, mirror-like verses of our own worlds or vast plains of alienesque gruesomeness simply too horrible to describe. It's the realm of the departed that's also *very* interesting, now… Eh. I seem to have gone into quite a tangent there, haven't I? Anyway. So. Thousands died in the fight against Alghuurl, and from the ashes of war two distinct organizations rose to power. The first was the Global Defense Force, GDF, consisting of only the highest ranking, most elite soldiers in the world. They were tasked to respond to any incident with a threat level higher than five in Type 1+ Awakening Events, but more on that later.

The second was a mysterious shadow organization called Haven. To outsiders, they are mostly known as the men in black, or not known at all. Their operations consisted of a more secretive approach, and they were often spotted in places where supernatural occurrences were reaching their peak.

After the Kraken wars, as they were later known, and the arrival of the GDF and Haven organizations, Earth went through what probably could be considered the most eyebrow-raising of changes: Humanity actually accepted their fate and adapted their current state of affairs… Simply put, they went along with their merry lives. The faculties of natural science rejoiced with the coming of uncountable new specimens in flora and fauna, and those delving into the realms of quantum physics really started to pick up the pace on their research after dealing with the one or two Dimensional Shambler incidents. Nasty buggers, but dealing with aggressive native wildlife after opening portals to other worlds is just part of the job description now.

Quincy was snapped out of his daze, where he'd been just staring at his apartment door, by his neighbor, Mrs. Silverstein, who was a terrible old lady with blue frizzly hair, nasty orange skin, just about three teeth left, and she usually sported the worst kind of bad breaths.

"Mr. Swansong," she cheerfully greeted into Quincy's right ear. "How is your sister, my dear?"

"Gah!" Quincy jerked back upon seeing the leathery old woman. "You startled me, Mrs. Silverstein. Ehm, Lilly is at work. So, probably fine?" Quincy reached for the door behind him.

"I see… well, we have to talk about Mr. Bhering's faulty doorbell up on fourth…"

"Oh okay, no thanks, bye!" Quincy shut the door behind him, leaving the old lady standing in the hall, still talking.

He shook off his jacket and flung it towards the coat rack. *Yikes*, he thought. The old lady gave him the creeps, and he'd seen *ghosts* today. Granted, most souls trapped on Earth could be considered less harmful than a crazy old bat giving him the stink eye, so let's not be too hard on Quincy.

Checking the contents of the fridge revealed nothing interesting or, at least, *edible*. Thus, Quincy took the liberty to decide that he and his twin sister, Lilly, whom he shared the apartment with, were going to order out… That is, if the pizza delivery guy was going to be on time. The last time they had ordered pizza, the guy that usually delivers on their block had apparently fallen into a whirling pocket dimension created by a real joker of a Pooka, which resulted in the pizza being delivered the day before it was ordered.

Quincy called and placed their usual order before kicking off his shoes and resting his feet on the living room table. Settled, he picked up the remote control and turned on the news.

~

There was a wall of sound inside the pet shop that was almost unbearable to sit through for any stretch of time, let alone eight hours a day. The constant screeching, barking, meowing, scratching, slurping, and general absence of anything resembling a relaxing atmosphere was oppressive.

Along the left wall were cages full of colorful creatures ranging from simple domestic pets to dangerous-looking slimy things. To the right-hand side of the store was a wall of supplies, carefully placed and priced with care and precision.

It was also *the* place to be in New Orleans to get exotic pets, and the line of customers often went around the block, just as it did today.

In the back of the store was a small desk and registry; behind it sat a girl. She had semi-long curly hair, pink cheeks, and a fair complexion. Her eyes were as blue as the ocean, and her smile was especially captivating. Still, there seemed to be a lingering darkness about her. She was often distant or dreaming, much to the dismay of customers when they went to check out or ask a question.

Today, she seemed extremely stressed with sweat dripping off her forehead as she tried to juggle the constant stream of phone calls, as well as the people who had been standing in line.

"Ma'am, you have to listen to what I am saying," she spoke into the phone, trying not to yell. "Primordial Wurms need to be released in the desert approximately three months before reaching adulthood and..." She bit back a sigh. "Yes? Yes, I know they are cute, ma'am. But... ma'am. *Ma'am.* Please listen, they have a tendency to *eat* people. Uh huh..." She rolled her eyes. "No, it doesn't matter if they are raised with love and care... ma'am. Please hold."

The girl pressed a blinking red button on the telephone device, took a deep breath, then said,

"Good afternoon, *Nawlin's Exotic Pets*, Lilly speaking."

"Hey, lady!" a man shouted from the row of people. "How

about you help us first, huh? We've actually taken the time to come to your store ourselves!"

"In a minute!" Lilly yelled towards the mass of people before putting the phone back to her ear.

"No, sir, we do *not* sell kittens for feeding purposes. Every cat we sell nowadays will require a comprehensive background check from the potential owner for current or past ownership of Cerberi... *Hello?* Sir? Damn!" Lilly threw down the phone. "Next in line!"

"Hey there, love, now I'm pretty sure you could help a man out with his... snake problem, can't you?"

The man that came to stand in front of Lilly was utterly gross; he looked dirty, and his skin was flaking off in more than one spot. Furthermore, his breath could bury a thousand ghouls back into the ground.

"Sir, please step back. I am *very* busy and am certainly not in the mood for this kind of crap." Lilly rolled her eyes and tried looking past the man for the next person in line.

The man's eyes shot to her name tag, and his face twisted into a crooked grin.

"Hmm, Swansong, huh? Perhaps you can sing me something as well, sugar." The man licked his lips, and drool dripped down towards the register desk.

Lilly shuddered.

"How about... *corpse walks into pet store and messes with the wrong girl?* You sick freak, get the hell out of the store!"

The man was taken aback but didn't look like he was about to take no for an answer. With incredible speed, he lunged over the registry and tried to grab Lilly by her collar.

"Listen here, you little shit, that's no way to treat someone who fought for this country, fought for the entire *world*! I'm the reason y'all are still alive today. I deserve to be treated with respect," he hissed.

· · ·

Something in Lilly snapped. All of the noise coming from the shop was drowned out, from the loud screeching of animals to the commotions of the people in line. With lighting fast and nimble fingers, she grabbed the man's hands and pulled his fingers backwards. There was a loud crack, and the man screamed from the top of his lungs; Lilly held tight.

"Listen up, scumbag. I've seen all the crap the world can throw at me; *I* was there, too. Nineteen at the time and as fragile as I could be." She lowered her head and glared. "But I remain unbroken. Do you think you can waltz in here and act like you can do anything just because *you* survived some tenta-cled freaks and ten thousand others didn't? You're a disgrace!"

Some of the other customers were now becoming visible agitated as well; most of them seemed to express disdain for the dirty man and appeared to take Lilly's side.

The man, burning with pain and anger, went on a rampage through the store. He was running around and yelling, knocking over food trays, empty cages, and even some of the other customers. Eventually, he took a tumble and smacked his head against the cages holding Carnivopods.

There was a crack.

"Oh! Oh no!" Lilly said, realizing then the full extent of what exactly happened. "Uh, don't panic. You there." She pointed at a rather pale-stricken man with sweat dripping down his balding head. "Call the police, or *if this gets worse*, see if any GDF troops are on standby. Anyone else… grab a net or something!" she gulped.

It was already too late for a net. The broken cage door creaked open, and the man's unconscious head was swallowed whole by a small gelatinous, octopus-like creature with three rows of razor-sharp, buzz saw-like teeth between its tentacles. He deserved it.

In the ensuing panic that erupted, the mindless noise of the customers and animals kept growing. While customers were running for the exit, Lilly hovered around the cage with a cattle prod, but every time she tried to get close to the creature, a tentacle slapped her away. One time, it even latched around her ankle and made her fall flat on her ass.

Eventually, the Carnivopod slowly crept back into its cage and shut it behind it. It even seemed to smirk before going to sleep.

Meanwhile, at the height of all the chaos, Lilly's boss came back from his lunch break and stumbled upon a panicked mob and a twitching man on the floor with his skin half-ripped off his head.

Lilly swallowed hard at the look on her boss's face.

"I can explain everything," she said through gritted teeth.

At that moment, a giant macaw leapt from its cage above the register and took… well, let's just say the balding head of Lilly's boss wasn't bald anymore.

Quincy was half asleep when the apartment door slammed shut. He jumped up and threw a pillow towards it. Blinking, he was relieved to see it was just Lilly coming home after her workday, the pillow landing at her feet.

She smirked.

"Dang, you scared me," he said, rubbing his eyes. "How was your day?"

Lilly sighed and threw herself onto the couch next to her brother. "Well… next to the usual stress of huge crowds and being understaffed, a guy got his face chewed off by a Carnivopod today. And my boss blamed me for provoking him." She grunted.

"Oh man, are you okay?" He frowned. "But wait… did you provoke him?"

"He came onto me first!" Lilly shouted. "It was another one of those veterans gone insane. I kinda broke his fingers, but still!"

"Broke his fi—"

"So I probably got fired today," she cut in, ignoring him. "Boss isn't sure yet; he's understaffed as it is."

"Damn…"

"The guy's chewed-up face, it was an accident; he did it to himself." She huffed. "I saw the same stuff he did, and I'm not crazy, am I?"

Quincy chuckled.

"It's okay. These things just tend to happen nowadays; it's not your fault."

"Thanks." She smiled. "How about you then, how was *your* day?"

"Same old smack, different day," he reported, twirling a drink coaster around on the table in front of them. "Teacher is a ripe old idiot, and lectures themselves border on mania. I'm thinking about changing majors, start studying at my own pace, maybe even taking a break from everything."

Lilly straightened.

"Well not everyone is as smart as you. If anything, I think you, of all people, would know what's best for yourself." She nudged his shoulder, making him laugh.

Both of them shot to their feet when the doorbell rang. Quincy held up a hand for her to wait and headed over to the door, looking through the peephole to see a big box of pizza.

· · ·

"Oh yeah. I hope you don't mind, but I ordered some pizza for us. We forgot to do groceries again."

"There is never a time when pizza is *not* a good idea," Lilly answered, overjoyed.

Quincy opened the door and was surprised to see that their regular delivery guy, Tom, was back doing his old rounds again.

"Hey! Good to see you, we thought you'd stop doing this route forever."

"Well, you'd think that getting trapped by one of those little trickster bastards would do that to a guy, but here I am," the guy answered sarcastically. "Gotta make a living somehow, eh."

During their exchange, Quincy saw Lilly had crept towards the door and now took the liberty of taking the pizza out of Tom's hands as he spoke.

"Thank you, Tom. You're the best! Bye!" She grinned at them then fluttered back into the room, calling over her shoulder, "Quince, pay the man!"

"She's in a good mood today, huh?" Tom asked, watching Lilly sink into the couch.

"The pizza was kind of a surprise."

"Oh, by the way," Tom started, "I caught your nasty neighbor stealing your mail again while I was downstairs. Here, I managed to snag it for you."

"Nasty old bag," Quincy hissed. "Thanks, Tom. That's really solid of you to do so. Glad you're back on the route, man."

"Eh, it's nothing really. Good customers are worth going the extra mile for," Tom joked then checked his address book.

"Next up is this family on Esplanade, but I always try breaking my record on getting out of there as fast as possible, haha!"

"That bad, huh?" Quincy handed Tom the fee and a generous tip.

"Yup, that bad." He shoved the money in his jacket pocket and grabbed his helmet. "Gotta go. See ya around, Quince."

Quincy waved, then shut the door and shuffled back to the couch, plopping down next to his sister. He fumbled with the envelope in his hands, eying the pizza in the meantime.

"Whash daath?" Lilly mumbled with a mouthful of cheese, pointing at the gray envelope.

Quincy shrugged, ripping the top of the letter open and scanning it - *Dear Mister and Miss Swansong, blah, blah, blah. Apologies… blah. Accumulation of assets.* "Hmm, apparently, it's a letter from a notary office about some kind of inheritance."

Lilly swallowed her bite of food and looked at him in confusion.

"An inheritance? From who? And why now?"

"No idea… Are you up for finding out? We could go there tomorrow if you'd like?"

"Well, it's not like I have to go work. The pet store's kind of closed for… renovation at the moment, so..." She looked mischievous, and he laughed.

"I'm not exactly dying for my next couple of lectures, either," he admitted before picking up a slice of the pizza.

Quincy looked over to see his sister shoving globs of cheese in her mouth and couldn't help but smile. There wasn't a stronger person in the world, he thought, than his sister Lilly. For everything they had been through, she had always come back stronger than before.

Over the past few years back, they had to grow up and grow up fast. While Quincy himself had taken on a more solemn route, taking up his studies and diving into books and research, Lilly just transformed, blossomed even, into this happy-go-lucky girl. She could laugh almost anything away and turn any frown into a smile. Even though she had this dark and tragic past, this was her way of dealing with things, and Quincy admired her for it.

Life at the moment, Quincy thought, *considering everything… yeah, still pretty good,* he decided. I wish things could have been better. Nonetheless, I am proud of you two.

Chapter 2

AGENT REYES STEPPED through the elevator doors with sweat piling upon older sweat, his brow shiny with moisture. His usual slick-back hair was greasy and pointy, and a slight five o'clock shadow stubble adorned his normally clean-shaven face. His right leg and left arm twitched nervously, and his mustache itched in the wind of the built-in fans that were set up all around him. Reyes noticed some of the brown, rusty stains inches off the fan blades and bit back a groan.

The base's architect had prided himself on the fact that giant metal fans were the way of the future… well, as far as eerie hideouts go in their dystopian, slightly post-apocalyptic-like future. Unfortunately for him, it was what eventually got him killed.

On a hot summer day, he had the misfortune of wanting to set the fan dials to a nice big breeze to keep the base cool—and instead had mistakenly dialed the fans all the way towards the wrong side. Basically, the poor guy got *sucked up, literally, and* thus the architect got himself remembered by the organization by having his name immortalized on the brand-new safety feature toggle that now adorned the control console.

Reyes, now at the end of the hallway, wiped his forehead,

took a deep breath, and knocked softly on the double office doors. Folding his shoulders in on himself, he tried to avoid eye contact with the two bulky men guarding the door. One on each side, they were near identical and wore the exact same all-black suit as Reyes did, wore the same black shades and had the same earpiece. However, something about them seemed off, in Reyes' eyes, but he just couldn't—

"Reyes! Quit moping around and get your ass in here, pronto!" a voice cracked from the intercom outside the door right before a

n automatic lock opened from within. Reyes flushed and looked away from the identical men, hurrying inside the office, somewhat relieved.

The lighting was abysmal, leaving most of the interior veiled in total darkness save for a small illuminated world map with several glowing red dots over on the right-side wall. In the center of the room, a desk stood drearily. And behind the desk sat a fat man, dressed in all black, with his face obscured by the creeping shadows.

Upon the first time he entered, years ago, Reyes had realized that the problem with the room was not a need for better lighting but the hints of *something* that swallowed natural light. He never stopped wondering what it was exactly that was wrong with his superior's office, but he never had the guts to ask either.

A shiver went down his spine; Reyes felt like something icy cold was sitting right beside him, but the other chair was empty.

His superior spoke in a slight off-putting, gravelly voice. "I assume, Agent Reyes, that the letter you were sent to retrieve has been intercepted as planned?"

"Well... uhm..." Reyes floundered, then took a deep breath. "The problem is that my agent, Mrs. Silverstein, she... uh..."

"Out with it, Agent Reyes." The man glared in displeasure, and

Reyes broke out in another round of uncontrollable sweating.

"She failed to retrieve the letter as requested—sorry—as ordered, sir."

"Hmm, disappointing, Agent Reyes." The superior tapped his fingers on the desk. "I am afraid that my faith in you has proven to be false. I will have to re-assign the case to one of your peers."

"No! Hold on! Please," Reyes stumbled. "The bugs we planted are still active, we can tail them tomorrow when they—"

"You know I don't like to break away from protocol. But so be it," the man interrupted. "It's very simple, Agent Reyes. I want you to retrieve the package and return it to me. Do not cause unnecessary harm or backlash—only if every and all negotiations fail... then the Swansong twins must die." His fingers tapped once on the desk. "Do I make myself clear?"

Agent Reyes swallowed hard.

"Yes, sir."

In that instant, it was decided that the Swansong twins' mettle was going to be put to the test.

The notary office was a rather beautiful building from the outside to look at. Dated back to the time of the first French colonies, it was remarkably well preserved with its wide arches at the bottom of the building, each sporting widely curved windows on the floor above them. The balcony railings seemed to be made from solid silver and gleamed in the sunlight. The building, as a whole, was a mixed batch of architectural influences; the top half had a much more Gothic feel to it. There were even some gargoyles, a classic staple in Eastern European architecture, looking down from the broken clock tower that loomed at the very top of the building. One of the gargoyles was scratching itself behind the ear like a dog.

Quincy and Lilly quietly admired the stunning building. It was different than most of the Creole and French colonial architecture they were used to. They had passed by a couple of times but never had any reason to go in until now—They were eager to find out what this whole inheritance thing was about. *I*, for one, am eager for them to finally delve into the true secrets of their mysterious family.

The inside of the office looked like the exact opposite of the building's exterior. In fact, it had more in common with a doctor's office than anything else—the walls were adorned with white plaster, and cheap plastic chairs filled an empty waiting room. At least, it appeared empty until Lilly and Quincy turned the corner and found an exceptionally old man asleep in his wheelchair behind a desk.

Upon hearing the twins approach, the receptionist woke up, snorted, and tilted his head downward, looking over his wonky reading glasses at them.

"Please state your name and reason for visiting."

Seeing the caution sign nearby, Lilly carefully maneuvered over the shining floor tiles towards the desk and caught herself on its edge as she slipped.

"Lilly and Quincy Swansong," she muttered. "We've received a letter concerning some kind of inheritance, but our parents died years ago. There must have been some mistake."

"Oh no. No mistakes at all," the man said but continued to look disinterested. "I'm pretty sure there aren't many *Swansongs* around anymore. Besides, we've gotten exclusive instructions from your parents to, in the unfortunate event of their premature passing, withhold your inheritance until the day of your twenty-first birthday. Which is—" The man shuffled through his stack of paperwork.

"Which *was* about three months ago," Quincy interrupted as he inched towards the reception desk.

"Ah, yes," the man replied with a shrug. "Do excuse our late tidings. Inheritances and insurances are pretty busy now that people seem to be dying a lot more. All these supernatural causes... Every death needs an investigation, and the paperwork alone..."

"Get to the point, Mister"—Lilly glanced at the man's nametag—"Bracken... Brackenwha... you know what, never mind."

He huffed. "Yes, if you would please follow me."

The receptionist led them to a small room with a table and three chairs. The twins said nothing and meandered behind the receptionist's squeaky wheelchair. Again, like in the waiting room, the whole atmosphere was clinical and depressing. The room was small and felt stuffy. There was only one very small window in the right-hand corner, and it was taped shut.

The twins sat down and exchanged a look.

"Well, this all feels very normal and totally not strange," Quincy sarcastically noted.

"I've been to funeral homes that were more alive than this place," Lilly added.

"I forgot you once worked at one." Quincy smirked. "What happened again?"

"Forget it!" Lilly murmured.

"Oh, come on!"

"Ugh, fine. We kind of forgot to order the tripled-furnished thick mahogany coffins, and the recently deceased kind of bloated up and oozed all out of it because of the humidity in the summer and yeah."

"You're forgetting the best part," Quincy pleaded when she didn't continue.

"The *worst* part about it was that the deceased, an old

Creole family of snobby Garden District buttheads too stupid to turn the gas off, threatened to sue for personal injury because the world we live in is so crazy right now that dead people can't just *stay dead!*"

Quincy couldn't help but to burst into laughter.

Lilly kind of felt offended at first, but the ridiculousness of the situation made her giggle all the same. I got a mild chuckle out of it, indeed. But you haven't had a real funeral unless your coffin's been thrown off a cliff down about two hundred and fifty feet below into the sea.

They fell silent when a tall, but very thin, man in a business suit slithered his way into the room. He held a suitcase in one hand and a shiny golden pen in the other.

"Ah, majestic! The Swansong twins in the flesh. Now, did you two know you are pretty hard to track down?"

"Well..." Quincy started.

"The last in the lineage of the great writer himself!"

"Yeah, but…" Lilly tried.

"Or should I say, the great prophet?" The man chuckled, only stopping after seeing their confusion.

"With all due respect," Quincy started, then glanced away from the thin man; he had the air of a slimy and disgusting car salesman. "We're not here to discuss prophecy. I believe you have some sort of package for us?"

"Ahem. Right. Now, let's not dally about. If you could both please sign this form here and here, oh, and here and then finally... there."

The man guided Lilly and Quincy through the process of making sure that everything was in order and that they *were* the right inheritors that came to claim the package.

"Your IDs seem in order," the thin man said with a grin before handing them back.

"What's this small print here?" Lilly asked then. *"Jackson Inc. is not liable for any personal injury or deaths occurring on any of the property owned by aforementioned institution through supernatural inter-*

ference or sheer force of will stemming from any persons or objects obtained through hereditary means after signing."

"It means we can't sue if our inheritance kills us," Quincy told her.

"Oh. Does that happen a lot?" she wondered aloud.

"Hmm. Not at all *that* often." The thin man smiled grimly. "It's a silly clause, nonetheless, can't sue when you're *dead*, am I right?"

"Right." Lilly threw him a wide, fake smile and then signed the last of the dotted lines.

Once the papers were taken from the twins, the man opened his suitcase and revealed two envelopes and a silver key. The key seemed old but was still very beautiful: The top half was smelted with markings that were embedded with turquoise, and the bottom half was as sharp and clean as any modern key could be.

Meanwhile, the two envelopes looked worlds apart from each other and the key itself. One was still very white and neat, the writing on the front spelling out their names—*Quincy and Lilly*. The other envelope was crumpled, yellowed, and seemed to have sustained water damage on at least one occasion. It was definitely a lot older, had different handwriting, and the ink was faded; it was addressed: *To the descendants*.

"That key is a pretty one, isn't it?"

The man gave a wicked smile, and Lilly shot him an annoyed look. She didn't like the way he had been acting the entire time, but now that they had their package, she'd like nothing else but for him to leave. Quincy often remarked that Lilly was easy to put her trust in people but only due to the fact that she could spot crooked or bad intentions from a mile away.

"Anyway, I will leave you two to it." The thin man stood up and backed towards the door as if he had felt and respected Lilly's wish for him to get out. "Take your time to sift through your letters if you'd like. You may do it here in private, or you can go. But, in case of the latter, please do not forget to notify Mr. Brackenwulf, the receptionist, of your departure so we may clean and lock this room back up." He paused. "Good day, Mr. Swansong, Miss Swansong."

After the man left, Lilly and Quincy sat there for a moment simply staring at the two letters in front of them.

"So which one are we going to open first?" Quincy asked. He had put both letters in front of him.

Lilly was fumbling around with the silver key. "Well, obviously, the one addressed directly to us. Right?"

"Obviously?"

"That old one could be from anyone," Lilly explained. "But that one"—she pointed to the left letter—"only one person in the world would dot his I's in that particular way… with an *x*."

"Dad." Quincy realized.

They both took a deep breath as Quincy ripped the envelope open and started reading aloud, his voice quivering slightly:

To our dearest son and daughter,

If this letter reaches you, it means the incredible burden has been placed on you of us having to leave this world before our time and before we could personally hand over the artifact and letter enclosed in this inheritance.

Know that the old letter reveals a terrible truth and secret that you must keep until you can pass it on to your children or until the time has come to act. Although we hope, and pray, that never to be the case.

Whatever happens, never give up.

· · ·

All of our love,
*   Emily and Tobias Swansong*

Lilly caressed the old, yellowed envelope between her fingertips.

"That's so sad. I mean… it makes me so sad." Her eyes filled with tears as she

looked at Quincy, noticing he was having a hard time dealing with the letter too. She reached for his hand, and together they sat in silence for a little while.

They had lost their parents to a plane crash on the day of their sixteenth birthday. Together, they swore that they would withhold from celebrating their birthdays from that moment on and traditionally saved the day to remember their parents. Emily and Tobias deserved more in life and a better life in general. But whatever troubles they faced, nothing but good can be said about how they had raised their son and daughter.

"I miss them," Lilly whispered, blinking away tears, her head resting on her brother's shoulder.

"Me too." Quincy squeezed his sister's hand and glanced over the letter once more. "A *burden*. I wonder what that means."

"I don't know," Lilly answered. She lifted her head and rubbed her eyes. "It's nice to hear from them nonetheless."

They both were lost in thought for a while until they heard someone audibly clearing their throat. A lady in a cleaner's outfit was standing in the doorway, looking at them in annoy-ance. Her hair was a mixture of vague red and bubblegum pink—both hair colors for which the lady was at least thirty years too old to have.

"Y'all done?" she rasped, sending an incredible

amount of spit flying out of her mouth. A record, surely, Quincy thought as he admired the lady's feat in slight disgust.

"Actually," Lilly started, "we still have a letter to read, so…"

"So... Yeah..." he chimed in.

A beat-up vacuum was placed in the door opening, and the cleaning lady leaned against the doorframe, loudly tapping her foot.

"Fine. I can wait."

Lilly and Quincy shared a quick glance before they stood up in unison.

"We can just, you know, read this outside." Quincy wove a fake smile onto his face that made his sister laugh.

Lilly held on to the silver key as Quincy made sure to collect all the letters and other documents, then they headed for the door.

"Goodb—"

The cleaning lady scoffed and turned on the loud vacuum cleaner.

The twins came back around to the reception only to find the receptionist, Mr. Brackenwulf, absent. A little sign on the desk read "*Will be right back. Do NOT ring the bell.*"

Quincy shrugged. "Let's just leave then."

Lilly nudged him on their way out of the office.

"So... this old letter seems important, huh?"

"Yeah, we're going to need to read this in a place with a lot more peace and quiet."

"How about the end of the world?"

The "End of the World" was the loving nickname for an exceptionally tranquil spot near the Mississippi where the river itself and the Industrial Canal met. It was just past noon, so the twins made sure they picked up some lunch at their favorite Bywater bistro before they sat down near a nice spot by the riverside, where they were treated to a great vista stretching out all across the riverbank.

From the middle of the river, a group of Devilfish stuck out their heads to investigate them. They were not the Devilfish like the majestic *Mobula mobular*, a near extinct species of eagle ray. These were quite literally hellish fish with great red gills, long pointy teeth, and a fork-tail, hence the name. The Devilfish was first seen along the coast of South Africa, a few months after the appearance of the Obelisk.

A group of night fishermen got the scare of a lifetime when one of their fishing nets contained a glowing red specimen—later discovered to be the evil cousin of the common piranha. The fishermen supposedly watched in horror as the fish ate half of the other fish in the net before burning through the net with flames from a still-unknown origin. After it escaped, it proceeded to swim to a nearby peninsula where sounds of horrid rituals can be heard on some unholy nights.

Luckily for the twins, this particular group of Devilfish didn't seem too interested in them, so they took their time to eat their lunch before taking the old, yellowed letter out to read. Their own fates were ready to be sealed, their lives forever to be changed.

"It's really crumpled up and folded a million times over," Quincy said, analyzing the paper in front of him. "Lil, look at this! The letter is from W.A. Swansong himself!"

"Really? That's just *great*. So our great-great uncle William has left us a weird ancient key and, according to our parents, some terrible old secret," Lilly responded sarcastically. "Somehow, I knew this would all come down to him. I only wish we wouldn't get suckered along every time."

Rude.

"It is very odd indeed," Quincy agreed, then frowned. "Hey, wait, what do you mean, suckered along?"

"Well... people coming up to you to say how they love your

ancestor's writing is one thing—even if we have nothing to do with his stories. But it's flattering in a way, and entirely innocent, right?"

"Right."

"Imagine three years ago when crap hit the fan big time. I was just done with boot camp, and all of a sudden, we get called out to Europe. Turns out all kinds of supernatural stuff is waking up all around the globe, right? Right, you know this. Anyway, as you are well aware, it turns out that our Uncle William didn't just tell stories, but somehow, he *knew* certain things, things he wrote about—they exist." Only after the worst has happened is when one realizes that some knowledge is better forgotten with the passing eons.

"I know. None of this is new information, sis."

"So... I was an eighteen-year-old fighting off monsters from a distant time and space, and my last name is Swansong." Lilly paused to wait for her brother's reaction.

"Oh," he muttered.

"Yes. The more creepy-crawlies started to appear, the more people seemed to link these events to our dear old uncle. In fact, they started to call him a prophet, as you know, and since he's *dead,* guess who was the number one spokesperson and apparent *know-it-all* for all things purple, full of tentacles, and monstrous? Me."

"I know that fighting these things is in no way the same as studying them on a scientific level," Quincy started, trying to choose his words carefully, "but know that I experienced the exact same expectation during my years at the university. When people are running around in the dark not knowing what to do, they apparently always try the source closest to the subject at hand. Our uncle wrote about this almost a hundred years before it was made fact that, yes, a lot of the things he wrote about turned out to be true."

"And we are the last Swansongs," Lilly finished gloomily. "So people turn to us for answers even though we have none."

"Maybe we don't, maybe we *do*." Quincy stared at the still-unopened yellow envelope, fiddling with the edges of the worn paper. Maybe he should just get on with it.

"Maybe..." Lilly snatched the yellowed envelope out of her brother's dawdling hands. Good.

"Lilly, no, wait."

"I can read too, you know! Time to find out what the old geezer came up with." She chuckled as she unfolded the letter. "Ahem. To the latest descendants of the Swansong family tree..."

Quincy scooted closer to her and looked at the age-old paper in amazement. The ink in the yellowed letter was faded and very hard to read in places. Some of the words became illegible over the course of what seemed like decades, while others, surprisingly so, still remained crisp and clear.

"To the latest descendants of the Swansong family tree,

It is with a certain malevolent strain upon the most intricate parts of my dwindling psyche that I must confide within you, the heirs of my legacy, the burden and responsibility to safe-keep and uphold a duty of secrecy concerning the shining silver key embedded in this inheritance and the terrible truths attached to it."

"Oh, here we go..." Lilly rolled her eyes.

"What? What's the matter?"

"He really had a way with words, didn't he?" She pointed at the top part of the letter. "Just look at this mess! Whatever happened to something like: *'It pains me to put you up with this sh*—'"

"Okay! Yeah. I see what you mean." Quincy coughed. "All these fancy words are pretty, but at the same time, his writing is nearly unintelligible."

"Right."

"It made our last name famous though!"

"Yay, and no fortune to speak of except for old, soggy

paper." Lilly pushed the paper into Quincy's hands. "Here, you read."

"In a most peculiar case of solecism, I must confer the trepidation that so heavily besets me and intromit this consternation immediately in reckless extravagance to you, the reader of this post-mortem."

Lilly groaned, and Quincy laughed before continuing. Looking at it now, it really was dreadful. Oh, how times can also change for the better.

"I ask you, the descendants, to abjure the inveterate train of thought and understanding of our universe and humanity's place in it as taught to you by your peers and listen to the information trusted upon me by the Great Race; and that you, the reader, will not treat these words with reckless abandon or profligacy now or in the near future."

Quincy looked up in amazement.

"The Great Race? Does he mean that same Great Race he wrote those early sci-fi stories about in *Strange Tales of the Unknown* magazine?"

"I'm not surprised at anything anymore," Lilly replied, turning to watch some seagulls dive into the Mississippi. "What I am more interested in is when this letter will get to the point."

"Well, we know one thing for certain, and that is that this is definitely one of W.A.'s letters."

"Uh-huh."

"Somewhere in the future, an event will transpire that will unleash a chain of disastrous happenstances leading up towards the sixth extinction

of humanity. Forces will rise up in puissance and will act with depreda-tion, hiding in the pusillanimous shadows of the deep bowels of the Earth and beyond. The silver key entrusted upon you will reveal..."

"I can't make out the rest," Quincy said, and Lilly cursed.

The rest of the letter was too faded to read properly, and the letters were simply illegible. It was done entirely on purpose. The only other words they could read were *"keep the key safe;" "The Shadow Beyond Time and Space"* with a whole string of numbers behind it for some reason; and *"with utmost regards, W.A. Swansong."*

"Are you kidding me?" Quincy rolled his eyes. "We were on the brink of discovering something new… and that's it?" He paused. "But at least we know that William *did* foretell God's abandonment *and* the emergence of supernatural beings."

"Let's not take it *that far* just yet. I want to know how this key fits into all of this and why we have it." Lilly inspected the silver key closely. "I mean, this letter says nothing. It might as well be a great coincidence and the ramblings of a dying man desperate to send his descendants towards the same sodding path of depression and darkness as he went under." She waved her head to the final lines *quite rudely again.* "And this? '*The Shadow Beyond Time and Space?*' Two thousand sixty-one, four thousand eight hundred eighty-six? What does that even mean; it's useless!"

"What do you suppose we do now then?" Quincy folded the letter and placed it back into its envelope.

"Absolutely nothing," Lilly replied with determination. "We honor the wishes of our parents and keep a hold of this key. That's it." She crossed her arms. "The last few years have been an absolute burden on both of us while all we want to do is try to lead a life that is as normal as possible in this crazy world. Let's try to keep that up, okay?"

Quincy took a good look around him. The End of the

World was peaceful and pretty, a place that made you believe that the world was not entirely shot to hell yet, and if the goal was trying to live a normal life, then the End of the World was a good place to start.

He hugged his sister. "Let's spend the rest of the afternoon living a normal, boring life picnicking along the waterway, okay?"

One of the Devilfish leapt out of the water, spit fire at—and roasted—a sparrow in mid-flight, and dove back down into the Mississippi.

"And let's try to ignore the occasional weirdness leaping out of the water as well."

Lilly laughed.

"What if we just burn the letter? W.A. Swansong's one, I mean," Quincy suggested a few minutes later.

"Ooh. Defiant. Rebellious even. Especially for you, Quince. We can't though," she pointed at the bottom of their parent's letter. "Mom and Dad specifically told us to keep it. So even though I'd like nothing else than to turn this thing into a bonfire, a little voice is telling me to keep a close hold on this ugly piece of paper and this key."

Quincy simply nodded. "Let's take the detour back home and tuck these things away. Somewhere safe and secret. A promise to Mom and Dad."

Near the waterline, a black car of a redacted manufacturer rolled slowly along the pavement, scanning the shoreline. Inside was a young but confident man dressed in a full black suit. Behind his sunglasses, he could stake out the entire northern waterline of the Mississippi while occasionally glancing at the picture displayed on his dashboard.

He noticed two solemn-looking figures wandering off back into the streets of the Bywater district and pulled out a round-looking walkie-talkie, pressing the button on its right side.

"Agent Reyes, come in. This is Agent Preston reporting. Over."

The walkie-talkie buzzed in anticipation. There was a thunderstorm brewing over New Orleans, and Agent Preston was convinced the electromagnetic particles in the air were screwing up his walkie-talkie, even as advanced as it was.

"*Khuuurrr krrrrr bzzzzz…*"

Silence.

"This is Agent Reyes. Go ahead, Agent Preston. Over."

"Agent Reyes. I have eyes on the bogey. Position *is* confirmed. Over."

A loud sigh came from the walkie-talkie. "You're not sitting in a fighter jet, Agent Preston. I assume by your colorful expressions that you have located the Swansong twins? Over."

"Affirmative, Agent Reyes. Don't worry. They'll be dealt with in no time. Over."

"Do *not* cause unnecessary harm, Agent Preston. If the twins don't have to be liquidated, don't do it. Over."

"Aww, come on, Agent Reyes. Why not? I've been trained for this. I—"

"That is an order, Agent Preston. Over."

In the meantime, the thunderstorm heading for New Orleans had arrived. Thick blots of rain started to splash against the windshield. Agent Preston, while meticulously having rolled the car back towards the residential areas, could hear the static discharge exploding over the walkie-talkie.

"Trigger-happy buffoon." *Krrrr zzzzbzzzzz khrrzz.*

"What's that, Agent Reyes?" Preston responded. "I did not quite make that out. Over."

After fumbling with the frequencies for a little bit, Agent Preston managed to get back onto the right channel, without too much interference.

"The chickens have entered the coop, Agent Reyes. Shall I proceed with the necessary arrangements? Over." He sloughed into his seat, making sure he didn't look suspicious in his unmarked shadow-government vehicle.

"The coop? What the hell are you... oh, you mean their apartment? Damn movies and stuff ruining everything, and no, by the way. I ordered Agent Silverstein to try one last advance at the twins. If the crazy old bat fails me again, I will give you the heads-up. Over."

"*Fine.* I'll stake out the building in the meantime. Over and out."

Agent Preston sat back with a growl, rolling down his window to let some of the cool air in. He glanced at his walkie-talkie before lighting up a cigarette and angling himself to watch the front door of the apartment building he sat diagonal from.

"You know what, *Agent Reyes*," he mumbled to himself, "I may take orders from you now, but once I've retrieved this package, I'm sure the tables will turn."

He reached into the glove compartment and pulled out his faithful Glock 22 and gave it a fast checkup. After he made sure the gun was loaded and ready to go, he smiled as he tucked the firearm beneath his jacket.

Chapter 3

THE CHAMBER WAS dark except for an eerie green glow lighting up parts of the interior. A faint humming groaned throughout the room, broken occasionally by small *blips* and *bleeps* from an unseen and strange machine as it processed some kind of data near the mess of jumbled cables and power outlets strewn around.

A slight breeze flowed through the dank chambers, creeping through little corners and crevices; it often sounded like low, unsettling whispering. In the back end of the chamber, partially uncovered by the green light, something moved —a mess of cables, feeding tubes, and restraints were holding something inhumane in place.

The light revealed little, save for a dripping, mucus-covered appendage coated with a membranous film. Then, from the dark, there came the most unholy of sounds: an utter alien, guttural clicking, the smacking of ooze upon flesh.

Next came a voice, a raspy voice that sounded almost electric, as if brainwaves were synthesized into Earthly speech.

"Can you feel it? Brother," the raspy voice wheezed, "it has been found. The key has...returned... returned to the rightful heirs."

. . .

A low mumbling came from the right next to the voice. Similar sounds of otherworldly origin floated through the chamber—it was something else trying its hardest to speak up, but nothing came.

"Conserve yourself… the heirs will come."

The strange mumbling finally found the energy to speak, although it did so with terrible hardship.

"They…must... They..."

The words stopped as the second voice hissed as if in terrible pain and agony.

"Yes... brother," the first voice agreed. "They must come."

Quincy slammed the door behind him and followed Lilly towards the living room.

"It's really not funny, Lilly! That old lady is just super creepy, all right? She's always following me, stealing our mail, killing me with her breath. *Killing me*, Lilly!"

"You should've seen your face!" She giggled. "Shouldn't you feel honored that girls her age still feel an attraction to a stunning young lad such as yourself?" She snorted at his growl before starting to laugh again.

"She was blatantly sifting through my pockets! I mean, the nerve of her, that fossil... that..."

"Oh, shush!" Lilly placed a hand over Quincy's mouth. "Come on, she's just demented or something. You must remind her of her husband; I don't know." She grinned, jabbing him in the side. "It's kind of funny, admit it!"

"I admit nothing. *Nothing!*"

. . .

Lilly laughed all the way to the kitchen, only being interrupted by gasps of air and coughing fits. Quincy glared at her before planting himself on the couch. He reached inside the inner pocket of his coat and found the letters safe and secure. *Man, what a day it's been*, he thought to himself.

Eventually, his sister finally stopped making fun of him and sat down next to him.

"Weird day, huh?" It was as if she could read Quincy's mind.

"Yeah," he responded, surprised. "I was just thinking that actually."

Lilly tapped the side of her head. "I know; we got that twin thing going on."

"I'm just glad we're not finishing each other's—"

"Sentences!"

"You did that on purpose," he exclaimed and watched Lilly get up and head back into the kitchen.

"No, really," she said sarcastically. "I don't mind being on the same frequency with you, but I also prefer to have my own thoughts and ideas." She returned with drinks and sat back down on the couch. "So, where were we? Weird day?"

"We've both experienced weirder. So I'd call it an average day at best. Except for the fact we got a letter from our parents. That's kind of cool, right?"

"We even managed to uphold their wishes for the entire day already!" Lilly grinned.

The doorbell rang, and Quincy groaned.

"Does Lady Silverstein just keep an open house all of the time or what?" Quincy shuffled towards the door. His feet were killing him; he had made the mistake of wearing his most formal shoes for the occasion today, which unfortunately weren't broken in at all. "I mean, whatever happened to using the buzzer downstairs?" He opened the door halfheartedly and stopped.

A man in a fully black suit with sunglasses, still on, and a snazzy earpiece stood in the doorway—it was a bizarre sight to behold. He had short, jet-black hair and an indistinct, clean-shaven face.

"Uh. Hi?" Quincy managed to utter, then glanced to see Lilly staring intensely at the odd figure from her spot on the couch.

While many people have reported seeing the men in black at the most volatile of paranormal hotspots around the world, never did Quincy and Lilly think one of them would show up at their front door.

"Evening, sir, ma'am." He surveyed the room. "My name is Special Agent David Preston, Haven spec ops personnel. We have reason to believe the two of you might be in severe danger. May I come in?"

"*Haven?*" Quincy repeated. "And uh, who or what gives you that idea? Agent... what was it?"

"Preston, Mr. Swansong," he replied coolly. "Please, let us sit down."

"Can I offer you a cup of coffee, Agent Preston?"

"Please."

During the exchange, Lilly got up from the couch. She eyed the secret agent with suspicion as Quincy led him into the room and offered him a seat on a rather spacious chair next to their couch and handed him a cup of instant coffee.

"So..." Lilly twirled the spoon in her mug viciously. "Aren't you secret agent types usually pretty damn wary of handing out your identity and stuff? Why come waltzing in here, floundering about your name?"

Agent Preston took a sip of his coffee and cringed at the horrible taste before recomposing and tossing a wicked-looking smile towards Lilly. "Obviously, Miss Swansong, the name with which I introduced myself is an alias, as my birth name is a secret to anyone except for the extreme higher-ups of our organization. Now if we can get to the matter at hand—"

"Why use a name at all then?" Lilly challenged, cutting him off. "Why not just use a number or just don't introduce yourself?"

"Being a part of our organization, Miss Swansong, is not a reason to drop any formalities," he reassured her. "Now about the danger you are in—"

"You look pretty young," Quincy offered, again cutting the agent off. "You can't be much older than we are. Does Haven recruit specially trained or gifted personnel from a young age? Or are you an exception?"

"Eh..." Agent Preston floundered. "We have agents of all sorts of backgrounds and ages, Mr. Swansong. Now, please, to the reason of my visit—"

"Do you have a badge? Can I see it? Or is it one of those ID cards like the FBI used to have?" Lilly asked, rambling. Her eyes narrowed; she got that air of mistrust again—felt the need to be wary.

"For *God's sake!*" Agent Preston slapped his coffee down on the table in front of him. "Was everyone in your family *this* curious? Now stop it with the questions and on to the matter of the artifact!"

Agent Preston stopped; he knew he made a mistake.

His hand moved down towards his left pocket.

"Wait." Quincy stood up; his hands were clenched, but his pose betrayed how nervous and out of his element he felt. "What artifact? Please state your business right now, Agent Preston, or we will be forced to show you out."

"We know about the item you procured from your inheritance. We have a database on all occult objects known to the agency at this time, and it is of grave importance they do not fall into the wrong hands."

"What's so special about it?" Lilly took a sip from her

coffee and nodded at Quincy to sit back down. She stared at Agent Preston without blinking, causing him to pull at his shirt collar nervously. "What danger could such a shoddy… item" —she chose her words carefully—"if it even *was* in our possession, possibly do?"

She could see the question caught him off guard and hid a smirk behind the rim of her mug.

Agent Preston hesitated for a moment to gather his thoughts on how to phrase his next sentence.

"It's, ehm... It's a beacon! Yes. The atypical woven material obscures a... uh... a special limestone that attracts Pit Fiends."

The story he'd made up on the spot wasn't a great success, and he bit back a groan. He instantly noticed the skepticism rising in Lilly as she looked to her twin. Quincy he wasn't sure of yet, but he tried his best to pull on his strings and not his sister's.

"Mr. Swansong, I implore you to not leave yourself and your sister in unnecessary danger. We *must* secure and protect the artifact."

"Tell me more about this limestone, Agent Pr—"

"My dear brother!" Lilly interrupted, her words harsh. "Could I please speak with you in the kitchen in *private* for a moment?" She paused. "*Please?*"

"Ehm, sure, Lil," Quincy replied, looking confused as he placed his coffee mug on the table. "Please excuse us for a moment, Agent Preston."

Lilly grabbed her brother, who was just a hair taller than her, by the shoulders and navigated him straight to the kitchen, cursing under her breath while deliberately trying to step on the back of his heels.

"Ouch! Watch it, dammit!"

Lilly slammed the kitchen door shut and moved to stand in front of him.

"What's your problem?" Quincy snapped, leaning down to rub the back of his feet. "What's your game, sis?"

"You tell me, Quince! I don't know if you already noticed the super secretive agent spouting nonsense in our living room yet, but *I* have, and I'm just about ready to shove him out of here," she whispered fiercely.

"Nonsense? Shouldn't we, like, at least hear him out? He said we were in danger!"

"Dude, *really*? He's obviously lying. There's something super important about this key, and I don't trust that guy at all." As she spoke,

Lilly nervously fingered the key inside the pocket of her jacket. She was glad she hadn't taken it out yet.

Outside the kitchen window, a flash of lightning lit up the entire room in a blinding flash. Thunder roared close to the twins' apartment seconds before a second downpour of rain began clattering hard against the window.

"Are we really going to send this guy out in this weather? You saw the news; it'll be like this the entire evening. At least let him wait out the storm and..." Quincy stopped and frowned as his sister pushed past him and towards the door. "Lilly? What are you doing?"

Lilly opened the kitchen door so that it was slightly ajar; she had a good view of the agent sitting in the living room.

"What, are we spying on the guy now?" Quincy crept up behind her.

"Would you *shut up* for once?" Lilly snapped. "Look!"

. . .

Agent Preston still sat quietly on the living room chair. He took a sip of his coffee, coughed because he apparently thought it'd taste better now that it was nearly cold, then pulled out a Glock 22 from his jacket pocket. He grinned when he pulled out a handkerchief and started rubbing it against the pistol.

"He has a freakin' gun, Quince."

"So?" Quincy shrugged. "He's a secret agent; they all carry guns, right?"

Oblivious to them, Agent Preston was still making himself comfortable. After cleaning his Glock to a miraculous shine, he reached back into his pocket and pulled out a handful of bullets.

"Quince, he is loading the gun. I repeat, he is *loading* it."

Quincy was pacing around in the kitchen, trying to keep himself levelheaded—*everything was normal and fine*, or so he kept telling himself.

"Well..." he floundered, leaning on the countertop, "of course he is loading the gun! He said himself that the artifact attracted monsters, right? He is preparing to defend himself, surely!"

"Oh yeah? Then where were all of the Pit Fiends when we ran around with that key all day, huh? Where were..."

Lilly stopped and backed away from the door, turning to look her brother straight in the eyes.

"Quince, he is holding pictures of us. Why is he holding our pictures? Where did they come from?" Now she was starting to get really nervous.

"You're grasping at straws here. It's only logical that he has our pictures. I mean, they were looking specifically for us, so it's no surprise he has some material to recognize us with. I'm sure it came from a database or something..."

While Quincy continued rambling, Lilly crept back towards the door and blanched.

"Quince," she hissed.

"What now?"

"He is pretending to shoot our pictures."

"Huh?"

"He is aiming his gun at our pictures and is going all like '*pew*' with his mouth."

Quincy looked over Lilly's shoulder, blinked, then grabbed Lilly by the arm and dragged her away from the door.

"Okay. You win; let's go."

"Convinced yet?" Lilly teased, sticking out her tongue, though she could see he was visibly shaking.

The sound of the thunder grew louder once Quincy shoved the kitchen window all the way open.

"You can go all '*I told you so*' later, okay? Get on the ladder; I got the car keys right here. Got your coat?"

"Never had a chance to take it off."

"Good. Let's move."

The twins carefully eased out of the window and made their way down the fire escape as stealthily as possible.

Glancing over the edge of the window, Lilly saw an angry Agent Preston kicking the kitchen door open in frustration seconds before she slipped down the ladder.

"*Dammit!*" Agent Preston yelled over the noise of the downpour. "Stop and get back here right now!"

But it was no use; the twins were already well on their way towards the parking garage.

Agent Preston came sprinting out of the apartment complex's front door and almost collided with Lilly and Quincy's Ford Fiesta as they pulled out into the street.

"Straight ahead! Just go, *go!*" Quincy yelled from the passenger's seat.

"What do think I'm doing? Cruising around nice and easy? I'm going as fast as I can here!" Lilly clutched the steering wheel, her eyes narrowed as she looked through the windshield.

. . .

"He's right behind u—"

Both Quincy and Lilly bolted upwards from shock when the loud pangs of bullets sounded seconds before the rear window shattered.

"Get down!" Lilly yelled, tucking her head closer to her legs.

Quincy glanced through the broken back window and saw Agent Preston climbing into his own car. The vehicle was as sleek and black as Preston's hair, and it roared right before its headlights illuminated the darkened streets.

"He's getting in the car!" Quincy yelled. "Now! *Drive!*"

The heavy rain and constant flashes of thunder made driving an exceptional feat for both drivers. Though, Quincy felt that Lilly had learned to drive around in all sorts of vehicles during her time with the GDF, so he was assured that her driving their Fiesta through a storm wouldn't be the biggest of issues.

"He shot at us! He just shot at us; what the hell did we do?" Lilly adjusted the rearview mirror. "Man, just *look* at this mess!"

Quincy turned to see water was now streaming all over the backseat. He went to comment, offer some sort of witty reply, but jolted to the side as Lilly pulled a quick turn across the wet pavement and the Fiesta tore narrowly through the curve, sending more than a few flowerpots up into the air.

"What do they want from us? Truly?" Lilly yelled over the roaring of the engine and the storm.

Quincy shook his head. "Still not really the time for that now!" He caught the reflection of lights in the rearview mirror and glanced back again to see the black car rapidly coming closer. "He's right behind us!"

Lilly accelerated and ran them straight across an intersection through a red light. A lone car that was also unfortunate enough to be stuck in this storm came to a screeching halt just inches away from Agent Preston's black car. Its honking faded away quickly in the ruckus. The road was barely visible from the rainfall, but the black car stuck close.

"I don't know what to do. I do *not* know what to do here!"

"Stop!" Quincy yelled. "That's one of the things someone would least want to hear sitting next to someone driving almost 88 miles per hour in downtown New Orleans!"

Meanwhile, Agent Preston drove on like a madman behind them. He lowered his window once he got a little closer and pointed his gun out of the car. He took a shot and missed, hitting the nearest lantern post. He cursed, fell back, and rolled his window back up.

"He's shooting again!" Quincy was sure his heart was almost beating out of his chest at this point.

In the flickering light of the failing street lamps, a lone figure suddenly appeared; he was walking across the street in a snail's pace.

"There's someone in the road, dammit!"

"No! Wait!" Quincy pressed himself against the windshield to see through the downpour. "That's just Old Man Walters!" His eyes were bright as he placed his hand on the dashboard. "Lilly, I have an idea. Get up to 90 and drive straight towards him!"

"Excuse me? I'm not going to drive over a poor old—"

"He's a ghost, Lilly! You can't harm him—just do it! If this works..."

Since Lilly trusted her brother one hundred percent, she crushed her foot down onto the gas pedal.

As if time itself slowed down, they watched the speedometer inching towards 90 miles per hour. Lilly squinted in fear seconds before their car ran straight through the old ghost wandering the wet road. The twins felt a quick jolt of static flowing through their bodies as they phased through the apparition. If the old coot had noticed anything at all, I'd be very surprised.

A split second later, Agent Preston came face-to-face with Old Man Walters and flew into a frenzied panic. He yanked the steering wheel to the left and immediately lost control of the car. The tires of the black vehicle screeched as the car swerved off the road and smacked into a nearby tree with incredible speed.

It was safe to say that not much remained of Agent Preston after that crash, but Quincy and Lilly weren't very interested in stopping to make sure.

Lilly glanced back in shock, adrenaline still rushing through her body.

"And now we pretty much killed someone."

Quincy looked out of the back window, trying to see the wreckage, but all he saw was flickering street lights through the heavy rain.

"He killed himself," he whispered while checking the map application on his mobile phone. "Just like the man in the pet store the other day, this guy sought out danger all by himself, and it turned and bit him straight in the ass."

"What are we supposed to do now, Quince?" Lilly slowed the car down, the brakes squealing in protest. "I mean, what are we now? Are we wanted felons? Where do we even go? We sure as hell can't go back home anytime soon. If they know our address…"

"It'll be a short time until another one of them knocks at our door, uh-uh... you're right," Quincy muttered, biting his fingernail.

As the silence grew between them, the thunderstorm subsided, and they merged onto the highway.

After a good hour and a half of driving, the twins stopped at a gas station to get their bearings and check out a map.

"We just passed Baton Rouge." Lilly traced a finger over the red interstate line.

"We can turn around and look for help. Should we call the police? Tell them we're being harassed by secret agents?"

"Even if we *could* convince the police that good old Agent Preston squashed himself against a tree by accident..."

"Which technically he did," he reminded her.

"Even if that is the case," she continued, "I'm pretty sure the police got nothing on Haven personnel. They'd much rather deliver us to them with a big bow around our necks than help us get away from them. I'm sure of it."

"So what are our options then?"

Lilly traced her fingertip over the plastic gas station map along the I-10 and smiled weakly.

"Okay, so it's about an hour and twenty minutes to Lafayette," she said. "I'd suggest us driving to the town outskirts, get a motel, and then try to get our bearings in the morning, sound good?"

Quincy nodded, following his sister's lead. It was no surprise she was a lot more confident in this harrowing situation, based on her military experience. So even though he felt uneasy, he knew he could count on her guidance and confidence to pull them through.

They hung around for a bit longer at the gas station, treating themselves to a good steaming hot cup of black coffee before they headed back on the road.

Verona Drive was quiet at the night. From a shadowy corner that led to an abandoned alleyway, a man in a military uniform came dashing down the pavement. His combat boots slapped clumsily across the loose stones, and he almost slipped when he reached the small military jeep parked at the edge of the lot.

"Come on, come on!" he hissed through his panicked breathing.

The man was fumbling around with an old radio. The thing popped and crackled so much that he was afraid it would burst into flames altogether. Finally a voice, albeit quiet and hard to hear through the noise, answered his call from the other side.

"We...ar...you sol..er, go...head." The radio crackled then with static.

"This is Sergeant Hicks from the preliminary GDF task force *Gray Hounds*, designated area of inquiry is Lafayette, Louisiana. That's Hotel, India, Charlie, Kilo, Sierra! Over!"

Sergeant Hicks sounded out of breath and panicked and was listening intently for an answer from the radio. His breathing became more erratic as the parking lot pavement beneath him started to vibrate as though an earthquake was just getting started.

"Ser...nt Hick...e...copy, ...at is you... prelim...ary assesm...t?"

His first reply was lost when an otherworldly and painfully loud howl pierced through the night sky. The quakes became fiercer, and Hicks noticed the screeching sounds of something rubbing hard against some kind of metal right behind him.

"Tell HQ to send help immediately!"

A sewer grate not far from the jeep suddenly jetted upwards from a great pressure or force. The pang of the grate landing on the pavement broke the tense silence. The street-lights around the parking lot all shattered before dying out.

Surrounded by glass, Sergeant Hicks was left staring at a thousand red eyes that eerily crept closer and closer; something burped.

"Tell them," he said with resignation into the radio, "Lafayette has gone dark."

Now I could tell you what happened to Hicks right after that, but there will be a lot more unavoidable descriptions of atrocities to come. Consider yourselves warned.

Chapter 4

IT WAS a little past midnight when Quincy and Lilly rolled their ashen gray Ford Fiesta into the Lafayette town outskirts. Upon pulling onto the town's main road, Lilly noticed a strange sensation hanging in the air. She explained to her brother that it felt like the buzzing of faraway electrical discharge and smelled like a combination of burning copper and old blood.

Quincy himself didn't notice, but, unlike his sister, he also lacked the basic field training a soldier would go through in order to get a good grip on a potentially dangerous situation out on duty.

"I wouldn't know," he responded. "Maybe some construction work went sour with the thunderstorm?" He tried his best, inwardly hoping the situation wasn't anything out of the ordinary.

"There's something wrong here," Lilly whispered when they drove past flickering streetlights on Moss Street and saw the utility poles upturned and broken further up ahead. Sparks of electricity were dancing around like fireflies.

. . .

A fallen utility pole blocked the street ahead, forcing them to drive onto the lot of a nearby RPM Pizza—which was closed. Against Lilly's better judgement, they decided to get out of the car for a little bit and figure out where to go next.

Once parked, they took the last of their gas station food out of the trunk and sat on the hood together. They tried to carry on a somewhat normal conversation, but they both were on edge, as if ready for the unexpected to happen.

"You think there was an earthquake?"

"Nah. It's not really the right time of year, besides, if it were an earthquake, who knows what else came with it," Lilly replied grimly.

"Guess so, you never seem to know these days."

Quincy looked up and saw a solitary figure standing in a singly lit windowsill. The moment he laid eyes upon it, the light popped off. "Nobody's really around." He glanced over his shoulder towards the empty, wet streets. "Do you think the storm was way more severe here? People seemed to be holed up inside."

Lilly seemed lost in thought and didn't reply.

"Lilly?" Quincy nudged her.

"Have I ever told you about the first time we were assigned regular patrol in the Carpathian Mountains in Europe? Right after I finished boot camp?"

Quincy shook his head. He had heard a handful of his sister's stories, but this one seemed unfamiliar. It was remarkable how much action she had seen in such a short time in the force.Being in the army after the Abandonment, all soldiers were required to get psychologically evaluated quarterly due to the intense stress that comes with fighting all matter of absolutely vile monsters and demons. Lilly had pulled through the first couple of evaluations, but the amount of battle proved too much for her in the long run. She was barely enlisted two years before she was dismissed, but her experience and valor in combat, even for such a short time, gave her the right to be called a veteran.

Quincy was incredibly thankful that his sister made it home safe and sound. He admired her for her bravery, but it was a mystery to him how she could be act so happy after having been thrown in so many horrible situations.

"Tell me, if you want to."

She straightened her back, her eyes shifting away. "Right. So we were fresh out of Nevada boot camp when the news came we were being relocated to Eastern Europe for a security measurement mission, which basically meant sitting on your ass all day until something happens —usually nothing does. I had my best buds Huxley and Lynch with me at all times, and after a few days or so, we were getting quite used to the country already. It was gray, rainy, cold, and the wind howled 24/7."

"That's sounds exactly like the opposite of everything you enjoy," Quincy teased.

"If only it stayed that way." Lilly looked at her feet, and Quincy's humor faded. "We were stationed there for about a week when the first disappearance happened. Hux went to bed, everyone saw it, and Lynch even slept beneath him in the bunk. Next day, he was gone. At first we thought he ran away because both Lynch and I often noted a certain sort of doubt within him, but all of his gear and rations were still neatly stashed away in his locker.

"Now that's not all. People then started to disappear nightly, and no trace of them was ever found. Others started having nightmares, sleep paralysis, and bouts of sleepwalking, and those were the lucky ones. When we, fresh and green wannabe-soldiers, couldn't figure it out, we called for reinforcements. They quickly arrived, far less subtle than we ever were, guns blazing and tanks strolling, and it turned into a massacre. Turns out, the camp was located on top of the necropolis of a Soul Sucker, an Elder one too!"

"Oh, that's not good. Not good at all." Quincy imagined

the textbook pictures he had seen of Soul Suckers and shuddered.

"The Soul Sucker and its minions had been gorging on our comrades for the past week, right after a small earthquake happened just before we were stationed there. Soul Suckers are attracted to weak-minded humans initially, so poor Hux was the first to go."

"What happened next?"

"To our biggest surprise, it was actually Haven agents that got us out of the jam we found ourselves in. The GDF royally screwed up by rolling in with the big guns, angering the plague of Soul Suckers immediately."

Quincy shifted uneasily on the hood of the car.

"You think they knew about the necropolis? Haven, I mean."

"I always had my suspicions," Lilly replied. "But after that chase earlier this evening, I know for a fact that Haven is up to something. I think they might have a way bigger influence on the state of the world than I initially suspected."

"The story. Why'd you tell it now?"

"Because…" Lilly stopped and swallowed hard. "That uneasy feeling I've been having ever since we drove into town…"

"Yeah?"

"I also felt it the night before Hux disappeared. And it never left me until I was out of those mountains."

"Something awoke here tonight?" Quincy shivered.

"Something may very well have."

Out of nowhere, an explosion to the east lit the sky above Lafayette aflame, and the twins rolled off the Fiesta hood as gunfire started ringing through the night air. The twins jumped into the car and drove off in a flash, right towards the gunfire—Quincy had no idea why Lilly had urged them to head towards all of the commotion. Perhaps it was an instinct sort of thing, perhaps she just wanted to help, or perhaps they were just stupid.

If Lilly's gut feeling was correct, then it would turn into another Soul Sucker situation unless she could help prevent it. Somehow.

She had no idea what she was doing, she knew that, but she just couldn't sit still in all of this. And Quincy would never leave her side even if she'd demanded it of him. So she didn't even bother to tell him to in the first place.

After a short spurt of speed, the car pulled in on the parking lot near Verona Drive, and both instantly wished they had turned around when they still could. Oh dear, how they wished they had turned around. Things weren't looking great, but, while you're here waiting in suspense, first another history lesson for you.

The events at Lafayette and the Carpathian Mountains are only two examples of what Haven and GDF forces describe as "Type 1 Awakening Events," which means an outside or natural occurrence led to a paranormal breach in a certain area. These events can be classified anywhere between "low threat level" to "global extinction threats," and as such, they all need to be approached with the utmost caution by whatever team or organization is leading the first response.

Another example that would be considered a Type 1 event was the outbreak of a laughing virus in Northern Ireland after a tsunami washed away an ancient faerie grove. The inhabitants of the grove were so angry that they lashed out against the local populace, infecting them with fits of laughter that never seemed to go away and was highly contagious.

At first the people didn't seem to mind it too much, and the village of Culdaff was promptly awarded with the title of "Happiest Place on Earth." This angered the faeries so much that they intensified the spell tenfold which resulted in the general populace literally *dying* from laughter as their bodies convulsed over and over.

Another one of these events occurred in Amsterdam

several months after Alghuurl's initial subjugation. There was an uproar in the city's red-light district where the local workers claimed that demons came to fetch them in the night. During the investigation run by a local GDF force, it was uncovered that a brutal quadruple homicide had taken place not long before the claims of these demons began. The remains of those murdered had been dumped in the city sewers, and later they rose from their stinking grave as ghouls, stalking the sewers and abducting, killing, and eating the foulest of human beings.

One of the GDF agents working on the investigation had said, "It was one of the most messed up cases I have ever seen. It's like a stinking and gory Ninja Turtles reversal."

There is also a classification for a Type 2 event, but as far as the common folk know, it has never happened before. The how and what on these theoretical events are top-secret, only known by the most prominent of world leaders, military commanders, and Haven's director. Considering the fact that a Type 2 event would exceed even a Global Extinction Type 1 event, the chances are slim the Earth would experience such an event more than once and survive to remember it.

Now back to Lilly and Quincy.

The streets ran red with blood, green with mucus, and silver with bullet casings. The twins hid behind their car at a fair distance from the action. In the middle of the parking lot stood a huge GDF tank that was struggling to move after one of its thick caterpillar tracks was slashed off by the most abysmal of creatures. Surrounding the tank were a dozen or so brave GDF soldiers firing their guns at the endless onslaught of terror that came to them from almost every angle of the lot.

The beasts' greasy hides were green and gray colored, and spikes protruded from their backs. They had bright red eyes which were sunk deeply into their melted faces. Yet the most terrifying feature of all was a huge gaping maw in which one could see nothing but the purest of blackness, a void containing nothing but the most unpleasant things on Earth and its billions of other dimensions.

"Lilly!" Quincy's eyes were wide and full of fear as he gripped her arm. "Can you please tell me whose idea it was to drive over here all heroically?" His grip tightened. "You see those things over there, right?"

"Shambler spawn," she said around a sigh; the hairs on her neck were on edge more than ever before.

"Ah! So I *did* guess that correctly," Quincy sarcastically replied. "What a wonderful day to die. First that guy from Haven—now *this*."

Quincy peeked over the hood of the car just in time to see a GDF soldier saw one of the spawns in half with his modified chainsaw gun, only to unfortunately get decapitated by another one of the monsters that had come up from behind him. Quincy yelped and stifled a scream while Lilly pulled him back and grabbed his hand.

Lilly dropped to her knees, watching the scene continue to play out from underneath the car as the soldier's head rolled towards them.

The twins held their breath for what seemed like the longest of times.

"So..." Quincy quivered. "What do you say? Low threat or..."

"Well, it's not quite global extinction," she said, deciding to dodge the sarcasm she was feeling. It seemed to at least calm Quincy down somewhat. "But considering these things we see here are technically only babies and that means there is a huge probability that a full-fledged Dimensional Shambler is on the loose, I'd consider the possibility that the threat level is at least continent-wide."

"Meaning this thing could destroy the entirety of North America?" Quincy yelled.

"Would you pipe down?" Lilly hissed. "I don't know what

to think yet. It could probably leave Canada alone, but the possibility is certainly there. I've heard stories of Shamblers eating up entire towns before, but I have no idea what these things can do if left unchecked." She frowned. "Did you know it's rumored that it was a Shambler that swallowed the town of Arkham, Massachusetts? It was so sudden of an event that…"

Lilly went off on one of her monster tangents, and Quincy was quick to zone out. He briefly heard the GDF commander scream at the top of his lungs, before he closed his eyes and drowned out everything else. He didn't hear the retching and smacking of the Shambler spawn, didn't hear Lilly rave about old writer theories, didn't hear the renewed gunfire.

All he heard was the voice of the GDF commander bellowing in utmost confidence, hopefully, *victory in the making.*

"Destroy their wretched hides! I want to see none of them alive, and so help me God—if He was here—if I see any of them escape into any of their colored little portals…" The voice trailed off.

"*Johnson*, get your ass out of that phone booth, son! *Now*! Do I need to call up your father and tell him his son needs to grow a pair? *No*. He died defending this country! Johnson, get…" Again the voice trailed off, followed by a sigh. "Well, there you go; I told that boy he needed to get out. Now look at him there…and there and—*Wilson, you idiot*! Poison mines aren't helping; throw it *away*! I have no idea how I came to lead such a sorry bunch of—"

"Quince! *Helloooo?*"

Quincy's eyes snapped open, and he brushed away his sister's finger poking him on the cheek.

"Did we win?" he asked, confused.

"Would you stand up already?" Lilly groaned and pulled her brother to his feet.

. . .

Quincy now noticed two people standing beside Lilly. One of them was a fit, young guy with brown hair. He wore a checkered shirt and a cap that read *Do the Dew!* The other man seemed to be in his fifties with matte gray hair and a nifty mustache.

"This is Sean," Lilly said, pointing at the young guy. "And this is *Uncle* Scooter," she introduced, pointing at the mustached man. "They seem to be in a spot of trouble like us, and since we can't really do anything here on the firing line, I suggested we team up and find a place to hide so this can either blow over or we die from starvation."

"We can always start eating each other, heh-heh-heeee," Uncle Scooter said, rubbing his belly.

Quincy eyed him; he couldn't tell if the man was serious or not.

"I see you have the most meat packed on you, so congratulations on being the first to go!" Lilly said, looking at the old man in disgust.

"I... uh. Can we *please* just go?" Quincy was exhausted.

Agent Reyes headed into his superior's office with the weight of the world on his back. Agent Preston had failed him, and the bits and pieces of him that were subsequently being scraped off the road weren't precisely able to talk details.

Now he was on his way back to get his ass chewed out again for not procuring the Swansong documents he was supposed to already have in his possession some time ago.

He gulped and squeezed his hands, then he went in.

"Agent Reyes," the man in the shadows whispered.

Reyes knew better than to speak up now; he kept quiet and would only speak when requested.

"Reyes, would you kindly explain to me how two young adults, barely managing to scrape together enough rent and food to survive month-by-month, managed to overwhelm one of our best agents?"

"Sir, I—"

"*Killing* him in the process? Driving away in a shoddy Ford Fiesta?"

"I—"

"Speak up then!"

"I have no idea what happened, sir. The twins must have known we were coming in some way or another, according to my intel—"

"According to *my* intel, Agent Reyes, these halfwits barely even knew we were active in New Orleans in the first place, let alone staking them out. I assume you have a next plan of action?"

"I will take care of them myself, sir," Reyes said with more pride than he expected from himself.

"Interesting, very," his boss supplied, dryly.

Reyes fidgeted, unsure if he was dismissed or not.

"Preston's funeral was the last one the department was willing to finance for now, did you know?"

"No, sir."

"You don't want to end up in a box somewhere in the desert, do you? In a mass grave full of unidentifiable remains of other *lesser functioning* agents?"

"Absolutely not, sir," Reyes whimpered.

"Then give me some info I can count on. Go ahead, out with it."

Agent Reyes scuffled around a bit before taking out his tablet and punching in some data before handing it over to his superior.

"It appears our targets were heading in the general vicinity of Lafayette, sir."

"So?"

"Our sources report a Type 1 Awakening Event erupted earlier, right beneath the center of the city. If the twins did plan to head through, there's a big chance they would be stuck there now. The city is in chaos; GDF troops already deployed, but they're not making much progress as of yet."

Although it was hard to see in the dimness of the room, at that moment Agent Reyes could swear he saw the eyes of his superior light up for just the smallest of moments. He knew this was just the piece of the puzzle he needed to get back into the good graces of Haven—or it would at least be his ticket on the way back there. That Haven lot is all the same. Each and every one of them would crawl over a mountain of corpses just to get ahead of their rivals. Sometimes, they'd get their literal *heads*. Disgusting, if you're not into that sort of thing.

"Well, would you look at that," Reyes' boss said, finally breaking the silence. "Perhaps you're not the totally useless sack of shit I was taking you for, Reyes."

"Thank you," Reyes replied through clenched teeth. It was a proper insult, and it pained him to hear it.

A little beep came from one of the many technological devices that were strewn about on the desk; Reyes looked up nervously as his superior seemed to skim some kind of field report that was being freshly comm'd through on a tablet.

"Congratulations, Reyes." The fat man looked up, and Agent Reyes could see him grinning from ear to ear.

"S-sir?"

"Not only are you going to capture two annoying children on the run with *my* information…"

"M-more leads, sir?" Reyes felt the hairs on the back of his neck stand up—this wasn't good; oh no, this would be terrible news indeed for him.

"You're going to trap and incapacitate a Dimensional Shambler in the process."

Lilly quietly closed the door of the small bistro behind her. Together with the help of the others, she managed to block it securely enough to let her guard down somewhat. Uncle Scooter passed out in the nearest booth almost immediately.

Lilly rested her head against the doorpost for a bit. When

she looked up, the defeated faces of Sean and Quincy were staring at her.

"I..." she stopped, and a wave of emotion hit her. She recalled the ghastly sight of Agent Preston crashing against the tree, the soldier's decapitated head rolling towards her, and then just about every horrific thing she experienced while on active duty. It was too much right now—for her and especially for her twin brother.

Tonight was reminding Lilly that she and her brother were still young and feeble, and she could see in Quincy's eyes that he was thinking the same thing. They just wanted to lead a normal life...

She brushed the thoughts away and looked around the bistro. The little café was empty, but, sure enough, the smell of freshly brewed coffee still lingered in the air.

Coffee, Lilly and Quincy often agreed, was like black gold. You could have the worst case of sleep deprivation in the world, but having just one or two sips in the morning could turn a dull and lifeless husk of a human being back on their feet and ready to take action. Quincy especially could appreciate a good cup of joe considering his academic endeavors often took him into the wee hours of the morning, and more than once he turned up for lectures with barely two hours of sleep.

"That smells incredible; I could really go for some coffee right now." Quincy moved to inspect the old jukebox standing next to the counter. "Hey, do you think this old thing still works?"

Ignoring him, Lilly figured there was no harm in getting some caffeine going, but she thought it best to cover and secure the whole building first, so she headed off into the back with Sean trailing behind her.

"So what's the story between you two?" Sean asked once the kitchen doors shut behind him.

"What's there to tell?" Lilly responded while inspecting the many pots and flavors the café kitchen had to offer. "Probably not much different than you and Scooter. Wrong place, wrong time?"

"I meant more like where'd you come from, how'd you meet and stuff," Sean huffed, straightening his cap and looking a bit flustered.

"What?" Lilly glanced at him and saw his flushed face. "He's my brother…" She snorted. "Oh, please don't tell me you're interested in hitting on me; I—"

"Not at all, jeez," Sean interrupted. "I just wanted to know a bit more about you guys since we're stuck together and all that."

Lilly saw Sean's cheeks flush more and forced away a smile. "Maybe we can swap life stories after we're not in immediate danger of getting our faces chewed off, all right? I mean—" Lilly broke off, her eyes narrowing on the stove.

"What's the matter?"

"This coffee pot on here, it's still warm."

"So?"

"So someone's been brewing coffee here not too long ago, maybe an hour tops, probably even less."

"We staked out the street for a while; nobody came in or out. You're imagining things…"

Sean's voice trailed off when a huge racket came from further back in the room; a wall separated the little preparation area and the rest of the kitchen.

"There's a backdoor!" Lilly yelped. "And it's probably open, *shit!*"

Strange noises and bangs began to filter in from the ventilation system above them.

"They're in the vents."

"What?" Sean stared up in confusion.

Lilly gaped at him before rolling her eyes. "I mean you're

a real dolt if you've never seen *Aliens* in your life, you idiot! Grab something sharp."

"What's all this racket in here?" Uncle Scooter appeared in the doorway, half awake and annoyed.

Before Sean and Lilly, two grizzly, bug-like appendages pierced through the ventilation shaft above Scooter and lifted him up towards the ceiling.

"Aaaah! Get them off! Get it off of me!"

Sean leapt into action, grabbing a frying pan from the stove and lunging towards the jittering claws. He hit Uncle Scooter a number of times before he scored a hit on the Shambler spawn—it didn't react.

"You're hurting me, you little shit! Aarrrgh!" Scooter yelled, the claws sinking deeper beneath his armpits.

"Quincy! Get in here!" Lilly yelled.

Quincy reached the doorway in time to see Uncle Scooter, yelling in fear and confusion but cursing all the way, disappearing up into the ventilation shaft.

Lilly cursed. "Quince, grab something to defend yourself with and get ready to blow this joint."

Blood began started to seep from the ventilation shaft, and Lilly knew it wouldn't be long before the beasts would return for fresh bait.

The trio, in shock but hyped on adrenaline and survival instinct, rushed back to the front of the café, only to meet by three wicked-looking Shambler spawn eager to eat.

One of them instantly launched itself towards Quincy, whose survival instincts reacted by whacking it with a frying pan he'd grabbed from the kitchen. The beast flew into the side of the bar, but it didn't look injured—only more agitated.

Meanwhile, Sean moved to stand in front of Lilly, wielding a couple of kitchen knives. He made some threatening gestures towards the two spawn heading his and Lilly's way. The black, gaping maw of the one closest to him seemed to tremble before releasing some sludge.

Lilly wasn't too keen on Sean trying to be her apparent

white knight, but then again he didn't know she wasn't a damsel in distress.

"Stop flashing those things and get to work with them, Sean!" she yelled, grabbing a barstool and flinging it over Sean's head towards the monster in the back.

Another loud *clunk* filled the air as Quincy once again whacked his opponent square in the sort-of jaw, and the beast fell backwards into the jukebox.

Lilly blinked in surprise. *W*

e might have a chance here, after all, she thought.

The force of the monster hitting the jukebox made the old music machine come to life, and the three makeshift monster slayers shared a quick moment of mutual understanding as they glimpsed the spawns' growing confusion from the noise.

"*Now!*" Lilly yelled valiantly over the music.

"Jeeeeesussss loves you."

Lilly took another barstool and slammed it down onto one of the spawns with her full weight. The stool knocked it off its feet, now lodged between its spikes.

"The Lord knows and sees all; He gives and takes."

Sean finished the beast off by jamming both kitchen knives hard into the top of its head.

"Hey heeeey!"

. . .

Quincy clambered on top of the bar and jumped before a spawn lunged at him. He hung awkwardly, twisted in the small lights above the bar, and pulled his feet up to avoid the razor-like claws of the gurgling beast below.

Lilly looked up at her brother in distress. To her right, Sean was fighting off the other spawn, but even in a weakened state, they were merciless and incredibly dangerous. Her mind raced.

Okay, if Quince took his time to show brawn, it's now my time to show brains. Her eyes flashed around the room before landing on the bar.

We're in the South… Rednecks everywhere, getting more dangerous by the second. Slack gun laws… That's it!

Lilly dove headfirst behind the bar, and her expectations soon met reality as she fingered the stock of a shotgun between her nimble fingers.

"Do good unto man, find your peace, and always pray."

Lilly jumped up and pointed the shotgun directly in the face of the Shambler spawn.

"Hey heeeey!" she sang with the song, then pulled the trigger.

A loud bang erupted, followed by gallons of green blood, slime, and other forms of mucus being sprayed across the bar.

Lilly heard Quincy sputtering above her. She shook her head and tried not to gaze upon the gruesome sight as she wiped some of the sludge off her face and retched. Regaining her composure, she nimbly launched herself over the bar just in time to see Sean using the last of his might to pull the jukebox off the wall and squash the remaining Shambler spawn beneath it.

.   .   .

"Hey heeeeee—"

The music abruptly stopped.

Shaken, but victorious, they gathered around and made sure nobody was seriously injured.

"Seems like we're all right." Lilly sighed in relief. "Although… Sean, I'm sorry about your uncle; it all happened so fast, we just couldn't react in time."

"Oh man. This is not how I planned to spend my day. *Damn.*" Sean lifted up his cap and swiped away some of the grime and sweat on his forehead. "I'm okay," he said. "Fine, really."

"No, it's not. I've seen a lot of death; it's not something you can shake off."

"He wasn't, like, my real uncle or anything really." Sean shrugged. "He was just some random guy I met up with on the street when things were starting to go to hell. He asked specifically for me to call him 'uncle.' Frankly, it was a bit weird and creepy."

"Okay… Is it all right then for me to feel a little less bad about Uncle Scooter now?" Quincy asked, looking slightly disgusted.

"Fair enough." Lilly chuckled, but she felt kind of sad. "Man, Sean, I've got to say you really held your ground there. I'm impressed."

"*You're* impressed? Color me all kinds of intrigued after seeing you handle this situation with the wits and skills of a…" He stopped and looked at her funny. "You're in the force, aren't you?"

"Yup, well, I was. Vet. Something tells me I'm not alone."

"North-East, 34th squadron, also known as—"

"The *Rad-Heads*," Lilly finished. "Yeah, I've heard of you. You guys were the first response team in New York when the Plague Children reports came, right?"

"Really?" Quincy stood up from the crooked barstool with

a groan. "The city was in lockdown for two weeks during that time. I was holed up in the New York Public Library for most of it. So in a way, I owe my life to you, *twice* now."

"Please!" Sean laughed. "Don't do that. I was just doing my job, back then and just now. History has a knack for repeating itself, so don't get too hung up on it."

"You're still in?" Lilly curiously stared him down; she guessed him to be around the age that most soldiers either retire or kick the bucket.

"I'm on leave for an undetermined time," he replied. "Docs are probably poking through my brain scans right now, determining if I still have the guts and willpower to go at it for another round."

Lilly could see he was really proud of the things he did, whether it was on or off duty. She recognized the gallantness of a spirited soldier, and in some way she was jealous. Nevertheless, she found herself glad to have Sean in their midst. To her, he felt trustworthy—at least somewhat.

"What do we do now?" Quincy took a quick peek in the kitchen and averted his eyes after seeing the carnage leaking down from the ventilation shaft.

Before anyone could speak, they heard voices from outside making their way towards the front door. Lilly was horrified to see that their fight had broken up the entire barricade they had built in front of the entrance. Figures appeared in front of the matted glass.

"Wonder if that coffee is done," a voice said from just next to the window.

"I could sure go for a damn good cup of coffee right now, sir," another one replied.

"Maybe some cherry pie to go with it. *Hmm.*"

The door opened, and Sean and the twins stood face-to-face with a high-ranking GDF commander and his two subordinates.

"What in tarnation is this?" the commander demanded.

In the wake of their triumph, Quincy felt a lot more

relieved than before. They had beaten the odds, and his body surged with adrenaline.

"This is what happens when you let stray civilians do your apparent dirty work... sir," he said to the commander. Ha! Only Emily Swansong could've taught her children flair and wits like that.

Lilly's mouth fell open. "Quincy! I..." She couldn't contain herself and burst into laughter.

The commander didn't seem to be in the best of moods after that, but he relented and glanced over the broken, squashed, and oozing Shambler corpses. While the troops were out patrolling and waiting for their coffee to finish, a trio of civilians managed to neutralize a significant threat.

At least, "significant threat" to these clowns, the commander thought as he watched Lilly making an attempt at stifling her laughter while Quincy tried to explain to her that it "Wasn't *that* funny!" and Sean was just hanging over a crooked barstool, taking in the scene.

"Just the three of you then?" the commander asked, eying them in suspicion.

The twins exchanged glances between themselves and Sean.

"Yes, sir" Sean replied, nodding.

The commander turned around to face one of his subordinates. "Aberdeen," he started, "we're taking these three to the library safe house. Afterwards, you report to First-Response Commander Honovi of the Gray Hounds. Give him your assessment of this block, and be sure to include the fact that there may be stray Shambler spawn about."

"Yes, sir," the soldier named Aberdeen said. He beckoned Sean and the twins to follow him out.

"A library shelter," Quincy whispered to himself.

"Like I said," Sean muttered, "history tends to repeat itself."

Chapter 5

THE GREEN CHAMBER still glowed with an unnatural hue; it was a damp, dark place where water could be heard trickling down on even the quietest of occasions. There was a mish-mash of strange machinery working nonstop now: vents, tubes, boiling pots, and flickering lights. A yellowed tendril snapped off its protective braces, and an inhuman howl could be heard all through the chamber.

"Why do you hurt yourself, my brother?" a raspy voice moaned, electric and distant. It was as if the voice was not directly present in the chamber itself but rather sounded as if it came from beyond a veil, millions of light-years away in an immense and hostile galaxy.

"I... refuse," another metallic voice boomed, "to be... enslaved."

"*We*," the first voice corrected. To an untrained listener, every articulation would feel like a knife stabbing in one's ears. "*We* must... have... faith..."

. . .

The slimy yellowed tendril landed with a blow on one of the glowing panels in front of the vises in which the entity was encased. An alarm went off in the distance.

"They," the second voice started, muffled in pain, "the heirs… are… struggling… must… help…"

The stalk-like appendage slammed into another one of the panels. The alarm screeched louder in the odd, obsidian black chamber. A huge shadowy form, like a gelatinous cone, erupted from the pod, and claw-like appendages began flailing around.

"No…" the first voice buzzed sharply as the sound of a million insects crawling around erupted from the other voice. "Brother. Do… Not… Do this…"

"They…" the second voice stopped and howled again from the pain of a thousand dead solar systems that had burned up in ancient times, many dark millennia ago. "They… must… Succeed… Brother."

The library was but a short and luckily uneventful hike from the bistro. The group had a bit of a fright when a set of garbage cans flew aggressively across the pavement, but it turned out to be a poltergeist. The sight of the GDF uniform made it realize its mistake, and it proceeded to scamper off into an alleyway, mumbling under its breath.

Upon entering the grand building, the twins felt relief for the first time in what seemed like ages. The Global Defense Force were a group dedicated to the safety of humanity and exemplary in their craft and were by no means affiliated with Haven. Haven's operations tended to be focused a lot more on harnessing supernatural power rather than fighting it, at least from what little Lilly and Quincy had heard of them. However, they hadn't forgotten their spat with one of their agents earlier, so the mysterious organization's reputation at least proved to be somewhat true.

The grand halls of the library were dark due to the power

outage, but field lamps powered by the GDF's generators made sure everything that mattered was well lit. Other sections of the library were boarded off due to being not yet cleared of hazards, one way or another, and there were those sections that were only lit by candlelight, providing the more introverted of civilians a place to rest their feet away from the ruckus of military strategy and overall hysteria.

When the group arrived, Sean went out to rendezvous with the active leadership on duty at the time. A soldier through and through, Sean wouldn't back away from a fight and was actively pursuing a chance to put on a uniform and get into the fray. Lilly watched him leave before she and Quincy overheard some soldiers mention that Haven personnel had been spotted in Lafayette and that they might be on the way to the library to check up with GDF intelligence.

It was clear by their reactions that most of the GDF higher-ups detested Haven, but their knowledge on certain aspects of supernatural and paranormal activity required the two agencies to work together on more than a few occasions.

After the conversation shifted to another topic, the twins quickly scurried off to a less crowded section of the library.

They ultimately found a lonesome corner in the lower right corner of the library's first floor. Quincy, being the bookworm he was, decided to pass the time browsing the local mythology section while Lilly stared out of the window. She still felt on edge as she replayed the events of the last twenty-four hours in her head.

"Why are we here, Quince?"

"Hmm, what?" Quincy lifted his head out of a book on bridges that were haunted by satyrs and yawned.

"How did it ever come to this? Why are we here?" Lilly repeated.

"Well, there's the thing with the Haven agent that came to us, our inheritance, guns… lots of guns and…"

"I mean *why*, Quince? Yesterday, we were both living a

semi-normal, albeit boring I admit, life. I worked in a pet shop, and you were in college. All it took was one letter, an inheritance, and, *voilà*, here we are, running for our lives, going nowhere apparently, and the worst thing is…"

"We don't even know why we're running in the first place," Quincy finished. He closed the book in front of him, picked up a candle, and wandered over to Lilly.

Quincy tried to wipe the dripping wax from his jacket as he spoke. "Look, I haven't got the faintest clue either. But don't let it get into your head. We'll get out of this. It's our inheritance they want, right? We have no idea why they'd want it, but the letter said we could never let it fall into the wrong hands. We made a promise to Mom and Dad."

"Ugh, I'm just…so *pissed off* right now. I actually *liked* that damn pet store, Quince." Her hands curled into fists. *"Dammit!"*

"Just relax for a second." He paused, looking around. "Listen, we may not know what the heck this key is for. But we didn't drag the thing along just to wait for who knows what. We're in a library, let me do some research on it. Let's see if *we* can figure out why this thing is so important."

Lilly managed to conjure up half a smile. "That's… actually not a bad idea at all."

"You look over there," he instructed and pointed to the left set of bookcases, "and I'll check these out. Just drop anything remotely interesting or relevant on the table there."

"Let's see," Lilly whispered to herself as she began reading titles. "*Tales From the Crypt*… no. *Essays on Chthonic Manuscripts*, yuck, no… *A Barbecue Fanatic's Guide to Midgard*, eh…"

A loud rumble came from one of the bookcases. It startled them, and Lilly's eyes flashed around, looking for the source. It sounded like it came from another room adjacent to theirs. But then more sounds started to ring out from behind the bookshelves in front of them. Oh right, I nearly forgot about *him*. How great.

"The weather is pretty bad in Midgard this time of year,

not many barbeques going on, so not much use for leg meat. Muahahaaaa." The voice was deep and creaky; it sounded muffled but still clear enough so there wasn't any doubt on what it just said.

What the fuck? Lilly shot her brother a look before saying aloud,

"Hello?" Lilly poked the bookshelf, not ready to lay her ear against it just yet.

"Hi," the voice said. "Did I frighten you? Did my voice chill your very bones to the core? Did you want to cry out to a godless heaven? Did it make you want to vomit up your smaller intestine?"

"Not…really?" Quincy raised an eyebrow. "You did make us jump though, just a little bit."

"Muahahahahahahahahaaaaaa!"

"So…" Lilly knocked on the wooden planks. "Who… *what* are you? *Where* are you?"

"I seem to be in a predicament of sorts," the voice replied and pretty much ignored the questions entirely. "Would you perhaps, if you'd be so kind, lend me some assistance?"

"I'm not sure if we're too keen on helping someone, *something*, that has any knowledge on how to best prepare a human leg," Quincy retorted, pulling up a chair and sitting back down at the table. He pulled a stack of books towards him with a sigh.

"Oh, go to your books, Quince." Lilly looked at him in slight contempt. "It never said anything about *human* legs. I, for one, am intrigued." She shoved some books from the shelf and tried to get as close to the wall as possible. "So how can I possibly help, oh ye invisible *force to be reckoned with*?" She shot a smile towards her brother when he snorted.

"You see the top shelf and second book to the right?" the voice vibrated through the wall.

"*Pins and Needles* by M.F. Goodsoup," Lilly confirmed. "That's the one?"

"Yes, pull it."

Lilly grabbed the book with two hands and pulled it backwards.

Nothing bad happened. What *did* happen was that a small door about four foot high off the ground opened in the book-case near the window on the opposite side.

Quincy walked up and pulled Lilly aside. "Are you sure about this? It might be a trickster, or worse."

"I know how to deal with them, and if it were any worse, this whole library would be blown sky-high already." Her eyes sparkled, and Quincy knew there was no talking her out of it. "Go back and read your books; I'll handle this. We're the last Swansongs. Weirdness is in our blood."

Somehow, Quincy got the feeling that it was his sister that this thing should be worried about and not the other way around. "Just be careful, okay?"

The small door led to a series of disorienting, crooked tunnels through the back wall of the library. The air was damp and stuffy, and Lilly found it hard to breathe at times. There was little in the way of light, and the single candle she brought with her provided less than adequate relief over the lingering darkness spread before her.

After ten minutes of scrambling in the dark, Lilly was relieved to emerge into a bigger room. She fumbled around before finding an old candelabra coated with wax and some usable candle stumps. She lit her candle's wick atop the sad-looking stumps and then took a good look around.

The tiny room looked old, ancient even. There were book-cases reaching all the way to the top of the chamber, and loose manuscripts, rolls of parchment, and paper were strewn all about.

Broken quills and empty inkpots littered the small space, not to mention the abundance of spider webs that made Lilly's skin crawl. There were also magnifying glasses, tiny fossils, big fossils, fossilized bones, rough gemstones, polished gemstones, gemstones that were in the process of being made into jewelry, and pretty much an entire collection of odd knickknacks and strange artifacts from bygone times.

It had all the makings of an office—it even had a window—but it seemed as if no one had been around here for a very long time. Lilly shoved some paperwork off the desk and carefully placed the candelabra and her candle down. She dusted off the old leather chair as best as she could and sat, her eyes darting across the room.

"So…" She tried shaking off the uneasy feeling the room gave her. "Where are you?"

An eerie gust of cold wind blew through the office; the old primordial bones rattled, and the bookcases shook violently. The wind scattered the parchments throughout the room.

"Stop playing games," Lilly huffed. "Show yourself. You're not impressing me with these silly tricks."

Though, she was amused. She grew up in a world where the mere sensation of such strange phenomena would send most people running for the hills. But not in their contemporary society, and certainly not for someone with her experience.

"Oh my, such a young face," something invisible in front of her whispered. "Did you know I was already considered old when the first of your kind started to hop out of the prehistoric oceans?"

"Buddy, I've heard this before." Lilly turned to scan the room. "Look, I'm sure you are *oh so evil*, but if you were a real threat, I wouldn't be here right now looking at how your old pieces of paper have superior dancing skills compared to me."

"Are you sure, little one?" The voice now came from behind her; it seemed to come from inside the back wall, just a little further from where Quincy was doing his research. "Aren't you in the least bit scared? Perhaps doubting yourself a little more each second? What if I *am* as powerful as I claim? What if I am simply playing with you? Toying around before I destroy your puny race once and for all?" A pause, then, "Muahahahahahahahaaaaa!"

"Show yourself, or I'm leaving."

The voice was now singing an eerie lullaby above her. "Look," she started, tapping her foot with impatience, "I came here because you asked us to help you. Since you didn't reach your grubby paws or whatever it is you have through the bookcases already, I'm inclined to believe you really do need the help. So show yourself, or I'm out."

"Just a little bit longer? Please?" The voice came from under the desk near her legs.

"No," she shook her head in defiance. "And *ew*? Get out of there, pervert."

From the top of the bookcase, the one just right of the window behind Lilly, came a noise that sounded like a big anchor scraping itself against the side of a ship.

Then, an old oil lamp flung itself off the top of the shelf and onto the desk—

"Boo!" came a booming voice from inside of the lamp.

Lilly yawned. On the inside, she could see a swirl of pink and indigo colors, like a sheet of soft velvet that was twirling around endlessly. The inside sparkled too, like many stars shining across some faraway nebula in a display of raw chaotic, and beautiful, cosmic force. Briefly, she glimpsed two glowing yellow eyes staring at her from the colored mass. They stared at her expectantly as if to say, *"Well? Go on!"*

"Oh…" Lilly sighed, unimpressed. "Ehm… *yikes*?"

"Muhahahahahahahaaaaaaa!" the voice roared. "No one can escape my unholy terror. Men, women and children, outsiders, and gods all bow before my might. *Bow* before me, mortal! Bow before Timaxoatilaciluzipta!"

"Yeah, no," Lilly replied with a smirk. "Wait, *what* did you say you were called? Timaxi… Ti…what?"

"Timaxoatilaciluzipta, annihilator of *worlds*!" the voice replied in excitement.

"*Riiiight...*" She blew a lock of hair away from her face. "Can I call you... Tim?"

A huff, then, "You may, I guess."

"Good. Tell me then, Tim, you're a *Fire Vampire*, aren't you?"

If there was one skill that Lilly learned in the force that she could then take with her to her next job as exotic pet store clerk, it was the identification: biological make-up and ecology of newly discovered exotic and extra-terrestrial species.

"How... how did you know?"

"Consider it natural instinct," Lilly lied.

Fire Vampires, from what knowledge she had about them, were extremely dangerous. If Tim had not been trapped in this oil lamp, she knew that he would absolutely be able to deliver on all of the promises of destruction he described. She also remembered them having a sort of hive mind, but, considering none of his kin had come to his rescue, it appeared to be either a myth or the unusual oil lamp blocked out telepathic communication. Either way, Lilly wasn't ready to find out yet.

"Are you going to help me or not?" Tim growled in annoyance.

"I don't know yet," she muttered and poked the lamp's side. "You're obviously very dangerous, and I don't see how we would be able to help you anyway."

"We?"

Shit, Lilly thought. *That wasn't necessary. Eh, better to play along for now.* "Me and my brother, you heard him across the book-case, remember?" She pointed to the other side of the room as if the vampire could see what she was pointing to.

"Ah. But I suspected the poor boy has died of fright from our initial encounter by now, heheheheheee."

"Keep your pants on, Tim. You're not exactly the most

intimidating thing in the world within this lamp. How'd you end up in there in the first place?"

"Foolish mortal! How dare you speak to me in that manner? Remind me to destroy your very essence the moment you unleash me from my cage!" The lamp shook. "Muhaha-hahahaaa!"

"Oh, I'm *really* inclined to help you now…" If her sarcasm had a smell, it would level an entire city block. "You didn't answer my question; speak up."

"I don't want to talk about it."

"Then I can't help you."

"Oh, please!"

"I need to know what happened exactly. Tell me all of the facts, then I can decide if I want to help you," she paused, "but only if you promise to let me and my brother go when we get you out, *if* we get you out."

"I'll make no such promises."

The swirling mass in the oil lamp flashed orange and blue for a moment.

"Okay. Goodbye, Tim." Lilly stood up and readied herself to go back into the tunnels.

"Wait! Okay, okay!" The oil lamp jumped up and down in panic. "You might be a stupid human, but you drive a hard bargain."

Lilly rolled her eyes but turned back around. "All right, talk."

"I was put here in this sorry state by a mediocre, perhaps slightly above average, sorcerer from your mortal plane. He summoned me from across time and space to this forsaken chamber and managed to ensnare me before I could get the word out to my kin."

"Aren't you a servant of Cthugha? The Great Old One?" Lilly remembered reading August Derleth in high school, another great author now proclaimed prophet. He was rumored to be a disciple of H.P. Lovecraft and some other famous writers from that era, including her great uncle W.A.

Swansong. *Ahem,* Swansong arguably being the most famous and best amongst them, *naturally*.

"Ah, pishposh!" Tim ticked against the glass in annoyance. "That weak excuse of a mage asked me the same thing. We are *not* servants. Cthugha was a living star, eons ago and many light-years away from your doomed planet. But there was another celestial, a great beacon of living matter, that clashed with her. They battled for millennia, each trying to earn their rightful place as the more powerful among the great kin of the cosmos. Cthugha eventually lost the battle, and she exploded into a great supernova, a fiery flash that was seen across the universe for eternity, up until this very day. We are the fiery bits of offspring that escaped the fury of destruction. We are not *servants*; we *are* Cthugha."

"Didn't you say your name was Tim-something?"

"Details. Something beyond your comprehension, mortal."

"And yet, you got yourself captured, by a human none-theless." Lilly couldn't help but laugh. "Who was he? Did he have a name?"

"Aleister Crowley."

Quincy closed the laptop computer, a grin on his face. Sean's contacts with the GDF really paid off in helping him acquire everything he needed for his research. When it finally clicked in his head, he prided himself on uncovering the mystery of W.A. Swansong's last letter and couldn't wait to tell Lilly.

He put some books away, then waltzed back to the table and pulled the candle closer to him. The only thing that was left was to uncover what William meant by *"stream."*

A door popped open in the back bookcase, and a panting Lilly came crouching out, holding a candelabra in one hand and an oil lamp giving off a strange purple hue in the other.

"Great, you're back!" Quincy sighed with relief. He'd been

glancing towards the little bookcase door every so often, hoping Lilly was doing all right.

"Hello, puny human. What is it like to come face-to-face with your worst fears? The total embodiment of all your terror? Muahahahahaaaaa!" Tim's wispy voice resounded through the empty library hall.

"Wha-what's this?" Quincy took a few steps back from the lamp.

"This," Lilly started, swinging the lamp onto the table, "is a Fire Vampire trapped over a hundred years ago by none other than Aleister Crowley."

"Crowley? You're kidding."

"Nope. It was apparently something of an experiment. Crowley cursed Tim—that's his shortened name by the way, don't ask. Anyway, he cursed Tim into forever being trapped within this device. Unless…"

"Unless?" Quincy asked, hovering closer to the remarkable lamp.

"Ugh…" The voice from within groaned.

"Unless," Lilly said with a grin, "he performs no less than three good, non-selfish deeds for the betterment and enhancement of all humanity."

Quincy chuckled in disbelief. "Well, sounds like you're screwed."

"Do not mock me, fool. I will tear up your world and bring you all down with me! I still have power within this shell of the damned! Beware, mortal, *beware!*"

"Feisty," Quincy teased and moved in to get a closer look. "Why did you bring him along?"

"Well, you heard him. He still has some power, and considering he can only use it for the betterment of mankind, I figured he may become useful," she said, her eyes sparkling with glee.

"Don't you think it's dangerous?"

"Well, not for us, not for now." Lilly's eyes fell on the

remaining stack of books on the table. "In other news, what did you manage to find out about our key?"

"Oh! Glad you asked. Sit down; this is great," Quincy said before pulling the chair next to him back and offering her the seat. Lilly threw herself into the chair in exhaustion and put her feet up on the chair opposite her. She edged closer to Quincy to nose over his notes.

"So Sean's buddies from the GDF were kind enough to provide me with a laptop and a strong battery to go with it. I then used the mobile hotspot from my phone to create a Wi-Fi point and, *boom*, internet." Quincy looked proud.

"Cool! Go on."

"So the first thing I did was to take a good look at some of the more distinguishing marks and features on our key. Turns out, it's real silver, and the turquoise gemstones are real as well."

"How do you know?"

"I took some classes in geology once for extra credit, and the GDF boys gave me this nifty-looking magnifying glass... Anyway, I traced the key's origins back to the Navajo tribe of Native Americans."

"Really? That's interesting. Some native tribes do appear in William's stories, but I don't recall the Navajo playing a big part."

"Right," Quincy confirmed. "Still, it's pretty cool, but wait until you see this!" Quincy clicked twice before a slideshow of pictures appeared showing all kinds of Navajo jewelry, then he pulled up a text document headed *The Shadow Beyond Time and Space by W.A. Swansong*. Lilly saw several words highlighted in the manuscript as Quincy scrolled through it. I've always been fond of these kinds of riddles.

"What? Swansong?" Tim interjected.

"At first, I had no idea what the numbers meant that were in William's letter," Quincy said, ignoring Tim as a smile manifested on his face. "But after giving it some thought, I wondered how large of a story *The Shadow Beyond Time and*

Space was in terms of word count, and it was then that it hit me."

He took out the old yellowed letter they had received and pointed to the first block of numbers. "Look, two thousand two hundred and sixty-one. When you use the text-processor program, it's super easy to find things regarding the word count. So it wasn't very hard to figure out that the two thousand two hundred and sixty-first word in the story was *take*."

"I think I'm starting to figure out what you're getting at." Lilly burned with anticipation. For all the bad luck the twins had in the last couple of days, this started to look more and more like a genuine mystery waiting to be solved, and she felt lucky she had a brother with the brains to do it. Like I said before, together these two could be unstoppable. Sometimes, they'd only need a little push in the right direction.

"The next word is the four thousand eight hundred and eighty-sixth, which is *key*."

"*Take key…* I'll be damned!"

"Let me have a look at that thing!" Tim pleaded; his lamp shook from one side to the next. Quincy shoved the laptop closer to his sister and pointed at the screen.

"The whole string of numbers in the letter…" Quincy pointed at the bottom of the letter which said "

The Shadow Beyond Time and Space 2261 4886 6092 1377 7101 4814 8007 3272"

and waited for her to nod before saying,

"The whole string translates into '*Take key. Go westward toward desert. Three stream.*'"

"Whoa," Lilly exclaimed. "This is exciting! So tell me, I get the first two parts of the message, but what does this last bit mean, '*Three stream?*' That doesn't make sense."

"That's the one thing that I've been trying to wrap my head around too. I don't have a clue yet."

"Don't sweat it." Lilly nudged him when he frowned. "We'll figure it out together. This is amazing though. We're like… on a quest, a quest given to us by W.A. Swansong himself."

Upon hearing the name again, Tim started to shine with an eerie red glow. "W.A. Swansong," he whispered again. "You know him?"

"He is, *was*, our great uncle," Quincy reluctantly replied, finally giving in to the Fire Vampire's desire for attention.

"My, my," the vampire said, and the lamp scooted a little bit closer towards them. "You *are* two very particular individuals, aren't you?"

"We try not to be," Lilly replied.

"A little late for that since you're staring right into the foggy dew of *death* himself, *me*. Particular indeed. Too bad you don't seem to grasp the most simplest of solutions when it stares at you right in your face."

"What do you mean?" Quincy asked. The lamp

pushed itself between them, drenching the faint candle-light and the darkness around them in a weird indigo tone.

"The Navajo have a strange way with words," Tim said in a hushed and grim tone. "They have one of the most unique syntax systems on your planet, but they don't have the biggest library of words in itself. Translating the word '*stream*' to Navajo would roughly result in '**tó nilįįh**.' But the Navajo don't have a word for '*stream*,' so it would pretty much translate back as '*small river*' or even just '*river*.'"

Suddenly the atlas in front of Quincy flew open to reveal an old 1920s map of New Mexico.

"There…"

"Three Rivers…" the twins said in unison.

Quincy picked up the laptop and did a quick search for Three Rivers. His eyes darted from left to right for a bit before he closed the laptop again and looked up at Lilly.

"Three Rivers was an old settlement in the northwest of New Mexico. It's situated right in the middle of the desert, and… Lilly, this is it."

. . .

Lilly nearly pushed her brother out of his seat from enthusiasm when he paused, studying the atlas.

"It's in the middle of the Navajo territory!" she realized, reopening the laptop and glancing at the screen. Her voice echoed through the halls of the library. You see? Just a *push* in the right direction is all it takes.

Tim's lamp shuffled from side to side in an offbeat manner that grabbed their attention. His yellow eyes popped from the swirling vortex and gazed straight towards the twins.

"You owe me a boon," he said. "I know how you humans work. Most of you are honest and just—you get a favor and are inclined to pay it back."

Tim sizzled with pleasure.

Quincy and Lilly exchanged glances before Quincy said,
"Sure, we will think of something."

Alarm bells started to ring throughout the building. In a matter of seconds, Sean came racing into the hall, looking very worried and sweating like crazy.

"We need to go *now*, guys! The Shambler is coming right for us! I have no idea what to do; the protocol is out the window with GDF is now taking orders from Haven agents." They gaped at him as he waved his arms. "Come on, we gotta move!"

Lilly swiped the lamp up from the table, and the twins bolted towards Sean. Quincy slid the key and letters back into his pocket as he ran. They had just reached Sean when a dark figure rose up behind him and smacked him on the head with a blackened club.

Agent Reyes stepped out of the shadows as they stumbled back.

"Ah. The missing children," he snarled. "Such a shame about Agent Preston, don't you agree?"

Agent Reyes sneered at his giant lackey beside him. He was a towering man, well over two meters in height and almost equally as broad. The only thing the meathead really lacked was a good pair of brains to go with it. But Agent Reyes liked him this way—dumb and resourceful.

"Take them away, Pauli," Reyes ordered. "Let us see if we can give them the riveting experience of seeing the insides of a Dimensional Shambler."

I absolutely do *not* recommend such an experience.

Chapter 6

A LITTLE OVER one hundred years ago, the townsfolk of Lafayette were simply overjoyed to see how well the construction of their new library was progressing. However, many of the folk who regularly wandered the vicinity of the new library during those more peaceful winter mornings would remember the day the unnerving, crooked, bald man was seen.

It hadn't been a particularly special day, but many good Lafayette citizens got the feeling that something wasn't quite right as they awoke that morning. Little bits of bad luck happened all around the city: from kettles that fell from the fire, to breaking stairs, to electrical failures across town. And then there was the tragic death of Bubby, a friendly raccoon beloved by many across the city.

Those who went on regular walks recalled seeing a strange, evil-looking man wandering the new library's construction site. He was seen whispering to the foreman and scooting through the unfinished corridors of what eventually would be the library's second floor. Upon seeing the man and making eye contact with him, many felt an intense feeling of dread creep up from within the very core of their being.

Others had heard his name whispered by the construction crew: "Mr. Aleister Crowley is permitted full access wherever he wishes to be. No, he doesn't need a hat. No, I don't make the rules, men."

Those that heard that damned name fell ill or experienced nightmares, night terrors, or sleep paralysis attacks for weeks afterwards.

But it was the case of Miss Rosa Blair that was the most tragic. She had been wandering about in the early afternoon, having just come back from her biweekly trip to the grocer. She had seen the bald man before on her first passing of the site and had heard the man's wicked name on her second passing. But on the third passing, she had bumped into him by accident when he had been crouching on the side of the road, speaking gibberish and nonsense.

That evening, Rosa Blair went to sleep and never woke up. And to this very day, it is said that she lies in her coffin, not alive but not entirely dead either. She is still dreaming, dreaming of the terrible bald man in the Lafayette streets and will hear his name screamed into her ears for all eternity as his terrible visage haunts her consciousness.

Most of all, she dreams of the man's insane ravings every night, from now until the end of all existence: "*This is it! Yes! The site of the first deed! From deep within the void of the world, from the dawn of the first sun, there comes the beast for which time and space has no boundaries. The first test, the first deed is nigh.*"

Yes, Crowley could be an absolute loon at times, but what he did here at the library, huh, even *I* couldn't predict that.

The streets outside the library were unrecognizable now. A deep purple sludge covered everything: houses, cars, plants—nothing was safe.

A little off in the distance, a towering behemoth of terrible nightmares loomed in the eerie shadows of the early morning.

Its howl sent reality bending, and to behold it was to see madness itself.

Four huge legs covered in slime, tentacles, and exoskeletal-like claws lumbered slowly towards the library. On top, the thing was a mess of eyes, talons, and blackness. And once in a while, there were other things, things that might or might not be real, things that seemed to flicker in and out of existence as it moved.

Agent Reyes and Pauli emerged onto the street with a dozen or so Haven agents in tow—all of them wore black and sported sunglasses, and all of them were armed to the teeth with guns, martial weapons, bombs, and some even had experimental energy weaponry.

"I don't get it! What could you possibly want from us?" Lilly pleaded as she was dragged forward.

Actually, she had a pretty good idea what Haven wanted, but she had already agreed with her brother that in the unlucky event of capture, it was best to act as oblivious as possible.

"Shut your trap, girl." Pauli raised his hand as if to strike her, but Agent Reyes cleared his throat.

"I think it's safe to say that you know damn well what we want," Agent Reyes said. "Why don't you give it up now so we'll both be spared from this mess?"

Quincy had kept quiet so far. The situation they found themselves in wasn't exactly his expertise, but his mind raced with scenarios and possibilities. He thought of everything they could possibly do or say to get them out of this mess, examined every possible outcome with precision, but none of them ended favorably. The only thing he could do right now was to hold on tight to the silver key in his palm, safely hidden away in his pocket, and not let go. Lilly clutched the lamp close to her chest. It appeared for all intents and purposes to be just an ordinary oil lamp.

Pauli pushed the twins down onto a broken car in the

middle of the road and tied them up. Lilly spat in his face, and his huge fist landed across her right cheek.

"Damn you!" Quincy cursed as he saw his sister lose consciousness. "We haven't done anything, we don't *know* anything, why won't you let us go?"

"Tick tock, Mr. Swansong," Agent Reyes mocked. "The Shambler spawn may be under control, but we both know that they are mere peanuts in comparison to their bigger half. Don't we?"

A horrifying howl came from the misty streets of Lafayette. In the early morning glow, Quincy could see the huge lumbering blackness of the Dimensional Shambler creeping towards them. From the corner of his eye, Quincy saw Sean racing towards them along the library's main walkway, but he was quickly halted by the Haven agents patrolling about.

"Sean!" Quincy yelled. "Help us! Get the commander, anyone from GDF, I believe this could be straight-out murder!"

"I can't do anything!" Sean yelled back, and Quincy could hear the defeat in his voice. "Haven's got this place on lockdown now. Stuff came in from the higher-up, and GDF is pulling out; I don't understand any of it!"

Haven agents started pushing Sean back into the building, when Lilly came to her senses, her eyes darting around before she leaned closer to her brother.

"Get that scrub out of here!" Agent Reyes ordered before he turned around. "Now, Mr. Swansong. I see your sister is starting to come back to us. Why don't you tell me where the artifact you inherited is before I ask Pauli here to cause some more damage."

"I don't know," Quincy pleaded, but something itched in the back of his mind. He glanced over at Lilly, and from what he could tell, she was thinking the same. He took a deep breath. "If you want it so bad, why didn't you just take it from us?"

Lilly started laughing when Reyes glared. "Because he doesn't even know what he's looking for!" She smirked. "You're calling people scrubs all around, but you're grasping at straws!"

"When the Shambler comes and takes us…" Quincy stopped and stared off at the incoming horror. He swallowed. "You won't even have anything to show for it. We're no good to you dead, especially not dead on another plane of existence."

Agent Reyes was visibly fuming at this point. The twins had cornered him, and he knew he had to put pressure on them quick.

A loud, audible groan came from above them; the Shambler was almost on top of them.

"Pauli," Reyes started and flicked his fingers, "search them. I want every single trinket on them delivered to me personally."

The big brute smiled wickedly as he lumbered towards the car. Quincy broke out in a sweat—he was all out of ideas, and their attempt at stumping Agent Reyes had only half-worked.

Lilly, on the other hand, had an idea.

"We don't have it *on* us, you idiot!" she lied. "Don't you think we'd store it in a safe place or leave it with a person we can trust? Especially when we heard your buffoons were knocking at the library door…"

"I don't believe you," Agent Reyes exclaimed, but he gulped audibly, and there was a sliver of a doubt in his eyes. Lilly picked up on it and prepared herself for the final gamble.

"Fine," she said, rolling her eyes. "Go and get Sean, the GDF soldier who was just here. He has it. Tell him to get the lamp over here now."

"It's that old oil lamp? Interesting."

Lilly hid a smile; she knew she had him. "And please hurry up! This thing is right on top of us!"

The vague outline of the terrible Dimensional Shambler was now a fully-fledged juggernaut; it was blocking the faint morning sunrays that managed to slip through the clouds and mist entirely. Its horrible ooze-covered and bubbling legs were less than a hundred yards away.

"Hurry up!" she yelped, panicked.

The horrific monstrosity was edging nearer, and the gruesome howls that came from it vibrated through the air. A nasty, terrible smell, a combination of sulfur and diamond dust, of moonlight and rotten eggs, started to drift through the streets. Quincy gagged.

Sean appeared from the library, holding the lamp with Tim inside close to his chest. He ran towards the car but stopped when Agent Reyes held up a hand.

"Is this what you wanted?" Sean yelled to no one in particular.

The noises from the monster were deafening; sounds of gunfire and yelling protruded the air as Shambler spawn started to fall off the giant monster and into the fray of Haven agents and scattered GDF troops.

"I'll take that!" Agent Reyes reached out his hand towards the lamp that Sean was clutching.

"Throw it towards the Shambler, Sean!" Lilly yelled from the top of her lungs. "Do it *now*! At its feet! *Go!*"

Quincy looked at his sister. If she was indeed planning to do what he thought she was doing, then she was more brilliant than he ever was. And brave, amazingly brave. He was also impressed, given the circumstances, how lucky they were to have found a trapped Fire Vampire with great power only to be used for good—well, at least for the moment.

Sean gathered his strength and threw the lamp as far as he could manage.

"HEYYYYY!!" Tim yelled as he flew through the air.

"Why would you do that?!" Agent Reyes grabbed his head in disbelief before sprinting towards the place where the lamp had landed. He giggled a little maniacally when he found it unscathed, but didn't seem to notice he was right underneath the gigantic body of the Dimensional Shambler.

Sean leapt to action and sucker-punched Pauli in the gut. The big hunk went down with a groan. Sean murmured something about "the bigger they are…" as he clambered on top of the car to cut the twins free.

Lilly slid to the ground and eyed Quincy expectantly, waiting for him to finish the job. He turned around, taking in the display of madness.

"Three feet. Six feet. Nine. Twelve," he counted to himself out loud. "Now, Tim, do it! Your first good deed!"

Agent Reyes looked up in confusion. "Wait, what?"

At that moment, a blinding flash lit up the entire township of Lafayette. Lilly, Quincy, and Sean closed their eyes, blinded by the light. The earth shook beneath them, and a low growling noise, an endless deep bass tone, vibrated through their bodies.

A last thunderous howl roared through the clouds, and for a brief moment, there was the sensation as if a thousand galaxies had opened up before them.

Then, in a flash, all was quiet.

The Shambler and its spawn were gone, as was Agent Reyes. Everyone who was on the street—be it GDF soldier, Haven agent, or civilian—all had a brief, terrifying glimpse into another world: a world of silt and green seawater, of barren rock and lifeless desert. A hostile world that in a billion years could never be inhabited by mankind, not by a long shot.

It was the place where Agent Reyes ended up breathing his last breath. He would not live long enough to give the situation any real thought, but he still cursed himself for one thing: He couldn't even make his superior pay for *another goddamn funeral*.

. . .

As the light subsided and Lafayette returned to a somewhat normal state, the daze that had overcome the crowd trickled away, but there was mucus and other nasty stuff everywhere. A lot of the buildings were half-destroyed or on fire due to the Shambler stampeding.

Lilly's eyes slowly regained their sight, and the first thing she saw was the old oil lamp lying unharmed in the center of the road ahead of them.

"One down, two to go! I like you, Swansongs! Muahaha-hahaha!" Tim yelled victoriously. "Now put me back the right way around; I don't like lying on my side."

Lilly glanced behind her and grabbed Quincy's and Sean's hands. "*Run!*" she yelled, and the trio sprinted towards the lamp.

Quincy lifted Tim from the ground, and they disappeared in the winding city alleyways before any of the leftover Haven agents were capable of reacting.

"Victorious, my... brother." The green and gray being shifted around in its prison. "They... are..."

"On... their... way..." The other metallic voice rasped. "Bless... the heirs..."

"May they... be... unharmed," said Abel.

"Until... we... meet," responded Caine.

To put it lightly, I am very disappointed by your progress so far. Agent Preston was a fanatic unfit for negotiation duties, and Agent Reyes was a blind lapdog who'd do anything to get ahead, including all the wrong things. I suggest you drop the imbeciles and apply heavier methods in order to procure the artifact. You know what this means. Do NOT disappoint me again.

· · ·

The Haven superior read through the email again, then closed the browser window and picked up his phone. "Get me the warlock."

Lilly, Quincy, and Sean ran. They ran as far as their legs could carry them across the early morning streets of Lafayette.

Quincy's usually slick hair was a mess of sweat and blood, and Lilly only now became aware of the many cuts and bruises she sustained when they were tied up. Sean seemed the least flustered of the three, but his eyes betrayed his demeanor, and it was clear how fatigued he was and how much the day's events had rattled him.

Rounding the corner, the trio came upon a parking lot and stopped to catch their breath.

"So…" Sean leaned on the hood of a car, panting. "I have no idea what you two are exactly about, but through all of the ruckus, I did hear one name that kept coming back: Swansong."

"That's right. We're Swansongs, the last remaining heirs, in fact," Quincy said through gritted teeth. "We're on a mission, we think; we're not exactly sure ourselves."

"We can trust you, can't we, Sean?" Lilly looked at him with pleading eyes.

"Absolutely," he said, nodding.

"We inherited this artifact from our parents, and if you delve a little deeper, you could say we got it from W.A. Swansong himself." She pointed at the key Quincy had taken from his pocket. "We're not quite sure what all the fuss is about, but Haven wants it, and they apparently want to kill us for it, if necessary."

"I don't know why you're tied up in this mess, but I trust Haven about as far as I can throw them," Sean spat.

"Don't get ahead of yourself; you seem to have a mean throw in you considering how far you threw Tim." Quincy chuckled.

"Yeah, about that… thing…" Sean stared at the lamp with an uneasy expression.

"Don't worry. That's a different story altogether." Lilly caressed the top of the lamp. The lamp groaned back at her in annoyance. "Oops. Looks like he's trying to sleep."

"I don't mean to pry. It's all good." Sean scratched the back of his head. "Look, I don't trust them Haven folks, and since you kind of helped save my life back in the café, I definitely trust you guys. If your… *mission*, as you like to call it, has anything to do with busting up any plans Haven has, I'm all for it."

"But, Sean, *we* don't even know what the hell we're doing," Lilly interjected and threw up her hands.

"Still, it was important enough for our parents to keep this silver key safe, Lilly," Quincy said. "By all means, I aim to honor that agreement."

"I agree, you know I do."

"What about me? Devilish imbeciles, do you have any idea who you're…" Tim groaned, half awake.

"Shut it, goodie-two-shoes!" Lilly tapped the glass. "We'll deal with you later."

The twins took a moment to put everything they had witnessed up until now into perspective and give it a place in their heads in silence. Sean filled in the time by strolling down the parking lot, checking out cars, and, much to Quincy and Lilly's shock, he hot-wired one of them and pulled up beside them.

"Wha… What did you do?" Quincy's head dove under the dashboard, and he got a chance to admire a mesh of jumbled-up cables.

"To start it, just push the two-colored cables together," he said. "You know, like they always do in the movies and stuff."

Quincy muttered something unintelligible under his breath.

Sean smiled weakly. "Listen, you told me your car was stranded somewhere all the way at the other end of town. You'd never make it over there without being caught. I'm helping you here—take the car and go west; go finish whatever it is these Haven creeps made you start."

The twins were dumbstruck.

"We're fugitives of one of the biggest organizations in the world, and they probably have a hefty reward on us, *plus* we got a dangerous, extra-terrestrial being trapped in a lamp by Aleister Crowley with us, and you're letting us go?" Quincy's eyes fell on the open road ahead of them.

"Yes. Now get the hell out of here. I'll try to persuade the remaining Haven agents that I was after you guys or something, tell them you escaped back to New Orleans. I'll try to give you time."

Lilly glanced at the car and dug into her coat pocket. "Can you do one thing for us?"

"What?"

"I don't like theft. Here's the keys to our car; it's that Ford Fiesta parked near Verona Drive where we first met. Please drive it over here when you have the chance."

"Lilly, are you serious?" Quincy motioned to the mess of burning buildings around them. "The owners of this car are probably dead; we're just surviving."

"What if they aren't dead and are scared and just want to get out of town just like us?" she retorted in anger. "Sean, please."

"Okay."

Quincy regained his composure. He held his hand out towards Sean. "Hey, uh, I don't know what to say... You saved us, Sean. We're indebted to you, heavily." They shook.

"Thank you. For everything." Lilly kissed Sean on the cheek.

"Goodbye, Quincy. Goodbye, Lilly. And uh… Goodbye, Tim… I guess."

A low growl rumbled from the oil lamp before it was put into the backseat of the car.

Lilly and Quincy were on their way in their brand "new" Ford station wagon. They had hurried out of Lafayette, taking careful measures to avoid the most obvious larger streets that ran out of the city and agreed that a detour through the southern suburbs was probably the best route. From there, they would follow the Interstate 10 up to Houston but, due to the events that had transpired the last couple of days, had decided to not venture into the larger cities because they had had enough of bigger cities for the foreseeable future. From the outskirts of Houston, they'd periodically stop and see how to best get to New Mexico as quickly and as discreetly as possible.

After discussing their plan of action, it was not until they were a good forty-five minutes out of Lafayette that one of them decided to speak again.

"Radio?" Quincy's hand hovered over the dial.

"Sure, let's see what's new around the globe."

"And learn where *not* to go."

News of the events at Lafayette were all over the radio, and the particular station they stopped on appeared to be heavily influenced by Haven. The newsreader slandered the GDF for not doing their job properly, resulting in massive casualties all over the city.

"If it weren't for the fine Haven personnel that arrived at the scene as quickly as they could and immediately dealt with the monster, who knows what may have happened?" the radio host rambled. *"In other news, a massive outbreak of giant insects is plaguing the Northwest, GDF forces…"*

Lilly flicked the channel and cursed.

"We know what happened, that's all that matters," Quincy reassured her.

"I want revenge," Lilly whispered.

From the radio now came the funky first notes of an old David Bowie song. Quincy looked over at his sister, seeing her mouthing the lyrics to the song and tapping the steering wheel with her fingertips. The song itself spoke of nightmares that came from nowhere and weren't planning to leave anytime soon.

"Creepy, isn't it?" he asked. "It seems… relevant, prophetic almost."

"Hmm? Yeah… I know. I like it." Lilly looked up to the sky. "Makes you wonder if David Bowie was, like, our great uncle."

"A prophet?"

"A madman."

They both laughed. I didn't think it was *that* funny, but okay.

Lilly slowed down in anticipation of the upcoming railway crossing. "What are we going to do when we get to Three Rivers?"

"I have no idea. A few days ago, I was just contemplating on switching my majors in college. Or even quitting altogether… Look at me now." Quincy shrugged.

"We'll figure it out," Lilly replied. "We're the last Swansongs; I guess being normal isn't in the cards for us."

Quincy watched the train flashing by. "At least not for now."

Lilly opened the glove compartment and took out her phone.

Quincy glanced over at her looking over the map application that she brought up. "So what's our next stop?"

"The middle of nowhere."

PART II

Trials of the Navajo

———————————

Chapter 7

———————————

"LOOK AT THEM OVER THERE, Harold. See them at the parking lot getting out of that rusty barrel of a car?"

Harold groaned. The two had been sitting on their porch all day, taking in the hot Texan sun and praising it thoroughly for warming their old bones. From their porch, they could see everything of note happening around the old crossroads as they were way off the beaten path and preferred it that way.

"Yes. Seems like they could be heading over to the next town for the convention. Don't you agree, Harold?"

Harold yawned without much additional response.

The two watched the young people meander over the asphalt towards the gas station convenience store; they seemed to be in heated discussion.

"Siblings, I'm sure of it. The curly haired young woman, she looks fierce, doesn't she? A real brawler that one, but a heart of gold."

Harold stretched his legs and groaned again, trying to go back to sleep.

"Don't shut your eyes and ignore these wonderful diversions, Harold!" Henry hissed. "Don't you see?" He nodded towards the two. "What about the young man? Slim, handsome, and unmistakably clever, very clever."

The pair eyed the young folk until they disappeared into the store.

"Do you feel it?" Henry asked and shivered. "A darkness follows them. They are being tracked by some malevolent fiend, I bet. It makes me dizzy." He blinked. "There is… an artifact. A blessing and a curse… no, perhaps just a curse. Oh, the terrible burden of forbidden knowledge, it hurts me to think it may have addled these brave young minds forever."

After a while, the young man and woman emerged from the convenience store with a big brown bag of groceries; the young woman was enjoying a scone, also.

"But perhaps, my dear Harold, they could be… the chosen ones?" Henry gasped, standing up. "Can they be the ones that the eldest of elders prophesied would come? Those who would emerge when the Earth was threatened to perish at the hand of brimstone and floods, ethereal and void forces, and extra-dimensional malady?"

Harold shrugged.

"The heroes that would uncover the deepest secrets of human history and plunge mankind into a new age of primordial conquest and simultaneous enlightenment. Could it be, Harold?"

Harold crouched and proceeded to lick his privates. He then stood up and dived down from the porch and into the shrubbery below.

Henry sighed at his friend. "Ah, I guess you're right, Harold. What do *we* know? We're just cats."

"Check it out." Lilly pushed the newspaper under Quincy's nose and licked the vanilla icing from her lips.

"*'Room for rent. Cheap and clean. Please, no clowns.'* What?" Quincy shoved the grocery bag into the trunk and scratched his head.

"Underneath that, doofus. Look." Lilly pointed at the tiny advertisement beneath the personal ads.

Quincy's eyes widened a bit. "Convention of Souls, huh."

"Apparently, it's a yearly gathering. The ghosts and specters of long-dead occultists, horror writers, and other macabre figures all gather at Bobby Mackey's Music World. It sounds super cool; we should totally go!" Lilly couldn't contain her excitement. "And by should, I mean we *will* definitely go, won't we?"

"Wait a minute." Quincy crossed his arms. "Rewind for just a little bit here; we need to talk about this." He got behind the wheel of the car and fumbled with the wires. "First of all, we already have a destination: Three Rivers." Lilly crept onto the seat next to him as the engine of the car roared awake. "Secondly…"

Quincy turned out of the lot back onto the road. The sun hung low and shone straight into his eyes. He snapped the visor down and continued, "Secondly, we're driving off the beaten path for a reason, remember? We're being followed by Haven and who knows what else; this could all be a giant trap."

"It's a yearly thing, Quince!" Lilly protested but still looked defeated. "Look, they've been doing this thing since 1983, see? It's just that nobody could really see them yet before a few years back. There's also the thing with Bobby Mackey's Music World, the world-famous, *literal* portal to *Hell*, burned down a year ago. So they rebuilt the place in Texas, and it's super near, like in the next town over and… Please can we just *go*?"

"Are you kidding me? So the old Bobby Mackey's *mysteriously* burned down, and now the convention just happens to be right on our path? That's all the more reason to find this super suspicious; you've got to agree with me on that."

"How could anyone possibly know we'd be here at this

time? The convention has been announced for months, and construction on the new Bobby Mackey's was started like ten months ago. It's the grand opening, in fact."

"Did the new Bobby Mackey's come with a portal to Hell included?" Quincy sighed and stared in the rearview mirror at the barren road behind him.

The sun's eerie glow was now obscured behind padded clouds. The air seemed to grow thicker, and the road seemed darker somehow, as if an invisible fog bank had just rolled onto the plains.

It had been about a week since Quincy and Lilly left the massacre that took place in Lafayette. They had taken careful precautions to exclude every possibility of getting caught by Haven, which they knew for a fact were tracking them down. The twins had narrowly dodged one of their elaborate road-blocks near Natchitoches, and when they'd rented a motel room in Sulphur Springs, they came back to find the place turned upside down.

This meant that driving along well-lit and busy highways was out of the question, as was staying in any major city or traveling in any straight line towards Three Rivers in New Mexico. At least little southern towns had their definite charms, the twins would admit to that, but they were also off the beaten path, and that could potentially be dangerous.

Paranormal happenings in big cities would be reported quickly and be taken care of in the blink of an eye—as the events of Lafayette showed. But if anything were to manifest in some hick town in the middle of nowhere, something seri-ous, they'd potentially have a big problem depending on what kind of activity it was.

Lilly remembered a tale one of her superiors had told her squad when she was first enlisted in the army. A special GDF task force known as "The Apothecaries" was called out to a small town somewhere in the northeastern part of the United States. The local inhabitants had all gone missing overnight, and all that was left was an unrelenting thick fog that engulfed the entire town, including the lake and the valley surrounding it.

When the task force leader had given an update to HQ that they were about to head into the fog, it wasn't long before the entire squad disappeared from the GPS and radar systems. In less than an hour's time, the entire Apothecaries task force was seemingly erased from the face of the earth and never seen again.

The town is rumored to still exist, but Haven personnel has been seen operating out of specially designed workspaces surrounding the town. The thick fog is usually absent, but several times a year it supposedly returns, and anyone passing by the town should think twice before heading down into that cursed valley.

Lilly shivered at the memory, thinking of what would happen if she and her brother got trapped in a similar situation. Unfortunately, they seemed to have a knack for being in the wrong place at the wrong time.

"Say we go," Quincy murmured, "what are we going to do at this 'Conventions of Souls'? What's our goal when we show up, save for chatting up some geezers that have been in the ground for decades?"

A low rumble came from the clouds overhead, and a splat of rain splashed against the windshield.

"I was hoping we'd run into our uncle, actually." Lilly stared at the drops of water forming on the window. "There are rumors that William showed up at several of the earlier conventions. He never spoke a word, but apparently his icy stare was enough to shut most people's mouths. People say he just looks around, as if searching for someone, and then leaves after about thirty minutes."

Absolutely dull, these kinds of gatherings. When you've met some of the strange people I have, take it from me that being dead can be a blessing in disguise.

"Dammit." Quincy groaned. "That's actually not a bad idea at all. If we find him there, who knows? He could help us out with our situation, like, a lot. Or not at all." He flicked on the windshield wipers. "What if he's not there? What then?"

"Then at least we tried," Lilly said, determined.

A clash of thunder came rolling from above; lightning flashed and adorned the sky in pink and blue stripes, a strange orange glow emanating from the heavens right before the rain came crashing down like a gigantic waterfall.

"If I may be so rude to interrupt your little tea party, my most humble bags of flesh and bone…" a voice called from the old oil lamp lying on the backseat.

"Hey, Tim! Have a nice nap?" Lilly turned towards the lamp and stuck her thumb up.

"Sleep is a meaningless term for a being standing so high above your petty mortal needs and emotions, girl." The lamp bobbed up and down until it sat upright on the seat. "Anyway, I'd like to point out the fact that I can feel an old presence very near."

"Who?" Quincy shot a quick glance at the backseat in his mirror.

"Crowley is manifesting about… five miles from here." Tim's inimitable garbled voice rose high above the noise of the clattering rain and the piercing thunder.

Lilly smiled at her brother. "Well?"

Quincy smirked and flicked the right blinker light.

After a couple hundred yards, the twins took the nearest exit that would lead them straight into the next town over, best known for two things: Satanic rituals and the new Bobby Mackey's Music World.

The most ironic thing in the world to say about the atmosphere inside the brand-spanking new Bobby Mackey's Music World (modeled one-to-one as an exact copy of the old one) would be it felt very *alive*. Truth be told, the place was packed with people, and there was a big ruckus going on. It's just that only a handful of these individuals were actually "alive" in the most basic sense of the word. Most of the bar's patrons on this particular day were see-through, had large echoes in their voices, and did not possess anything close to a corporeal body.

Still, considering the ghosts of many an occultist, black magic practitioner, or the likes in between were present, the general ambience was pleasant, and, some might even say, welcoming. The chatter was friendly between individuals who had never met in their lifetime or who weren't even alive in the same decade.

However unconventional the idea, when Quincy and Lilly Swansong entered through the front door of the establishment that was filled to the brim with the ghosts of the past, it was one of the first moments in a very long while that the twins did not feel like the odd ones out. They actually felt very comfortable, and even Quincy dismissed some of his fears about Haven finding them here.

The twins felt a strange sense of belonging in between the specters of old, felt a sense of respect and a recognition of their heritage and bloodline.

Quincy passed a group of men hulking around an old black-and-white television set and couldn't withhold a smile.

They were watching one of those ghost hunting television shows that were all the rage before ghosts became a completely arbitrary part of the world. Apparently, the group of apparitions had once "lived" in a certain Louisiana mansion for a long time, and they were reminiscing about the time this TV crew came around and how they scared the crew out of their wits by doing the most mundane things around—such as turning a doorknob or saying "hello" into a microphone. The group of specters was laughing with every "Did you see that?" or "What was *that*?" coming from the TV.

Lilly watched with delight, laughing just as loud, but a sudden vibration from the oil lamp clutched between her arms made her shiver. A voice rose up from behind the couch, and the TV set flickered off with a trail of smoke rising from the back of it.

"Playtime is over for now, boys. Skedaddle along to the bar and get some drinks; I believe I have a matter to discuss with this young Swansong lady, who appears to be in possession of my lamp." The lamp started to make little bubbling noises, but so far Tim had stayed quiet.

Quincy turned around and stepped over to Lilly's side as she took two steps back, still holding the lamp close to her chest. The ghost of a wicked, ugly, bald man stood in front of the twins. He wasn't the tallest of men they had ever seen, but there was no denying the air of mysticism and dread surrounding him.

"Oh, pishposh, stop gawking at me and sit down," he ordered. "Allow me to introduce myself—Aleister Crowley." He smirked. "A pleasure."

Ergh, A necessary evil, that bald smirking git. I only hope Lilly and Quincy take extra caution around him.

Outside, the dry Texan heat rippled through the air like radio waves. Unknowing passersby stopped to look for a few moments when an odd feeling washed over them in a particular spot on the road, but the abnormal manifestation and the unusual sensation it brought drove them on before long.

A little distance from the new Bobby Mackey's front door, a green glow started to emit from nowhere. It started churning into a huge oval shape, and from deep within its core, a black void began to grow bigger and bigger. From the center of the void emerged a stranger, a dark individual wearing a robe as black as midnight; he was clutching a likewise pitch-black cat which was wrestling to get out of the stranger's grip.

Within mere moments, the dimensional portal closed behind him, and the stranger stared longingly towards the roadside café where the Convention of Souls was taking place at this very moment.

"Perhaps you did not cheat me after all, vermin," the stranger said to the black cat in a low, gritty, and vibrating voice.

"May you rot in the deepest depths of Ulthar's dungeons; you shall not get away with this!" Henry, the black cat, screeched before he swatted the stranger along his face.

The hooded figure yelled in pain and released the animal, who quickly disappeared into the dried bushes along the main road. The stranger dabbed along his eye and flicked the drops of blood gathered on his fingers onto the ground.

"I have bigger game to catch than mere housecats at the moment. But let it be known that Kraal never forgets." He pulled his hood down tighter, then lumbered over to the front door of Bobby Mackey's.

"Enough with the formalities and the gaping maws, children. Let us sit down," Crowley insisted and pulled up two chairs. He stared intently at the half-obscured lamp for a spell.

While an echo is common in ghost voices, Crowley's voice had a sort of inherent delay that was booming and unnerving. Still, out of real options to turn tail and flee, the twins decided to play along for the moment. So, they sat down and reluctantly agreed to have a conversation with one of the most wicked men to ever have lived. They didn't even know how his death had fared him nor were they in a particular mood to find out.

"The Swansong twins in the flesh, and luckily so!" Crowley's dark eye sockets widened slightly. "I've heard of your little exploits in Lafayette, and I must say it was absolutely smashing. Well done."

"Thanks?" Lilly stared at him in confusion. "But we don't go around celebrating an event in which innocent people lost their lives."

"Rightfully so." Crowley nodded. "Alas, that has been the way of the world since forever. Way before you two were born, and even way before that." He cleared his throat. "Now tell me, do you know how long these paranormal debacles have been... *'pestering'* as you could call it, our planet for? Hmm?"

"It's been a little over three years ago now, I reckon," Quincy replied, taking the bait.

"Aha, but you see, young master Swansong, it has been going on behind the veil, in the shadows for over centuries now. From the lowliest of poltergeists and risen dead to the most abhorrent of intergalactic plagues, the Earth has been in the midst of it ever since time itself began and even before that.

"Why, your great uncle himself took a peek behind that veil once or twice. Can you imagine what he *didn't* get to see? Let me reassure you, however, that this simple factoid does not make your mission useless by any stretch of the imagination. We are entering a new age, and the *key* to enlightenment is, in fact, in your hands." He paused, his head tilting to the side. "Can I see it?"

"Ooookay, hold it right there," Lilly demanded. She wasn't entirely sure if it was because he seemed to know a great deal more about them than he should or because his voice was grating and giving her a headache, but either way— she didn't trust him.

"You seem to know a great deal, Mr. Crowley. But you haven't exactly given much reason for us to trust you. Either you tell us everything you know, or we're just going to walk out of here and you can sit here talking to your fellow undead nutcases for the remainder of the convention, okay?"

Quincy kept quiet. He couldn't explain the sudden feeling he was having, but despite all of the otherworldly members of society present, he felt as if an intense malevolent being was staring at him—not at his body, but deeper, staring into his soul, picking apart his weaknesses and calculating how best to use them against him.

It wasn't emanating from Crowley, though, but from a different force somewhere within Bobby Mackey's altogether.

Quincy wiped his sweaty hands against the inside of his jacket and pulled his collar nervously.

"Watch your tone, Lilly Swansong!" Crowley hissed. "I may know a lot, but as your dear departed grand-uncle used to write in his lovely pulp magazines, you should know that it is both a blessing and a curse. If I'd told you everything I know, both of your feeble brains would melt before I'd even end with the prologue of how the universe *really* came into existence."

"Hee-hee, tell 'em, Master," Tim called out from the oil lamp, which began to shine a little bit brighter. He had waited some time to make his grand entrance, looking for the perfect timing to garner as much *shock value* as possible.

Lilly almost dropped the lamp.

"Master?" she whispered "Well, *shit!*"

"Ah, good of you to join us finally, Timaxoatilaciluzipta, don't think I didn't see you swirling around in there." Crowley sneered. "Your Fire Vampire's rude interruption actually leads nicely into my next topic of discussion…"

"Wait, *our* Fire Vampire?" Lilly raised an eyebrow.

"It'll also show you, young Swansongs," Crowley went on, ignoring Lilly for now, "that I am on *your* side."

Quincy had trouble shaking off the dreaded feeling, but he couldn't keep quiet any longer.

"Show us how?"

"Relax," Crowley answered, less forceful this time, perhaps even with a genuine air of compassion. "Yes, I know a lot, and no, I can't tell you everything for reasons I have just explained. Let me just say that I am here to help you, and exhibit number one in that regard is that oil lamp, and its contents, you hold in your hands, young Miss Swansong.

"I summoned Timaxoatilaciluzipta long ago, before my untimely death even, with the express purpose of enslaving him and bending his will so he'd be a powerful ally whenever the time came for the Swansong heirs to find him.

"Now, some call me a prophet, and when asked, yes, I *do*

meddle in divination and can predict the future here and there, but what I did *not* see was my unfortunate and untimely passing before getting the Fire Vampire under control. Luckily, I see you are doing a pretty good job of that yourself." Crowley bared his teeth as his mouth curved into a wicked smile.

"No way." Quincy felt his mouth drop open before he shook his head. "You can't possibly have known that one day we would make a run out of New Orleans and by way of interdimensional harassment be holed up in a library in Lafayette *just* so we could find your lamp and meet Tim. That's nonsense."

"Friendly reminder, Quince, but we are currently sitting in a roadside café surrounded by the specters of some of the most renowned historians and occultists the world has ever seen. Perhaps the most well-known of which, Aleister Crowley, is at this very moment talking to us about stuff and events we *just* experienced which he never could've known about." Just reciting it out loud gave Lilly a headache.

"Stranger things have happened," Crowley agreed.

"Spare me, please." Quincy grabbed his head and moaned, his skin pale. "Listen, this is just too much for me now, or something is very wrong here, but I feel like I'm being drained. I feel weak and nauseous. I think I need to head outside for a moment."

Crowley turned his head and took a look around the bar. Lilly followed his gaze and watched him focus on a particularly unsavory-looking character in a black hooded robe, drinking scotch in a corner booth.

"Excuse me for just one moment," Crowley said, sounding wary. "Whatever you do, keep Quincy inside at all costs!" He floated off towards the robed figure.

"Quince. I don't trust Crowley for one bit. We need to get out of here *right* now," Lilly urged as soon as he left.

"I... can't," Quincy whispered. "Something is keeping me

here; I'm being forced on this chair with what feels like the weight of a mountain."

"What? What do you mean?"

"I feel like if I'd stand up, I'd die."

"He's bound to a particularly nasty work of black magic," Tim whispered. "What a sight to behold."

"Damn that Crowley, if he weren't already dead, I'd—"

"It's not him," Quincy interrupted. "It's something else I…" He blanched suddenly. It was as if a veil of shadows was lifted from right in front of him. He stood up and looked around. "Wait. It's gone."

"You're scaring me, Quince."

In a flash, Crowley was back at their table. Gone was the playful smirk he had on his face earlier; all of a sudden, he looked very grim, perhaps even troubled.

"The laws of the Convention of Souls state that no one, be they alive or dead, may be harmed during the entire duration of the event in any place within the convention's walls," he said. "That hooded figure in the corner there, do you see him?"

"Yes." Lilly nodded while Quincy groaned.

"His name is Kraal. He's a very dangerous black mage, a warlock, and he just got his first and final warning, considering our convention laws. Kraal was using a life-drain spell on you, Quincy."

A perverse ritual it is, indeed, to twist the minds of young, susceptible individuals. Kraal may prove too hazardous to take head-on.

"I feel fine now," Quincy reassured Lilly when she reached for him. "Why would a warlock be after us, though? Why does it feel like everyone in the world is *hounding* us night and day?" he added angrily and pounded his fists on the table. It made Lilly jump; it was a side of her brother she rarely saw, and for good reason too.

"The only thing I can think of is that he is working for Haven. You, my dear Swansongs, have a very big problem on your hands. Within these walls, Kraal cannot possibly hurt you; our rules forbid it. However, take one step outside, and we are all powerless to help. The convention's laws bind us to the building and only for as long as the convention is taking place. Once it is over, we simply disappear to another plane of existence."

"Why not just get Tim to zap us out of here?" Quincy wondered.

"Who says I wouldn't rather just take in the pleasure of watching you consumed by necrotic fire? I still owe you very little. In fact, you might as well say you owe *me*," Tim hissed.

"Well, that's just great." Lilly let her head fall back with a sigh. "So, we're sitting ducks here with this Kraal guy, just waiting the convention out until you lot up and disappear so he can evaporate us on the spot?"

"Hmm, ducklings, hehehe." The oil lamp shook with mirth.

"Most likely," Crowley confirmed.

"Lilly." Quincy tapped her on the shoulder. "I know you can't possibly comprehend what I'm going to say right now, but after experiencing what I just did, I'd take a dozen Dimensional Shamblers over this guy any day of the week. This guy is seriously bad news."

"Oh, great. Really helpful, Quince!" She threw him a fake smile before growing serious. "Mr. Crowley, what are our options here?"

"Follow me up to the smoker's lounge; I'll explain it on the way." He floated off quickly.

The robed figure watched the twins and Crowley dart off to another part of the café from underneath his hood, which was stitched with patterns of unknown symbols and runes.

After waving off an invitation to join in on a card game

with Edgar Allan Poe and L. Ron Hubbard, Kraal took a simple white crayon from his robe pocket and started drawing symbols onto the table in front of him, forming half a circle first. After the drawing was completed and the spell was written down, he lit a candle and placed it on the outer edge of the semicircle. Next, he clapped his hands and watched the vision spell take form as the tiny figures resembling Lilly, Quincy, and a see-through Crowley manifested in front of his eyes.

Kraal reached for the earbuds from his iPod and stuck them in place.

"You will reach Santa Rosa in time, where you will meet a Navajo native named Paw Hathale. He'll know of the place you seek, and he'll help you." Crowley hobbled up the hallway.

"How do you know this?" Lilly asked.

"I have divined a lot about you Swansongs. Unfortunately, now is neither the time nor place to tell you about the rest of your lives, nor is it my place to tell you either way." Crowley jiggled a door handle. "Here, this room should be sufficient; let me prepare for a moment."

The vision spell wore off, and Kraal pulled the iPod plugs from his ears and took his smartphone out. His grin stretched from ear to ear as he typed out an email in haste. Afterwards, he headed for the front door of the establishment.

"That fellow looks like bad news," one of the ghostly patrons whispered to his neighbor as the black mage passed them.

Kraal grinned.

"How do we even recognize this Paw fellow?" Lilly asked while she fought her frizzy hair, trying to pull the locks back into a bun. "Besides, you do know how far Santa Rosa is, right? How will we ever get there?"

Lilly stopped and eyed the symbols Crowley had drawn on

the wooden floor. "Say, how can you manipulate chalk that well if you're a ghost? Does it take a lot of energy?"

"Oh my days, child. Do you always ask this many questions around your dead superiors?" Crowley sloughed on the ground. "Now I know how this sounds coming from me, and given the situation of the past few years but, have faith will you?"

He stood up and dusted off his ghostly fingers, probably out of habit more than actual practical use. He then lifted his hands into the air, and a flurry of horrifying sounds and guttural speech came out of his mouth. The words were too terrible to reproduce or imitate, and Crowley's voice was even more unsettling than usual, but when he was done, a black doorway stood in the middle of the room.

Pitch-black and perfectly still, it zoomed in and out eerily in the room's bad lighting.

"What's this?" Quincy asked, looking apprehensive.

"Your ticket out of this place." Crowley waved them closer. "It took almost all my energy to summon this portal… Now be aware that it probably won't stop Kraal from tracking you down, but it will give you a *hell* of a head start." He sighed when the twins just looked at him.

"Now get in there, quickly! This thing won't last forever!"

"How can we thank you?" Quincy eyed the ghost with newfound appreciation.

"Just make sure Timaxoatilaciluzipta does what he needs to. Now go!"

"One moment," a new voice said. It was now the time for me to reveal myself.

Quincy and Lilly both turned their heads at the same time and dropped their jaws in amazement. There I stood, a solemn apparition looming quietly and unmoving in the corner of the back room of Bobby Mackey's Music World. My face was, as often described I guess, stern, cold, and calculated but unmistakable. It was me, W.A. Swansong.

"Quincy! It's him!" Lilly ran towards me, her long-dead

ancestor, and tried to grasp my hand, only to have her fingers slip right through my cold, non-corporeal form.

"We have so many questions!" Quincy went over to join his sister.

"My dear heirs," I said, "you hold in your possession a key to enlightenment. Do not let it fall into the wrong hands."

"My power is waning!" Crowley cried, now flickering in and out of focus. I had to hurry. "Lilly, Quincy, there is no time!"

"It's really the old coot Swansong himself," Tim cackled. "Look at him all dead and wrinkly, muahahahahahaaaa!"

The little chamber was shaking; the foundation beams above them could be heard creaking and moaning by the sheer force of the magical anomaly present in the room.

"What should we do?" Lilly pleaded at my shadowy outline. "Please help us!"

"There is no time, child," I admitted. I wished I could take their burden, but I could only intervene as much as this. "Remember this: When you lose your way and nothing can help you get back, think—*as above, so below!*"

"What does that even *mean*? Dammit!" Lilly felt tears prickling behind her eyes.

"Classic old Swansong, no answers but only mysticism and bulls—" Tim's voice disappeared as Quincy threw him into the portal ahead of them.

The portal was now flickering heavily, and the beam across the ceiling shifted with a profound crack. Crowley had all but disappeared.

"There is no time, Lil!" Quincy called out, grabbing his sister's hand and pulling her towards the portal.

"Help us!" Lilly reached for me one last time as she was yanked into the portal by Quincy at the very last second before it disappeared from the room.

Then there was nothing.

I am sorry.

Chapter 8

THE SUN-BLEACHED, rickety shed had seen better days, but it would've lived for at least a few more years were it not that two youngsters and a talking oil lamp had fallen from the sky and demolished it entirely on their way down.

Paw Hathale took a deep breath and sighed.

The desert air on the outskirts of Santa Rosa was never *not* dry, but it was clean, cleaner than city air could ever be again, and he liked it that way. Paw also preferred the way the world was before a bunch of young people could randomly fall from a black hole in the sky onto one's private property.

He recalled fondly a time when the world was innocent. When rituals to invoke ancient spirits of the land were a special and sacred occasion, a great privilege. Nowadays, to speak to old spirits one could simply walk over to the nearest grocery store and find at least one ghost harassing customers.

Paw often longed for the old days. He was proud of his Native American heritage and always tried to stay true to his ancestors by living off what the land provided him. But he always gave back in return, for every tree he cut down for the wood to expand or repair his home, Paw would plant a seed that years from now would sprout a new tree. It was his way of life and that of his ancestors, the way of the Navajo.

A loud cough emanated from the rubble of the destroyed shed, and Paw stood at attention.

"Why are you even coughing; you're literally made of dust! *Stardust!*"

Paw saw a woman in her early twenties shuffling from the wreckage. He was glad to see that she hadn't sustained any serious injuries. She was, however, yelling at something shining in the nearby shrubbery, which was a tad odd, at least from the Navajo's perspective.

Paw didn't go in for a warm welcome just yet, as a man now rose from beneath the splintered boards. Like the woman, a few cuts and bruises seemed to be the worst of things, so Paw let out another sigh of relief. This man seemed to have his wits about him at least and looked smart and refined, albeit caked in a layer of sand and dust.

For a minute or so, the twins and the old native simply stared at each other.

Paw noted their curious expressions as the twins stared at length at his long gray hair, his feather ear jewelry, and then his turquoise and silver rings. Lilly smirked a bit at his Hawaiian shirt with neat flowers and tiny hula dancers printed on it.

To Paw's surprise, he wasn't the one that decided to break the silence.

"Uh, aloha," Lilly greeted, then shook the dust out of her hair.

For a brief moment, Paw felt insulted before he looked down and burst out in loud, infectious laughter.

"First you destroy my precious toolshed, and now you come to me with this meaningless Polynesian babble!" He laughed heartily. "Look around you, young folk, there isn't anything around here but sand, rocks, and cacti. But, if you really wish to know where we are, and from the look on your confused faces I'd wager you do, I can tell you we're just a couple of miles from Santa Rosa, New Mexico."

"I… We, uh…" Quincy stammered and looked at Lilly for help.

She placed the lamp on the ground, wiped the sweat off her brow, and shrugged.

"First things first then," Paw said, "I'm Paw Hathale, and you've stumbled onto my ranch."

Upon hearing the man's name, a cold shiver crept down the twins' spines. Crowley had been right. *As much as I despise him, I admire Crowley's tenacity in helping my family. In life… and death.*

Let us have another history lesson, shall we? Many years before the Abandonment, in 1947 to be exact, a fiery object was observed shooting across the night sky in the desert nearby Roswell, New Mexico. Onlookers described it as a shining disc of metal, like a round airplane but moving unlike any plane they'd ever laid eyes on. State troopers were called to the scene, and, with the help of government forces, the so-called *Roswell UFO incident* was quickly debunked as a weather balloon that was malfunctioning.

Though, locals of Roswell didn't forget easy, and to this day the oldest of living eyewitnesses and their offspring stand convinced that the object was definitely *not of this earth*. In fact, ask any local old geezer at a bar or shady truck stop in or around Roswell, and he could fill an entire night telling tales about the town: Electrical devices going haywire for no reason, cows falling over dead, strange lights in the sky, and sinister government agents dressed in all black hanging around the town asking abnormal questions.

The men in black, as Roswell citizens liked to call them, appeared soon after the reported incident. What most people don't know was that the Roswell incident sparked one of the first "public" appearances of the organization some people know nowadays as Haven.

The team at Roswell was led by a man known only as Beckett. Beckett was a high-ranking US Army officer who'd secured himself a medal of valor after a raid on one of the Nazi's most notorious hideouts in World War II: the SS experimental research lab and medieval castle *Schloss Alterblut*. Soon after the war was won, Beckett was recruited by a top-secret government agency to hunt down, neutralize, or capture supernatural activity.

Beckett quickly rose through the ranks, and with it, his power rose as well. In the early 1980s, he became head chairman of the board and redubbed the organization to Haven. However, soon after, he disappeared under mysterious circumstances.

The truth of the matter is that the organization was already ancient even during the days of Roswell. But alas, the true lineage and how the organization rose in power throughout the centuries is lost forever. You can blame the late medieval trend of burning books on anything even remotely resembling occult content on that one. Oh, I can only imagine the rich pools of history and knowledge forever lost to the strands of time. How I've wept for the idiocy of our ancestors.

Lilly had trouble containing herself—she wanted to just pick up the steak dinner with her hands and rip the meat off with her teeth. The feast Paw Hathale had prepared for them made them feel like they hadn't eaten anything for at least a week. As a matter of fact, if you don't consider terrible gas station food or sketchy roadside diners real food… they really hadn't eaten anything for more than a week.

Paw's home was small but very cozy. The wooden walls were adorned with old monochrome pictures of Native Americans, all wearing the same impressive-looking jewelry as Paw did but excluding the snazzy hula shirt. An abundance of cacti, both small and large, stood in clay pots all over the living room, and an impressive skull of a North American bison hung graciously over the front entrance.

Although not entirely sure if or why they should place their trust in Paw, as they couldn't account it to be by Crowley's promises alone, the twins had decided to explain their entire conundrum to him as soon as dinner was served.

During and after they had finished telling their tale, Paw sat at the table, staring in front of him. Once in a while, he took a bite to eat, but he seemed to be off somewhere in deep thought or wrestling with strong emotions.

"A dreadful tale," Paw remarked eventually as he stood up. "Unbelievable one would say, but that word has long since lost its meaning, wouldn't you agree?" He looked grim but determined. "I have not heard of this Haven you speak of, but the legends and myths of the men in black have always left a sinister trail in these parts. Ancient Navajo tales speak of similar strange and shadowy figures skulking around places of power or holy sites. Not only here, but all through the country and beyond, from the icy shores of Alaska, along Chichen Itza on Mexico's Yucatán Peninsula, all the way down to the Nazca lines."

"Excuse me, did you say Navajo?" Quincy glanced over at Lilly, and she nodded.

"Yes, I did. The Navajo are my tribe; I wear their colors and my inherited adornments proudly."

Lilly blinked, then took out the silver key that was still in their possession. She laid it on the table, and Quincy swallowed nervously.

"It's beautiful." Paw gazed at it with a mixture of disbelief and admiration. "So, this is the artifact you speak of?" At Quincy's nod, Paw leaned over and pressed his face closer to the table, his crooked nose just inches from the tip of the silver key. "There are many secrets hidden in its grooves, can you see? Ancient symbols adorn the sides. What stellar craftsman-ship. Look!"

Lilly and Quincy bent over the table to see where the old Navajo man was pointing at. "Yidiists'a'! That means *to hear*." Paw carefully picked up the key and held it to his ear.

Lilly and Quincy stared at each other in mild confusion until Lilly spoke,

"Right!" She tapped the oak table. "Is there anything else you might be able to tell us?"

"No." Paw handed the key back to Lilly. "But if this is indeed the precious artifact you are tasked with to bring to Three Rivers, then I shall be your driver and guide." He laughed in relief, as if he had finally found new meaning in his less-than-stellar, and declining, existence. "That key is the purest of Navajo craftsmanship I have seen in my life. It would be an honor for me and for my ancestors to help you on this task."

"We would be truly grateful…" Quincy started but swallowed his words after Lilly jumped to her feet and stormed outside.

"Damn!" she called out as she disappeared through the back door.

Quincy and Paw exchanged glances and stood up in unison. They followed her out back where she was wandering off towards the broken shed.

"What are you doing?" Quincy yelled to her while attempting to maintain his balance on the uneven wooden porch.

"We left Tim out here all day!" she called back. "He must be furious." She nervously laughed.

Paw looked over at Quincy. "Is Tim the vaporous entity in the oil lamp you had mentioned before?"

Quincy just nodded.

It wasn't before long that Lilly returned with a dented oil lamp full of fresh coyote claw marks and even a slight spat of poo.

"You bunch of idiotic bags of useless tissue! You have no idea the horrors I have went through!" The lamp flashed blood-red and deep crimson in disgust. "My handle could've been broken; I could've been stolen, killed even!" Tim raged on.

Lilly could barely contain her laughter as she cradled the lamp as if to sooth a small child. She felt a bit guilty but only just a really small tad. Quincy scratched his head at the odd scene before turning to Paw.

"Once again, what I tried to say was that we're extremely grateful for your help and…"

"Don't mention it." Paw reached for the door and gave a soft wink. "We'll leave at dawn; I'll get your rooms ready."

Sean frantically closed the laptop as it began to emit a dangerous amount of smoke—his *third* one. The other two lay broken down in the corner of the room, both their motherboards fried in the attempt of getting access to the super-secured and encrypted databases of Haven. Third time's the charm, however, and he managed to get in.

One minute and thirty-seven seconds, that was all the time he got to find out just how much Haven knew about the twins before his unauthorized access was detected and he was booted off the server. The laptop gave up soon after.

"C'mon, c'mon, Lil, pick up!" He fought the urge to throw the phone against the wall as it rung and rung. Considering it was 3 a.m., give or take, it wasn't too strange for Lilly to not pick up her phone, but this was urgent.

He dialed again. No response.

A hard knock sounded on the apartment door.

"Sean Cooper? Open up, son. We know you're in there, no use resisting. Let's not make this hard, okay?"

Sean heard the familiar sound of a handgun magazine clicking into place and jumped to his feet.

"*Shit!*" His fingers slid over the locking mechanism of the phone again, but this time he opened his text messages.

The pounding on the door intensified, and with his back turned towards it, Sean shivered as he heard a loud crack as the wood gave way.

"Cooper! We know what you did, and there's gonna be hell to pay! You're going to see some *shit* making you wish that Pthnymerian Spider Queen would've finished the job! Open up NOW!"

Sean typed faster, feeling as if he was wading in a pool of his own sweat.

He hit send.

Then, as quickly as he could, he forced his strength on the outer edges of the phone until it snapped in half. The device made a sharp cracking sound in perfect harmony with the door slamming to the ground in a splintered mess. A group of men in black sunglasses and suits stormed into the apartment; Sean was forced down on the ground at gunpoint.

The agent that had been addressing him from the other side of the door grinned as he held his head close to Sean's. Sean saw his teeth were dirty, yellow and brown, and his breath stank like aged coffee. The point of his gun pricked painfully against Sean's temple.

"That's right, Mr. Cooper." The agent was taking immense pleasure in his moment of triumph. "We know everything there is to know about you. Every. Little. Thing. What makes you tick and what gives you… conniptions. Are you going to be a good boy and work with us? Hmm?"

"How about taking a breath mint first, you creepy, goddamn *lizard*," Sean hissed.

"Shame." The agent raised an eyebrow, and the strange speckled skin beneath his receding hairline wrinkled. "Fine."

The agent took his gun off Sean's head and fired a shot.

Sean gave a bloodcurdling scream as his right middle finger was blown off, evaporated from the brute force of a bullet so close to its target.

The agent stood up from the floor and kicked Sean in the stomach. "Take him away, agents." He grinned as he turned his head back to Sean. "Look alive, *Sergeant*. You're entering a world of *fucking nightmares*."

Buzz. Buzz. Buzz.

Lilly opened her eyes and yawned. The phone going off was lighting up half the room. She looked at the Austrian cuckoo clock, another one of Paw's eccentric pieces, and groaned.

"3 a.m. What the…" She stretched her arm out and reached for the phone. Her face darkened as she noted the missed calls from Sean. She opened the text message and gasped at what she read:

They'll find you everywhere!!!! Santa Rosa? MOVE! They are COMING!! GO NOW! DESTROY THE PHONE!

"Oh no, oh f—" Lilly bolted from the bed and made a rather poor effort of getting her clothes on straight.

"Quince? QUINCY! Dammit!" Lilly kicked open the guest bedroom door and strode across the hall towards Quincy's room. She threw open the door, and the hard bang of the wood hitting the wall made her brother jump up and fall flat onto the floor.

"Lil? What the f—" He struggled with the words, still half asleep.

"Shut up!" Lilly blew the label sticking up from her reversed shirt away from her mouth. "I just got a text from Sean, says Haven already knows we're in Santa Rosa and we gotta move right now!"

I knew I liked this Sean fellow; he's got a heart for the right cause.

Quincy got up from the floor and sat back down on the bed. He grabbed the pillow he had been using and pressed it against his face in exhaustion.

"Right now?"

At that moment, a low rumbling began to emit from beneath the foundations of the house. It started softly at first but gained momentum pretty damn fast. Glasses and lights clinked together, and furniture creaked and shifted. A gigantic shock wave next rippled through the house as if a truck had driven straight into the parlor. Quincy grabbed the edge of the bed while his sister clung to the doorframe.

"I'm guessing *right now*, yes!" she snapped, shaking dust out of her hair.

Another huge bang came, the whole house creaking in dissatisfaction. Paw's stylish paintings on the many artistic expressions of the moose came crashing down to the ground, their frames shattering with a pang in the hallway.

"Do you think it's an earthquake?" Lilly raised her voice to be heard over the roaring of the shaking building. She struggled to keep her balance. "You're smart, Quince, do earthquakes happen often in New Mexico?"

"How would I know?" Quincy fought to keep his balance as he pulled his pants on one leg at a time. "I didn't *major* in geology!"

The shaking got so bad for a minute that the twins swore the left side of the house just sank a few inches deeper into the ground.

"What in the name of the Infinite Abyss is going on *now*?" Tim's lamp flashed on with bright summer colors. The lamp slid off the nightstand, but Lilly managed to catch it in time.

"Wait, is this floor still straight?" Lilly's mouth fell open as she saw the debris of the painting frames slide casually from the right side of the room to the left. Down a slope. "Aah, Quince, the house is *sinking*!"

Quincy grabbed the handful of things he had laying around and threw his backpack around his shoulders. "Don't have to tell me twice!"

"By the cold, harsh flicker of my neon flame, something wicked this way came." Tim whispered in an eerie tongue.

"Are we going fishing? Hehehe. I'm afraid the *bait* is a little bit out of your league."

"What the hell is *he* on about?" Quincy snarled through his teeth. "If he hasn't got anything helpful to say, tell him to *shut* whatever part it is that the noise is coming from!"

"Got all your things?" Paw came running towards the doorway, looking pretty shook up. He was wearing leather motorcycle attire, goggles, and a nifty brown leather cowboy hat.

The twins followed Paw as he flew through the house at incredible speed getting his things: a flashlight, a rifle, some supplies. Now and then, another huge bang shook the house, and the floor was growing more uneven by the second.

"So how bad is it?" Quincy turned to Paw, trying his very best to keep up with the immaculately fit old-timer.

"Oh, it's very, *very* bad, Quincy."

"Like, tell us more… Richter scale-wise, what are we looking at?" Quincy was panting between every word; power walking wasn't his forte.

Paw stopped in his tracks and turned around, looking Quincy dead in the eye. "*Richter* scale? Earthquakes? Son, we've got at least *three* full-grown adult Primordial Wurms hammering at the foundations of the house from beneath the soil." He yanked the front door open and pushed the twins through, pointing at the pickup truck on the sandy driveway. "Go, go! Go as fast as you can!"

"*Primordial Wurms?*" Quincy threw his backpack in the back of the truck and opened the door. "Are those what I think they are?"

"Delightful," Tim slurped. "I have always wanted to see one up and close.

Paw pulled the driver's door closed and started the engine. "Well, I'm not giving you the chance!"

About ten feet in front of the car, a giant wormlike monster emerged from the soil with a deafening roar ending in a mad shriek even though it had no visible mouth to speak of, just a face full of jittering insect-like mandibles with green acid-like fluid it drooled from its clacking jaws. The giant thing was golden brown, covered in slime, and looked very pissed off.

"Too late, old man!" Tim cackled in triumph. "Muahaha-hahahahaaaa!"

Paw crushed the gas pedal as hard as he could, and the car jolted in reverse, out of the driveway, and away from the hulking monstrosity.

"I should've never told all those people to release their pet Wurms into the desert when they start to reach an arm's length." Lilly cried, her hand tightly squeezing the brilliant silver key she didn't want to lose.

"I shall try to get back to you on that, since I would very much like to know what that statement means!" Paw said before focusing on driving. His nimbleness with the car's gearshift was extraordinary, and Lilly and Quincy were convinced that the old Navajo's driving skills would be the only reason they would get off the ranch alive.

The car shot straight through the ranch's wooden fence onto the paved main road. The rumbling seemed to follow them away from the house and towards the open plains.

"Don't get your hopes up." Paw's eyes glistened in the rearview mirror as he looked behind him. "Lots of the Great Wurms make their home in the desert, but they usually stay dormant far beneath the surface. Something or someone agitated this pack into attacking us and…"

"And once they are disturbed, the average Primordial Wurm will never cease their assault until their prey is abso-lutely decimated," Lilly finished, remembering the standard instruction she had to memorize while working in the exotic pet shop.

Quincy looked out of the window. "They can't get through the paved asphalt, can they?"

"They can if they really want to, but I wouldn't worry about it that much," Paw replied.

"How so?"

"In about a mile or so, all there is left is dry, dirt road."

"Oh."

Chapter 9

"WHAT'S THAT? Do you see it, Quincy?" Paw adjusted his rearview mirror and pointed.

Lilly opened her eyes and sighed loudly.

The morning sun had risen quite fast over the outstretched wastelands of the Chihuahuan Desert, and the heat had become unbearable. Paw's old pickup was a fixer-upper with no AC, but in regards to outrunning the giant underground Wurms rumbling about Paw's ranch, it did the job admirably. Only a slight tremble could still be felt beneath the wheels of the car, and that was including the generally rocky terrain.

But now a new problem had surfaced.

"It looks like we're being followed." Quincy glanced out the back window before his eyes met his sister's in the backseat. "Black vehicles, looks like Haven has caught our scent."

Lilly slammed her hands hard against the back of Quincy's seat. "*How* can you be so calm about all of this?" she cried angrily, visibly distressed. "Just one day… I'd really like to just make it *one* day in a semi-comfortable place without having to worry about being followed or eaten or killed." She pulled up her knees towards her face, and a tear rolled down her cheek. "I'm tired of running. I want to go home."

Quincy could understand her pain from the inheritance to the sudden and violent departure from New Orleans to the memories of their parents that all came flooding back. He couldn't even imagine the kind of strain Lilly was under. She had seen these violent events before.

"Listen, sis, you're the strongest person I know. If anyone could see this thing through to the end, I'd put my life savings to the odds that you'd be that person." He struggled to keep his own tears in check. "Furthermore. You are pretty much the only person keeping me sane." He grabbed her hand and smiled. "I need you in this, Lil. More than anyone else. We'll get through this together."

Lilly smiled slightly, wiping her face. He could be such an odd fellow sometimes, but when push came to shove, he could be as caring and as emotional as the lot of 'em. "If we're gonna end up dead, I'd want no one other than my own stupid brother to spend eternity with." She laughed when he rolled his eyes.

"That was truly touching," Paw chimed in, "but dare I say we truly *do* have a problem on our hands here."

The black unmarked all-terrain vehicles and combat-outfitted Land Rovers of Haven came sliding into view. High in number and probably better outfitted for the dry desert, they appeared to have no trouble outrunning the functioning but battered pickup truck.

"What are we going to do?" Quincy held fast to his seat as the car swooned over a large bump of dry vegetation.

The truck took an involuntary sharp turn to the right as one of the enhanced Haven Land Rovers crashed into their truck bed.

Paw struggled to keep control of the wheel and pulled the truck to the far left, just barely avoiding another collision with a gun-outfitted quad bike. "I don't know! I really don't! Ideas, any ideas are welcome." He pulled a hard right, and one of the black Land Rovers raced past them.

Lilly quickly glanced behind her. "Paw! What's underneath these blankets in the back?"

"Guns," he replied. "But we don't have much ammo for them, and I'm not in the habit of shooting people, just wild animals that happen to be too close to the ranch." He stomped hard on the brakes, and one of the ATVs flew past; he then slammed the gas pedal and crashed into its back. The Haven soldiers, outfitted in black SWAT-like gear, held on for dear life. However, one unlucky sod managed to careen out of the back—there was a bump and a sick crunch.

"Well, there goes my reputation of being a kind soul," Paw complained.

"We could use this stuff!" Lilly yelled over the noise of roaring engines. "We could fight back and…" She screamed and dove forward; seconds later, gunfire from a trailing quad bike broke the back window, and glass flew everywhere.

Paw made another sharp left turn, and the truck spun hard, kicking up sand and dirt. Immediately he went right and kicked the brakes, leaving more clouds of sand behind.

Lilly reached into the back of the pickup through the shattered glass and started piling the bricks and larger pieces of wood onto the seat next to her. Every once in a while, she had to stop for her own safety, as Paw was fighting to outmaneuver their pursuers.

"Can I just say you're an amazing *kick, effin, ass* driver?" She smiled when Paw chuckled a bit.

Quincy just felt nauseous. This business wasn't his forte at all. He'd rather be back in Lafayette figuring out how to send a Dimensional Shambler back to its home-plane; at least they had a tendency to move a lot slower. After giving it a bit of thought, he realized that that line of thinking was an absolute lie. He sank into the seat.

"Quincy!" Lilly yelled. "I need you here!" She was

stacking the bricks up next to her and handed one of them to her brother. "Weight?" she asked.

Quincy broke out of his painful self-pity session and straightened his spine. He took the brick carefully.

"Uhm…five to six pounds, maybe," he answered. "Why?" Quincy gave the brick back and held on as the truck took another hit and dipped to the left-hand side.

Lilly gave him a curious look. "I need your math skills," she said with a grin. "Give me an angle, the timing, the amount of bricks, anything!"

Quincy ran the quick calculations through his head. Most of it was purely speculative, but it had to do for now.

"Okay," he started and glanced over at Paw then at Lilly, "this is mostly guesswork, but…"

"As good as it's going to get, bro," Lilly reminded him.

He gave a quick smirk and turned to Paw. "Paw, on my signal, hit the brakes full-on for about three seconds, then go back to top speed." Paw nodded in understanding. Quincy then looked back to Lilly. "When I say go, throw two bricks out of the right window, try to aim for the tires."

"Wait, what do you mean? The *right* window as in the right one depending on where the quad is going to veer off to, or the right-hand side window? From which side? Yours or mine?" Lilly intervened. She stared at the bricks beside her in confusion.

"Uh… Crap, I hadn't thought of that. Take the… You know what, just go with your gut; I trust you."

"Dear Lord." Lilly puckered her lips. "After all these years, still trying to lay the blame on me if things would go wrong," she teased.

Quincy looked ahead, then back, then to the sides. He alternated this for a few minutes until he was sure the quad's ammo magazine was empty and needed to reload; that would be their window to strike. The other vehicles, two Land Rovers, two ATVs, and another quad, surrounded them for now. They must've decided it was less of a risk to simply let the truck run out of gas, then come grab them.

Quincy took a deep breath. "Okay… ready?" He held up his hand towards Paw. "Now!"

Paw slammed the brakes hard for exactly three seconds.

The trailing quad and its driver came flying towards the truck first. Its driver was so preoccupied with reloading the mounted gun that he nearly slammed right into the back of the pickup. At the last moment, he veered right, and Lilly was waiting for him.

"Go, sis!"

Lilly released the bricks out of the window. They neatly bounced off the dry dirt once and proceeded to perfectly lodge themselves underneath the body of the quad between the vehicle itself and the ground. In an instant, the quad's back flew up into the air, and the driver was launched off… But, in an unforeseen turn of events, he managed to snag the right side of the pickup's back at the last minute and held on tight.

"Veer left, Paw!"

Paw pulled on the wheel. The cursing and moaning of the Haven agent could somewhat be heard over the noise of the entire spectacle—the agent held on firmly. Even worse, he improved his grip.

Lilly threw a brick that hit the agent right in his face, which was obscured by a ski mask and goggles. She heard his cries, but still he held on. She threw another one and another.

"Why. Won't. You. FALL?" Lilly grabbed at the empty space beside her, realizing she was out of things to throw.

Paw had to dodge an oncoming formation of boulders, making the truck veer sharply to the right. This gave the Haven agent, bloodied and bruised as he was, just enough momentum to throw himself into the back of Paw's truck. He idled for a few seconds, trying to get his balance sorted out, before taking the gun out of his holster and pointing it straight at Lilly.

Lilly could only stare at the deep, dark hole of the gun barrel. She was done fighting; this was it. She would die a miserable, unimportant death in the middle of nowhere.

Everything had been for nothing.

As the black-clothed Haven agent prepared to pull the trigger, a significant tremor deep beneath the ground made him struggle with his balance, almost losing his footing again. He shot and missed, the left side mirror of the truck exploding into fragments. The agent cocked the gun again but fell to his knees.

The desert floor seemed to be cracking and shifting, the rumbling worsening. Once more, the Haven agent stood up, determined to finish his mission. Alas, just as he had pointed the gun back to Lilly, a humongous, slimy, and jittering monstrosity leaped from the side of the truck right into him, leaving nothing but a spray of red mist and a pair of feet in black boots.

It happened so suddenly that Lilly could barely comprehend what just happened. She felt a trickle of blood hit her face and screamed.

"*Holy shit!*" She turned towards her companions.

"Don't say anything!" Paw cried, gripping the wheel of the truck tighter. "We both saw it!"

"The Primordial Wurms are back. We're screwed," Quincy groaned, dismayed from the turn of events that always seemed to be a tad worse than before.

A little to the right of the car, the trio saw one of Haven's ATVs sink beneath the rocky desert floor, and within seconds a geyser of blood and shiny metal car parts spurted from the newly created fissure.

A little black dot appeared on the horizon—first as incomprehensible as a green pea in a meadow, then it rapidly started to grow, and in less than a minute, the dot had transformed into a shadowy robed figure riding a spectral horse along the cracks in the dry ground.

"It's Kraal. He found us!" Quincy cried and turned to Lilly. "What now?"

"Who?" Paw chimed in.

"It's the black mage that Crow—" Lilly started, only to join Paw and her brother in a terrified chorus of screams as six or seven adult Wurms rose up all around them. Eyeless, the long tube-like hulks of mucus-drenched terror swathed around wildly.

When one of the Haven vehicles drew too close, unlucky victims were lifted up from their seats and dragged into the beast's fleshy maw by one of the vibrating and oozing mandibles protruding from it.

"FOR THE HATRED OF A MALIGN COSMOS, WHAT IN PURGATORY'S NAME IS GOING ON OUT THERE?" a voice cursed from within Lilly's backpack.

Lilly pulled out the oil lamp with shaking hands and saw that it was pulsing a bright mix of orange, purple, and pink.

"I understand you'd go *mad* at even the *thought* of having me around all the time, flesh bags. But I could've choked to death in that dark and humid contraption!" Tim complained, causing the lamp to rock back and forth.

"Again, you're literally *vapor*."

"I am more than you can possibly imagine! Muahahaha-ha!" Tim chimed victoriously.

Quincy groaned loudly and reached for the lamp. He held it firmly between his hands and snapped, "We are *not* in the position to be cracking jokes right now, stupid purple ink stain!" He rattled the lamp like it was a Magic 8-Ball. "We're surrounded by Primordial Wurms and are probably within moments of *death*. Help us!"

"*Primordial Wurms?*" Tim exploded in laughter. "You are still dealing with Primordial Wurms? You should've called upon me earlier, as always, stupid humans. Now..." His booming voice turned into a whisper. "Turn down your engine, stop what you're doing, and stand perfectly still!"

. . .

Lilly raised an eyebrow. "What?"

"They don't have eyes, dimwitted female specimen," Tim roared. "They hunt for prey through vibration and sound. They won't find you if you don't move and make absolutely no noise whatsoever."

Quincy looked at the horizon and noticed that Kraal had disappeared. Quincy thought of him as a menace, a force to be reckoned with, but with what Crowley told them, Kraal also seemed to have a massively inflated ego and apparently put too much trust in his pets. "Paw, shut it down," he said.

"Excuse me?" Paw protested. "You're seriously doing what that, that *thing* tells you to you? He's one of them!"

"As much as I hate to say it, Paw, this *thing* has already saved us once. As a matter of fact, it does seem logical that the one thing humans wouldn't be able to comprehend would be to *not* run away from giant flesh-eating worms."

Paw cursed loudly. "Damn it all; tonight was bowling night."

He shut down the car.

"Yes. Of course, it's done." Kraal swept the single bead of sweat from his brow, looking satisfied in a grim way. "Once the beasts are done, they'll report back to me and disappear back into the earth. I'll get the key afterwards. What? Yes, we'll call it an earthquake, tectonic plates shuffling about. If someone saw one of them, it's no matter; everyone knows they dwell beneath the Chihuahuan." Kraal rested the cruddy flip phone between his ear and shoulder, flicking his hands. From a puff of smoke, a clock manifested before him.

"Yes, sir, yes, this line is 100 percent secure." He rolled his eyes. "There is absolutely zero chance of them escaping, sir. Your men? I cannot guarantee them *not* getting in the way. It's on them." Kraal puffed his lips, blowing the vaporous clock apart. "You what? You'll have my head otherwise? Uh-uh, okay. Goodbye." Kraal slammed the flip phone together, and the device emitted red and green sparks before disintegrating in his hands.

Frustrated, the wizard got back on his ghostly horse, a gift from the Grim Reaper himself, and kicked the beast between its cracked ribs—the echo of its eerie neighing could be heard reverberating across the entire valley. Kraal rode off.

"Have my head… Ha! Not before I'll have yours first, you slimy, bloated bastard."

The sand beneath the tires of the truck shifted and rumbled. In the distance, the agonizing screams of the Wurms' unfortunate victims filled the air.

"So, this is kind of working, what do we do now?" Lilly asked Tim, shuffling about nervously.

"Ssh! Stop talking, are you nuts?" Quincy whispered, his eyes were popping out of his head.

"I think the gurgled cries of all those people literally being eaten alive right now should at least *help* cover up some background banter, wouldn't you *think*, bro?"

Tim let out a hearty giggle at that.

"We're still sitting ducks for those things as long as we stay here and can't move anywhere!" Quincy protested. "It's only a matter of time before they're done with their Haven morsels and remember there are three other snacks waiting."

The sound of an incoming engine silenced the twins' banter. Paw, Quincy, and Lilly peeked out of the cracked truck windows, trying to make as little noise as possible… even though there was an entire ruckus going on just over the rocky outcropping to their left. The helicopters flew into view, and Lilly immediately recognized the sandy color of the GDF special desert operative choppers, a mixture of tan and bleached bone. More noise was added to the mix as from the southeast there came the similarly colored rough terrain buggies and modified cross motors.

It appeared as if the GDF was coming to save the day.

"This doesn't make sense."

"Huh? Why would it ever not make sense?" Quincy took a sip from the water canteen and frowned at his sister. He couldn't hide his relief at seeing the special forces gather around the giant worms thrashing about.

"Who called this in?" Lilly shook her head. "GDF only responds to activity having a severe threat to humanity, places where there's a risk of many victims, in big communities or metropolitan cities. Haven would never stoop as low as to call them for help; they'd rather let their agents die with dignity from a significant supernatural threat. Furthermore, the Wurms aren't harming anyone else; we're in the middle of nowhere.

"Nobody knows we are here. And hell, even if they did, they wouldn't march out to save two stupid twenty-one-year-olds and an old man who disturbed the giant worm monstrosities of which they should've known would be in the desert."

"That's horrible," Quincy muttered. "I thought the GDF was created for this exact purpose."

"To neutralize significant anomalies that threaten cities and continents—the entire planet." Lilly sighed. "This whole thing should *not* be worthy of their attention, even with Haven's involvement."

"If the Global Defense Force's goal is to neutralize big threats, then what does this Haven, the men in black, do exactly?" Paw kept a close look at the war zone beginning to unfold just a mile or so to the east.

"Haven is bad business," Quincy explained. "Nobody knows exactly what their end goal is. I bet three-quarters of the planet don't even know of their existence. And neutralizing doesn't seem to be a term used often by them. When discussing the supernatural, they'd rather talk about study, containment, or worse… weaponizing."

Lilly nodded. "So, then why is the GDF here…?"

"*Deus ex machina*," Paw mumbled.

Lilly looked up. "Excuse me?"

"The Latin phrase… 'God in the machine'? It is used often to describe an event of divine intervention." Quincy turned to Paw. "What on Earth are you on about, Paw?"

"When all possible explanations have been expended and disproved, we must look towards the impossible." Paw turned the ignition key, and the truck roared back to life. "We don't know why the soldiers are here, but look." He pointed to the east. "They're driving the beasts off. Impossibility somehow saved the day. We're getting the hell out of here; Three Rivers is close."

"You two," Tim whispered, "have a *very* unusual knack for survival… *Accidental* survival. But I tell you if it were just you two in the Great Library of Celaeno with a Stargazing Shrieker, then things wouldn't be so—"

Tim's ramblings disappeared when Lilly stuffed the lamp back into the backpack.

"See ya later, Tim."

With the sounds of gunfire, hoarse screaming, and thunderous engines' roaring still raging, the twins, Paw, and Tim rode off as fast as they could in the exact opposite direction.

The strange conical shape shifted on its axis. It released its elongated three-fingered claw from the exposed wire that lead right into the heart of the central server. The black metal bonds dug hard into its green, rubbery skin. The shape's breaths were uneven and sounded laborious as it tried to twist into the least painful position of its prison.

"Is it done, brother?" Caine's voice drifted through the flickering green room like lighting conducting off an antenna.

"It is done," Abel acknowledged with a metallic, rasping moan. "They are…"

"…on their own now…" Caine finished and coughed. Flecks of what seemed like stardust drifted to the top of the room. "Thank you."

Chapter 10

THE GDF, or *Global Defense Force*, originated when several of the world's most elite military and special ops teams joined forces during the first Type 1 Awakening Events that took place not long after the Abandonment. The consequences of dealing with a newfound Eldritch truth shook many world leaders to their core. So it came to be that after the preliminary threats were neutralized, a worldwide elite military force would be established.

Would-be soldiers of the GDF were trained under the harshest of physical and mental conditions to prepare for whatever would lie ahead in their newfound career. Thus, only the best of the best could apply, and only those who would rise even beyond that would serve time in the GDF.

Outside of the quarterly psychological evaluation, every six months a rigorous test of physical prowess would determine if a soldier was fit for another quarter or half a year of service. If not, the soldier would be dismissed and return to live their life as a civilian with the pride and glory of having served in the GDF—and living to tell the tale.

The organization prides itself on its strict code and procedures yet maintains a distinct freedom among its many chapters. About a year or two after the Abandonment, special ops teams were trained for specific threats, and code names were given to all of them. Each chapter or task force of the GDF got their orders from a centralized hub somewhere on Earth, but the manner of executing their orders would vastly differ.

A particularly devious task force known as The Crimson Ghosts were dishonorably discharged not long after they had completed a mission in a city somewhere near the capital of Oslo, Norway. The team, led by their captain Otto Vanhoorn, had been called in to investigate and disrupt a lesser demon prowling around in the city. The demon supposedly turned many of the town's inhabitants into meaty lumps of flesh that would crawl across the ground, spitting acid. The wicked mounds of bloody blobs could infect other townsfolk—turning into a pandemic. Thus, the event known as the Liquid Zombie Apocalypse started.

After dispersing the demon and destroying the remainder of its unfortunate victims, something went very wrong inside Otto Vanhoorn's head. Whether it was the demon having possessed Otto at the last moment or simply the snapping of the last strings of his sanity is still unclear to this day. The Crimson Ghosts were ordered to purge the entire city, with anyone refusing their orders shot the second they revealed their doubts. The city was set ablaze, and Otto led an exciting, albeit short, life as his self-proclaimed new alter ego *Red Specter* while he danced around the smoldering ruins. A second GDF team in the vicinity of Oslo, the Fire Starters (kind of an unfortunate name given the situation), answered the call to eliminate the new threat of a chapter gone wrong.

Fortunately, the tales of GDF wrongdoings are few and far between. The organization has prided itself on its experience and knowledge of dealing with the now ever-looming supernatural threats.

Take the Tomb Prospectors task force, for example, who

solved the mystery of the shape-shifting maze within the Copenhagen metro system by locating and destroying the Abysswalker that was luring unfortunate victims to its lair. Or the Vampire Killers, who got their task force name by single-handedly ridding the Paris catacombs of an entire coven of Nightstalkers led by an exceptionally dangerous Tepessite. Even recent events have made their way to the mouths of the masses. Stories of the Gray Hounds task force have already been going around, them having recently rid the city of Lafayette from the claws of a huge Dimensional Shambler.

What was curious though, there were no mention of any Haven agents… or meddlesome twins made in those tales.

The Navajo settlement of Three Rivers, New Mexico, was a highly visited trading post back in the day when the offspring of the first English American settlers rode west in search of new lands and gold. Three Rivers got its name due to the three streams of pure, clean water emanating from its surrounding rocky hills that ran through the land. It was an oasis of immaculate, fertile ground and a beacon of light for weary travelers in an otherwise harsh and unforgiving desert. The ancient Navajo chieftains prided themselves for being able to provide such blessed land for their people, and every year great ceremonies were held to please the now unknown gods and spirits the age-old tribe worshipped.

Nowadays, the settlement appeared to be completely abandoned. Circles of stone and rotten wood were strewn about, giving only subtle clues of the quaint buildings and huts that used to adorn grounds alongside the rivers. The rivers themselves were all dried up, leaving only the traces of crackled soil and petrified fish bones to indicate a beautiful stream of water had once flowed there. The lands were swallowed up by the desert and lay lonely in the shadows of the surrounding mesas.

Strange desert plants now grew alongside the dried

riverbeds. The Death's Head flower was recognized partially by its bright red petals that indicated danger, but mostly by the fact that a human skull was nestled on top of each stem. To try and wander through a field of Death's Heads is said to be the equivalent of playing Russian roulette. On one hand, the plants could do absolutely nothing but follow you around with their empty eye sockets and permanent grins. On the other hand, it could sprout thorny vines and ensnare its living prey. The victim would be caught with no way out and be slowly drained of blood by the thousands of microthorns pricking into their skin.Many Death's Heads even liked to play with their victims, giving them just enough substance to live another day, thus making the grueling process last for days, weeks, or even months. Eventually, the victims would expire, and their bodies served to feed the soil the Death's Heads occupied.

"But then the worst is yet to come… It is said that victims of the Death's Head flower would eventually become one themselves, and, if you listen closely near a field of them at night, you can still hear the tortured cries of the souls that fell victim to these horrific flowers." Paw looked away from the flowers in disgust. "So much beauty in this world, now gone rotten."

"Creepy story." Lilly blinked and looked towards the sun. It was high noon, and the temperature had risen considerably.

Paw nodded and wiped the sweat from his brow.

The group had been wandering through the broken-down structures and piles of rubble for about an hour and a half now. There didn't seem to be anything noteworthy around for miles except for the few stories Paw could tell about the land and its history.

"The thing about the plants. I didn't know about all of that," she said, watching her footing while traversing over uneven rocks.

"Well, I did, and I kind of hoped I never had to come this close to them." Quincy stared at the bright red cluster of petals in disgust. "I've heard enough of these stories from the biology majors in college. Apparently, there was an organized field study a few years back that went horribly wrong."

Tim's lamped bobbed up and down in Lilly's hand. "That sounds like a right bit of fun, Master! Please do tell more. Muahahaha."

"I'd rather not, I…"

Lilly's eyes grew wide, and with a smile she tapped the lamp, making it slide off the smooth rock she had just planted him on.

"Ow!" Tim complained, hitting the ground. "In Chatturga's name, why?"

"Did you just call Quincy '*Master*'?"

Quincy raised an eyebrow, realizing he had heard the Fire Vampire right.

Tim glowed a slightly orange, as if it was his personal way of blushing. "I… uh, you must have heard wrong, my Mistress, I…"

"*Mistress*?" Lilly nearly fell off her rock from laughter. "I knew it!" she yelled. "You *like* us, Tim! You like us so much; you just think we're super swell, don't ya?"

"I… 'Tis but a duty I have for Mr. Crowley, I…"

"*Mister* Crowley, huh?" Quincy looked at his sister and grinned. "Wasn't it *Master Crowley* before?"

The lamp shook nervously. "It… Is it hot here or what? The sun, so grossly incandescent today, it must have some kind of negative effect on me. That's it, surely. Ha-ha-ha. Ha."

"You're the offspring of a space god *made of fire*!" Lilly howled.

Quincy massaged his jaws, trying to hide a smile. "It's okay, Tim. We like you too."

"That's okay, Master, I…"

Lilly cackled loudly. "I can't take this!" Tears were welling up in the corners of her eyes. Even Paw started chuckling now, only half-understanding the situation.

Tim flashed an angry red mixed with violet and indigo. "Bah! I say one thing to accommodate you bags of insignificant blood and bones, and this is how you repay me? By mocking *me*? I am Timaxoatilaciluzipta! *I* am the one who mocks!"

Lilly covered her mouth and held her breath, trying to control herself and stop another outburst, but that proved to be harder than escaping Lafayette or dodging secret agents in a desert full of giant leeches, because soon she was doubled over with laughter.

"Okay, okay," Quincy began, "it's getting too warm for this nonsense." He grabbed the oil lamp from the sand and sat it on his lap. He then untied the jacket from his waist and used the sleeve to clean the glass; Tim glowed a satisfied pink. "So, great Timaxo… Timolaa…"

"Timaxoatilaciluzipta! He who rends the flesh from the carcasses of PLANETS, HAA!"

"Okay, great Timaxoatilaciluzipta." Quincy saw Lilly and Paw's eyes widen as he pronounced it correctly; he shrugged. "As you can see, your unfortunate Master and Mistress appear to be in a rut of some sort. We did everything as instructed by W.A. Swansong and Aleister Crowley and yet here we are, dumbstruck."

"Here you are," Tim echoed.

Lilly understood what her brother was going for and chimed in. "Oh, great one! Magnificent being that came from the far cosmos in order to help *us*, sorry excuses of carbon-based life-forms, *humanity*, which you so rightfully mock."

"Hmmmm, yesssss!" Tim buzzed with glee.

"What should we do now?" Paw wondered aloud. The trio moved to sit around Tim's lamp, causing him to bask in glory.

"Let me see that key of yours, Mistress." Tim swirled around behind the glass, green and turquoise sparks popping up from deep within the core of the otherworldly entity.

Lilly dutifully held the shining silver key up towards the lamp. "I'd prefer you just call me Lilly, by the way," she said. "It was fun for a while, but *Mistress* makes me very uncomfortable."

"This writing here," Tim said, ignoring her, as he splashed a bit of crimson in the lower corner of the glass, indicating a spot on the key, "it mentions a test. Navajo, what does it say again?"

"Yidiists'a'," Paw answered. "It means to hear."

"To *hear*," Tim repeated just half a second behind Paw.

Lilly and Quincy looked at each other.

"Very good, Navajo."

"I prefer Paw."

"What?"

"You call me Navajo, generalizing me and boiling me down to a single set of facts about my people and race and—"

"All right, all right, *jeez*... *Paw*," Tim hissed. "Now, with the powers of extreme, superior intellect invested in me, I will relay my answer to you, the forever-inferior species."

"Get on with it," Quincy pressed.

"I hear..." Tim's voice started to take on a strange rattling sound. For such a powerful being as the trapped Fire Vampire was, and as hilarious as Tim proved to be, he could almost be considered unnerving right now. "Water."

"You hear water?" Paw looked around. "That's impossible."

"Three distinct streams of water flow deep beneath the earth. None are as mighty as what once was, but still, they flow." Tim bathed them in yellow and silvery streaks.

"Three streams," Quincy announced, the pieces falling into place. "Take key—go westward—toward desert—*three stream*. The riddle *does* make sense. I was so afraid we had been heading in an entirely wrong direction!"

"And again it is *I* who points you in the right direction, Master," Tim chimed in. "Somewhere west of here, the waters collide, and..." Tim paused as if in thought, his colors flickering. "…they drop down. Deep, deep down into the Earth."

"Right." Lilly stood up. "I've heard enough." She began to sift through the rubble of a nearby ruin.

"You don't believe me, my Mis— uh, Lilly?" Tim sounded confused.

Lilly came back, breaking little twigs off a nice long branch she had spotted earlier. "Oh, I believe you 100 percent." She took the lamp and hung it at the tip of the branch, which she moved to hold at chest-height pointing forward.

Quincy and Paw stood up, both chuckling.

"Lead the way, my all-powerful dowsing device!" Lilly yelled happily, and Tim sighed.

Kraal walked away from the smoldering graveyard of metal and half-devoured carcasses that piled up in the middle of the Chihuahuan. The air was quiet, and the ground was still. Kraal held the hand he used to streak the blood off the desert sand to his nose and gave it a good smell.

It lacks young blood;

The black mage screamed in anger at the realization.

Behind him, great pillars of fire rose from the earth, and the smoking pyre was again ablaze. Flustered, Kraal tried to calm himself down and moved to stroke the green, algae-like mane of his spectral steed. Raising his head, he inched closer and closer to the undead horse's muzzle.

The mage's mouth puckered, and he whispered soft words into the ghostly ears,

"Disappointing. Isn't it?"

The horse exploded.

"Over there!" Quincy pointed.

After gathering some supplies from the truck and about a

half hour's hike along the wall of the mesa, the group stumbled upon another area of ruins. However, these seemed more peculiar since they were tucked away discreetly beneath the shadow of two overhanging cliffs. It looked like a good spot to hide things from even the nosiest of desert dwellers. The derelict, waist-high walls seemed to crumble at the touch but didn't look like anything more out of the ordinary than the previous encampment ruins they were just at.

"Something sleeps below." Tim swooshed around in the lamp at the end of the stick Lilly held. "The streams converge here, deep beneath the surface of this dry plain."

"Something what? Sleeps?" Lilly protested and shook her head. "Why can't things just be easy for once?"

Paw let the bag of guns, torches, and other supplies fall off his shoulder. "The spirit of the lamp is right. I feel something old, something ancient stirring. These aren't just ruins…" He looked around, noting curious Navajo symbols carved into the rocks nearby.

"Look." His fingers traced along the image of a man, perhaps a primitive Navajo ancestor. The man's arms reached into the heavens, while below him a large open space was depicted just below the surface. A line of rectangles was carved underneath, together with various old depictions of animals. "The sacred buffalo, the lizard, and the tarantula." Paw sighed. "This is a tomb."

"Now hold on just a minute," Quincy protested, "a tomb of what exactly?"

"I'm afraid I do not know."

"All I see are the same beat-up old walls we've seen in Three Rivers so far. For the life of me, I just can't seem to figure out what we're missing here. What is supposed to be hidden out here?"

"A secret," Lilly reminded Quincy. "A riddle no one is known to have ever solved. Remember what the ghost of W.A. Swansong said…" Lilly delved into her pocket and revealed the silver Navajo key. "It's the key to enlightenment!"

She held the key high up towards the sky, and a

n ill wind began to flow between the cracks of the cliffs and the mesa walls. It was as if a final piece of a grand and intricate clockwork puzzle had just fallen into place.

Sunlight danced off the sparkling silver key, its reflected light shimmering against the red rocks surrounding the group. The heat of the day gave birth to a humid but chilly fog. It drifted up from the ground to about shoulder height, after which the irregular wind swept it away towards the now cloudy sky.

Lilly gasped and lowered her arms while Quincy and Paw looked on, puzzled, as the sand beneath their feet shifted away. It didn't drift away with the wind, however, but it parted evenly, a couple of yards to each side.

Between the old Navajo walls, which now lay broken down and forgotten by time, there was an intricate silver plate. The plate was decorated with all kinds of symbols and ancient hieroglyph-like drawings, as well as beautiful turquoise gemstones. By all means, the plate seemed to be a trapdoor, and smack-dab in the middle of it was an opening. There was a lock, the diameter and fitting an unmistakable match for the twins' artifact inheritance.

The place was as beautiful as I remembered it. I had only ventured there once, when my curiosity was still possible to satisfy. It was there I learned the truth, and it was in there that it was thrust upon me and my family to keep it a secret.

The trio huddled closely around the gorgeous silver plate. Even Tim was flashing with excitement as Lilly held up the key and shoved it into the lock with trembling hands.

It was a perfect fit.

Quincy held his breath as she turned it slowly to the left with precision, but about a quarter way it got stuck. Lilly twisted it once more. Stuck again. She cursed and turned it again, all the way to the right this time. A satisfying click emanated from the mechanism somewhere behind the door. The few grains of sand left along the edge of the plate and blew towards their feet. Suddenly, the whole thing lifted up about a quarter of an inch.

The key sank into the lock and disappeared.

Silence.

"That's it?" Lilly said, dismayed. "All that drama with the light and the wind and the strange fog and this is all we get?" She plopped down in disappointment.

"Lilly, come on!" Quincy inched a bit closer to the opening. "What did you expect?"

"I don't know, something more spectacular maybe?" she complained.

"Quit arguing over nothing, you two, and help me with this," Paw snapped, leaving both Lilly and Quincy a tad mortified. They had seen him worked up before, but he hadn't seemed like the angry grandpa type. Then again, they had only known him for little over a day, so what did they know?

The twins each took a side and lifted the great silver door upwards. It was surprisingly heavy, but three times the manpower and the enthusiastic shouting of a disembodied entity in a lamp made sure the job got done.

Lilly's breath caught, her eyes widening in awe.

Quincy gulped twice when he noticed the dark and ominous passageway leading down into the darkness below. He knew this would be the last stop of their quest, whatever that quest might be: To go down into the caverns, these caverns out in the desert westwards, where three streams became one.

"Help me prepare the torches," Paw requested as he dragged his duffel bag full of goodies towards the opening. "I have a feeling we're going to be needing as much light as we can carry."

Sean opened his eyes wearily and looked around the dark and empty room. He tried sitting upright, but his head was swirling all over the place. He slumped with a groan and shivered from the cold. Waiting for the dizziness to pass, he glanced up and down and from left to right.

The room was a bizarre architectural mess with walls that consisted of abnormally angled edges and odd twists. Some corners were black and spiraled into an intricate detailed mess of grooves, unclear to the naked eye. Others were flat, straight and light. There was no logic behind the design of the cell, yet it seemed to be created with the utmost mathematical precision.

A cell. Yes, that's what it was.

Sean laid there, quiet, his hand hurting like hell; his eyes flickered around again. The fact that he couldn't perceive the cell as one entity, one simple square space, disturbed him, and it made him angry. He tried to close his eyes, but he didn't dare go to sleep, likely ending up with what was probably a nasty concussion earlier.

Haven had him in their dirty claws, and he still had no idea why the twins were so important to the organization, but he was convinced he couldn't let them fall into the dark agency's hands.

They hadn't broken him.

Yet.

Quincy blinked away the beads of sweat prickling his eyes as he lifted the lit torch closer to the stone brazier adorning the wall. Paw and Lilly did the same, and the small stretch of stairway lit up with a soft orange glow.

Countless Navajo carvings adorned the walls. Perhaps they told an epic story about the earliest among the tribes, or perhaps they were simply shopping lists or cooking recipes. However unlikely that second option was, most of the symbols seemed to be too worn to tell.

Paw nevertheless halted at one of them. He looked grim but chuckled soon afterwards.

"What's so funny?" Quincy walked up to him, holding his touch closer to the wall to drop some extra light onto the carvings Paw stood in front of.

"See these, Quincy, Lilly? Oftentimes, these carvings are the subject of ridicule and wild speculation."

"How so?" Lilly asked.

Paw's hand wiped some of the dust and cobwebs from the wall. "Their true meaning is lost, even to the likes of me, but many fake scientists and conspiracy theory nut jobs link these ancient drawings to other native cultures such as those in Mexico, Chile, and Peru. See this one here?" He pointed at a carving of what looked like a half a moon rounded off to one side and ending in a sharp point on the other. A man was inside the moon, and he was surrounded by what seemed to be stars.

"Chariots of fire riding across the sky!" He laughed. "An ancient astronaut? Space travelers from ages past? Preposterous."

"Anything is possible," Quincy told him and drew the torch back from the wall.

"You say that, Quincy?" Paw answered in confusion. "A man of science?"

"Science, as it once was, is out of the window, Paw. Ever since a stupid black column of misery rose up from the deserts of Egypt," Quincy retorted. "You, on the other hand, I thought to have at least somewhat of an open mind. Being a man raised by the land and the spirits that closely watch over it."

Paw grunted and continued walking, leaving the twins following a bit behind.

"Aren't I an ancient… astronaut as you call it?" Tim called up to Lilly. He bobbed patiently, comfortably attached to Lilly's belt now.

Lilly patted the lamp. "Shh. Not now," she whispered. "I

don't know why Paw is down here helping us, but I get the feeling a part of him doesn't want to be here at all."

Tim mumbled something in a vague yet menacing extraterrestrial tongue before fading to silence.

The descent down into the bowels of the Earth was arduous. In between studying the ancient graffiti lining the smooth cavern walls and making sure nobody tripped on their feet and tumbled down, the trip definitely took longer than expected.

In fact, what were they expecting actually? It was a question that often popped into Quincy's mind on the parts of the trail that were dark and cold, where the walls started to get coarse and the steps uneven. He figured everyone present must've asked themselves the same question once or twice now, yet they all seemed to have the drive to go on.

For Quincy and Lilly, it was their promise to their parents and long-dead ancestor.

Paw, on the other hand, seemed more reluctant, but even he couldn't shake the feeling of excitement creeping over him. He had plunged himself headfirst into a sacred place linked to his own ancestry and must've been the first Navajo to do so in perhaps hundreds of years.

And Tim, well, he was simply there because he had no other place to go. Having no feet and being trapped in a lamp, he secretly hoped that some cosmic force would keep the twins alive just long enough for him to elope to greener pastures—or brighter nebulas, if you will.

"These particular three animal symbols keep coming back." Lilly pointed at the three distinct images of a spider, a lizard, and a buffalo.

"It was, in ages past, a test for young warriors." Paw moved his torch away from the collapsed bit of stairs that had reached. "Watch that," he said, distracted.

"Tell us more, please?" Lilly asked. She was a sucker for this kind of thing.

"Very well." Paw held his breath for a moment as he

stared at the ancient artwork. "The animals represent three legendary Navajo warriors and their strengths. Years ago, young Navajo men were expected to pass three trials, each linked to one of the warriors and their animal aspects."

Paw pointed at the spider. "The first trial tested the warrior's instincts. Like the great tarantula, it is important to always know where you are going and whether you stand a chance to win a fight." His hand glided over to the lizard next. "The second trial was the test of cunning. Whether he be big or small, to outsmart your adversary was a great feat. Old chiefs used to say being as sly as a lizard was an accomplishment as praiseworthy as being able to hunt the biggest bull in a pack of buffalo." Paw's hand shook, and he hesitated for a second before moving to the drawing of the buffalo. "Which brings us to our last trial. The buffalo. Physical prowess like no other: pure strength, plain and simple."

Quincy noticed the offbeat way in which Paw was talking and grabbed his arm, noticing now how badly he was shaking. "Paw, what's wrong?"

"Are you all right?" Lilly sat down on the steps a little bit higher up. She saw the old man was leaning against the wall and having trouble breathing, but she didn't dare get too close in fear of him feeling crowded.

"I'm fine!" Paw protested and brushed Quincy's hand away. "It's just…" He sighed. "I grew up hearing many a tale about the three trials, and, believe it or not, most of them did not end very happily. They used to scare the living daylights out of me." He wiped the sweat from his brow and gave a nervous smile. "I guess I still have a bit of youth left in me. It all came back to me for a second."

"Are you sure you're fine?" Quincy pressed after Paw took a deep breath.

"Oh shucks, let it go already."

Meanwhile, Tim was impatiently rumbling in his lamp. The colored light kept fading from bright to dim, and he seemed to want attention.

"Hmmm, Tim? Go ahead." Lilly tapped the glass.

It was a bit of a trick she had pulled on the Fire Vampire, but considering he had to obey their commands, usually, and Lilly was kind of enjoying the silence during the descent, she had ordered him to only speak when spoken to during their time on the staircase. She couldn't believe it actually worked. Seeing him now glowing brighter than ever before, she wondered why they had even bothered using torches in the first place.

Overall, Tim seemed to be an excellent survival tool.

"Go ahead!" she confirmed again.

"…nngggh! SHARPEN YOUR EARS, YOU IMBECILES!"

Lilly sighed; his attitude still needed some work though. I agree wholeheartedly.

"Stop jabbering on about pointless Earthling tales for just one second and *listen!*" The lamp swayed from left to right, clinking against the rocks.

"Extremely rude, but the lamp is right," Paw agreed. "There's running water nearby, which means we can't be far from an open cavern."

"A good thing too." Quincy planted his hand on the low ceiling, which was littered with sharp rocks. "I've been keeping an eye on this tunnel for a while now. It's getting narrower every dozen steps or so."

And so the group pressed on, and it didn't take them very long to reach the source of the rushing water Tim had heard. They seemed to be very close indeed. However, nothing could have prepared them for the spectacle they witnessed upon reaching the end of the long stairwell.

The last step of the stone stairs widened into a small plateau, only a couple of square feet wide. A magnificently huge natural cavern opened in front of them. Enormous torches with large flames burning orange, red, gold, and green hung from the walls of the gigantic space. The light of the flames danced off the crystal-lined rocks, which reflected the light back into the darkness. Beneath them, they heard the rushing of a waterfall.

Stepping closer to the edge, they could see ripples of water shimmering against the walls from an underground pool far below. It was as if they stepped into the great wide nothingness of space itself.

The trio stood there, stunned. There was no possible way to tell how big this underground space really was. The flames of the wall torches spread out as far as the eye could perceive, miles and miles into the cold darkness. The biggest surprise, however, was both the most wonderful and most terrifying thing they had ever laid their eyes on—looming right ahead of them was an ominous stone bridge lined with flickering orange braziers.

And the bridge led towards the center of the cavern, where a colossal inverted pyramid hung from the unseen ceiling, basking in a strange glow. It was impossibly huge, like a great underground skyscraper with smooth across all edges. Its faces were blank, no ancient artwork or carvings of old adorned its outer facets. The broad side was held aloft somewhere way up, while it got narrower as it came down. It is still the most marvelous thing I had ever laid my eyes on in both life and death.

At the end of the bridge, in the center of the megastructure, was an ominous stone archway leading inside.

They stood there for a while in complete silence, each of them awestruck by the overwhelming splendor of the megastructure.

Lilly was the first to act. She inched forward on the plateau, testing its weight limit, then untied Tim's lamp from her belt and held it in front of her. She took one very brave step onto the bridge.

"Shine," she whispered to the lamp, and Tim obeyed, the magnificence of the crimson, purple, and indigo glow appearing from the lamp and soon amplified by the millions of crystal rocks surrounding them.

"What the hell are you doing?" Quincy sputtered. He was shaking in his boots.

Lilly turned her head towards her companions and pointed at the giant inverted pyramid.

"End of the road." Her smile had a touch of sadness.

Chapter 11

"OUT OF ALL THE stupid things I might've done in my life, this might be the grand winner of it all," Quincy complained. He held his torch firmly as he eased onto the stone bridge, his legs still twitching beneath him.

"It's not like it's a rope bridge swaying around in a hurricane, Quince!" Lilly called back. She was a little bit ahead of Quincy and Paw. "This thing is solid as a rock." She jumped up and down for a spell, laughing.

"Xelothat's entrails! Stop that!" Tim called out, his lamp swinging around in Lilly's hand.

"Not what I mean!" Quincy shouted at her. His voice echoed a million times over in the wide, open cavern. "I mean all of this, this is ridiculous!"

"It's what you signed up for, though!"

"Signed up for? *When?*"

"Did you think you were heading for a lovely and bright unicorn-filled forest glade when you saw that creepy stairwell leading beneath the earth just a few hours ago?"

"Well, a *giant upside-down pyramid* wasn't exactly the first thing that popped into my mind!"

Paw lifted the barrel of the gun he held into the air and

forced it down upon the bridge, hard. The smack was incredibly loud and reverberated back and forth between the cavern walls for a good while. "Would you two *pipe down* for just a minute?" he hissed angrily. "We have no idea what we're up against here, but a shouting match isn't going to help!"

His eyes flashed between the twins. "One thing I've learned, pyramids are built for the dead…. Now for the love of God, let us not disturb them."

"Well, that gun made the loudest noise of all…" Lilly muttered.

"What's that?" Paw snorted.

"Nothing."

The group moved in silence for a while.

About halfway up the bridge, the reflecting crystals were now but shimmers in the faint glow of the distant wall torches. And when they stopped again and stood alone in the darkness, the only light was the carefully planted bridge braziers, the pink hue coming from Tim's lamp, and the unnatural glow that emanated from the pyramid itself.

"I don't think I've ever heard tales of pyramids in Navajo legends," Quincy said, glancing to Paw. "I thought this kind of architecture was only found south of the border, way down in the Southern Americas?"

"The Navajo did not build pyramids, Quincy," Paw replied with a shiver; he looked sad and defeated.

Lilly felt for him. It was one thing to have your day ruined by two kids falling on your shed, shouting about some kind of mission. But it was another thing altogether to almost lose your life on multiple occasions on the same day. Same goes for finding out way more mysteries about your heritage than you might've expected or wanted.

At least they were things they had in common, but she and her brother had been forced into this—an unsure adventure with an unsure outcome. Paw had been swept up into all of it. He wasn't wanted by a secret organization. He wasn't even as much as a blip on their radar and could've lived his life in peace on his ranch until he died.

Too late now though; he was in.

"Sorry for the ruckus earlier," Lilly said, turning to Paw. "Actually, sorry for everything. This is all our fault. You're an innocent bystander sucked into a ridiculous scavenger hunt by a couple of fugitives from New Orleans."

"I don't believe in coincidences, Lilly." Deep shadows appeared in the creases of his skin as Paw smiled. "Something larger, larger than life, brought you to my farm. It was something that wanted me to find whatever we'll encounter in there." He pointed at the stone archway leading into the pyramid. "Don't be disheartened, young Swansong. We all have a part to play, I'm sure of it."

Lilly gave a weak smile and turned to Quincy. They were walking again, but he was trailing behind a little bit, and when he caught her eye, he waved her over.

"You sure about all of this?" Quincy looked at Paw, at the oil lamp, at the cavern around him, and at the pyramid before finally landing back on Lilly.

"Quince… I'm not sure about anything right now," she admitted. "I just know that we don't really have any other place to go. I have no idea what awaits us, but please understand that I *need* you by my side here."

"I trust your instincts, always have and always will." He averted his eyes. "But you're the only family I have left, Lilly. Understand my concerns as well, rely on my judgement too. Okay?"

Lilly embraced her brother right then and there, on that dusty stone bridge deep beneath the earth, leading them towards an unknown future. "I'm sorry," she admitted in a whisper. "I may have been acting wild and sporadically, and I really am sorry. It's just that…" she trailed off.

"Just what? It's me, Lil, tell me."

"Ever since we got that package with the letter and the silver key, our lives have turned into utter chaos, agree?"

"You can say that again; there's absolutely no denying it."

"But don't you feel like, ever since that day, you have an actual goal in life, other than wasting away doing nothing and looking at how the world is turning to *shit?*"

"I was in college before all of this," Quincy retorted, slightly offended.

"Which you were ready to shake up or leave altogether, remember?"

"You're right," he admitted. "And yes, I do feel like we should see this through to the very end, but I'm sick of not knowing what the end of it all looks like."

"I know what you mean. But let's figure it out together, okay?"

Quincy and Lilly shuffled over the bridge side by side after that, talking about anything not pertaining to their current situation—like how Lilly would love to get a pet alligator if they'd ever get back to New Orleans, where then Quincy went on to explain how bad of an idea that would be and how she of all people should know that with her exotic pet experience.

At one point, Quincy told Lilly about how he'd love to travel through Europe and Asia someday. He wanted to visit the truly old world, see all of the medieval castles in Ireland and Scotland, and stand in awe before the Great Wall of China. Lilly offered, then, tales of the times she was stationed in Europe and Eurasia and spoke of the terrible things that hide in the oldest of buildings there, beneath the second and third layers of the deepest of cellars and dungeons.

Ultimately, they decided that if they ever got out of this mess, they'd just move back to New Orleans, get an old tomcat from the shelter, and name him Howard. That would be a great place to start.

If they ever got home.

The stone archway leading into the belly of the structure was now looming just some twenty yards ahead. Lilly took a step forward, but Quincy reached out and grabbed her by the shoulder, pulling her close.

"Wait, one last thing," he said, then pointed at the oil lamp.

"We've used Tim's powers to do a good deed just once now. But we could've used him to get out of that mess in the desert. I just thought about that. Why didn't we?"

"I have no idea," Lilly replied. "I thought about it, perhaps a million times, perhaps even more than I thought about fearing for my life. But back in Lafayette, I had this gut feeling that we needed his help; I can't explain it." She looked up at Quincy. "Besides, we did it together. It was as if we both knew what to do instantaneously." Lilly grabbed his hand. "When it's time for him to do his thing, we'll know; we'll both know."

The group had reached the end of the giant bridge and were standing on a tiny plateau around eight feet in diameter. A single tiny brazier rested in the corner, but its flame was nearly extinguished. Looking back, the twins noticed the bridge disappeared into total darkness about three-quarters of the way through. The wall torches weren't even visible anymore.

The caverns play tricks with the light, Quincy thought. There was no natural way to describe the phenomenon, nor was there any need to.

"I don't know about you, but I'm hungry as all heck." Paw grimaced before pulling some sandwiches and beef jerky from his pack—which Quincy and Lilly eagerly accepted. As they ate, Paw took a peek inside the giant open door ahead of them and gulped.

"Prepare your calves; there's another stairwell going down."

Indeed. If there was one thing taking away the splendor of this stunning structure, it was all the damn hiking that came with it.

Sean wasn't even surprised when another group of black-suited individuals marched into his cell. *However, today was different,* he thought. Most of the Haven agents looked identical in every way to emphasize their anonymity. But the fat man in the middle, he was different. He had this weird aura around him, Sean noticed, and the smell surrounding him was horrendous. Sean caught but a whiff of it as the fat man cleared his way into the chamber, and it nearly made him vomit.

He couldn't quite put a finger on what exactly was wrong with the man. He also didn't know if the smell was merely his imagination or something else.

Sean felt more dead than alive at this point. There was no excessive torture, nor was there much in the way of brutal interrogation. The route Haven had picked was a lot more wicked. It had been a couple of weeks or maybe even just a few days... he couldn't tell the difference anymore. They'd chosen to let Sean slowly lose his mind. They'd give him water, but not daily, and never enough to fully satisfy his thirst. They'd feed him, too, but it was never enough, and it was never anywhere near edible.

Sometimes a pair of particularly ugly agents would come and stand in his cell, staring at him for hours, but they'd never say a word; they'd simply look at him. Other times, it was the terrible lizard-like agent that first arrested him. He'd taunt him for a while before just grinning like a madman for thirty minutes, then leave. To Sean, it seemed as if none of the agents that came to visit him ever blinked. But once again, he didn't know if it was real or if he was truly starting to lose it.

. . .

The fat man inched his way forward, and without any sign of remorse, he pushed one of the lower-ranking agents out of his way. The agent tumbled to the side of the cell, and his head landed on one of the sharp points sticking out of the uneven wall. There was a quick murmur between the remaining agents as the agent slumped halfway to the floor, his forehead still stuck to the wall.

"Is that supposed to intimidate me or something?" Sean asked before wheezing but kept his held high. He was standing his ground, trying not to look at his new cellmate, when internally he thought something more in the line of *Holy shit, this guy is terrifying*.

"I hope not. I'd expect the GDF to train their soldiers to endure horrors far worse than merely unfortunate accidents such as that." The fat man's voice was deep, as if he had eaten a fistful of gravel. His bald head shone bright from the light source high above them. In the light, his face was ugly, wide, and he had huge lips, like a fish. For a moment, Sean thought he saw the flapping of gills on his neck slightly protruding from his collar.

Keep it together, Sean. Dammit. "You know what you remind me of?" Sean coughed, pointing at the man's head.

"Enlighten me."

"Did you ever see that one cartoon with the mutant alien mice and the bikes and the enormously fat, horrible-smelling, barracuda look-alike mother*fucker* of a bad guy?" Sean gritted his teeth. "You'd *wish* you'd be half as intimidating as that guy." Sean braced for the impact he'd likely receive from such insults, but the hit never came.

The fat man just stood there, laughing, and somehow whenever he opened his mouth, the smell would get ten times worse. "Oh, you amuse me, Mr. Cooper." The man snorted between cackling. "I'd like to keep you around a little longer, at least until we can show you what we'll be doing with the twins once we've secured the remains."

He blinked at Sean then, in a very weird way. It was very

slow, and the eyelids seemed to stick together, the separating of which came with a nasty smacking sound. "In all of the graphic detail," he added with a smirk.

"You'll never find them!"

"We already have. Those idiots have entombed themselves up in the desert with nowhere else to go except straight to hell."

"But *why*?" Sean cried in desperation. Did Haven actually manage to break him? "What is the meaning of all of this?" Sean's anger was rising.

"Enough!" The man licked his lips. "We shall continue this conversation later. Maybe. In the meantime..." The man stopped and winked over at two of the tall, thin agents. "Men, make sure that Agent Richter accompanies Mr. Cooper for a little while longer. Let's say we collect him... in bouts of... forty pounds at a time?"

"Yes... sir..." The leftmost agent acknowledged before he turned around towards the door.

The fat man gave Sean a mocking bow as he turned around and headed out of the cell, followed by the rest of the agents. "Oh, and, Agent Samhain?" Sean heard the fat man say just outside. "Let's not tell Mr. Cooper what's on the dinner menu for the time being, hmm?"

Hundreds of miles away from Sean's cell, the twins and their sort-of guide, Paw Hathale, happened upon a whole other sort of problems.

They had entered the great and mysterious underground pyramid that was hidden away beneath the desert of New Mexico; however, traversing it, even without a clear idea of where to go, proved to be a difficult and confusing task. The tunnels inside of the pyramid ranged from dark and tiny to well-lit and very wide. And the walls could be adorned with all kinds of Navajo art or other illustrations of a strange, alien nature.

They had been walking for a few hours but hadn't yet found never a clear sign of where to go—it was all completely random guesswork, and it got them nowhere. They had been walking up and down stairs, crossing narrow pathways, and even at one point had to avoid or kill some dangerous critters along the way. Sometimes they needed to stop for breath, or there were times they ate some of their meager trail rations or drank some water.

The further their journey led them, the more confusing the giant maze became.

Discovered were doorways leading to enclosed walls and stairwells leading to nowhere, or worse, abruptly ending in a dark abyss. Quincy had dropped a coin down one of the holes they stumbled upon, and after waiting ten minutes to hear it drop to the floor, the group decided that *not* falling into one of these holes was now one of their top priorities.

Meanwhile, Lilly became increasingly agitated at the situation. She felt responsible for the mess she got her two companions in, even though she knew that it wasn't just her fault. She was and always had been a woman of action. If there was a job to be done, she'd plan it out and see it through. It was one of her many perks that Quincy often applauded her for, and it was exactly the reason why she felt so helpless now.

Quincy and she had a quest, a job, to see through to the end. But somehow, all of this didn't make any sense.

When the group wandered past a distinct, lavish, man-sized obelisk, they knew they were going in circles.

"That's it. We're officially, 100 percent, totally lost," Lilly grunted and planted her butt on the waist-high clay wall in frustration. "Any bright ideas? Quincy? Paw?"

Both shook their heads.

"Tim?"

A quiet grumbling resonated from the lamp.

"Hello? Mr. *Destroyer of Worlds*?"

"Oh, leave me alone," Tim snapped and exhaled, somehow, without functional lungs. "I've got nothing."

"Nothing at all?" Lilly raised an eyebrow. "Not even a snide comment or a slick insult fitting the situation?"

"Fine, have it your way," Tim said. "I've got nothing, you useless particle from the speck of dust they call humanity."

"What's eating you?" Quincy raised an eyebrow in genuine confusion. "I thought we were becoming friends."

Paw coughed at that but stayed silent.

"Only by lack of another means," Tim grunted and flickered an angry red. "I am done with this trifling business. I was meant for greater things. I was not meant to be treated like some household object, lighting the way for you to get lost in some tunnels deep underground until you either die of starvation or exhaustion. Sure, it'll be a good laugh at first, but afterwards there will be nothing left for me; not a single soul will find me here in this place."

"Wonderful positive thinking," Lilly countered. "You were locked up in a library for years; how would this be any different?"

"At the library, I could at least scare people into thinking I was a ghost, hehehehe."

"So you can't help us at all? Not even if we ask you to use your powers?"

"I could teleport you out of here, if I wanted to, but I get the feeling it won't be for a *greater* good, so our little agreement wouldn't work, I think."

"Isn't rescuing us a definite act of kindness?" Quincy sounded a bit insulted at Tim's skepticism.

"For you, perhaps. But not for the Earth, which, coincidentally, *I* could not give less of a Nightgaunt's fart about were it not for that bastard Crowley."

Quincy straightened his jacket and padded off some of the sand that had collected around the shoulder pads. "Somehow, I get the feeling you know more about our mission than we do. Has Crowley told you anything?"

"Nothing you don't already know in some way or another," Tim grumbled. "And now, I am done with this pestering business. I'm going to take a good long rest, and when I'm done, I expect to find you either dead or at our destination… either way is fine with me. Wake me up when you've found your enlightenment."

"Hold the phone!" Lilly yelled. Her eyes widened, and she had a wild look in her eyes Quincy knew all too well. She grabbed the lamp and shook it around violently. "Hey!" She pressed her forehead against the glass. "Say that again! Wake up, you stupid, horrible, inexplicable excuse for a demon!"

The lamp lit up for a second. "I'm not a demon, you dumb cow!"

It faded again.

"Lilly, what the hell is going on?" Quincy interjected and grabbed her shoulders. "Sit the lamp down, sis. Let's talk about this!"

"He's playing games with us, Quince! He knew all along; he just wouldn't tell us straight up."

"What are you talking about?"

"Enlightenment!" Lilly boasted. The look on her face was a mixture of contempt for Tim and excitement for her revelation. "The ghost of W.A. Swansong told us that we held the key to *enlightenment* in our hands. A *literal* key."

"Uhm…"

"Swansong gave us all the hints we needed in here. We knew it all along!" Lilly started to pace back and forth. "Quick question, why did the ancient races of the Earth build pyramids?"

"To bury their dead?"

"And?"

"They… they built them so high up in order to get closer to the gods!"

"Right, and if you find God, you find?"

"Enlightenment?"

"Yes!" Lilly smiled. "*As above, so below*—it was the sentence we had to remember if we ever lost our way. Swansong was talking about this exact moment! We have the key to enlightenment. If God is above… and the pyramid is inverted…"

"We've got to get all the way down!" Quincy said in awe. "Lilly, you're a genius! All this time, we've been walking in random directions, up random slopes and random stairs. We've just got to head into whatever direction is down."

"My brother's calling me genius?" Lilly laughed. "Guess there's a first time for everything."

Quincy turned to Paw. "Paw, are you getting all of this?"

Paw sat on the little wall sticking out, smirking. "You two are really something," he said before laughing. "I could never really grasp if you were a pair of stupid youngsters that got themselves way too deep in shit or simply misunderstood and brilliant." Paw rested a hand on Lilly's shoulder. "Like the marvelous tarantula, that was a fantastic display of pure and raw instinct, Lilly. Many a Navajo warrior would be jealous of such a feat." His eyes fluttered to Quincy. "If it were the trials, you two would be off to a great start."

Kraal was furious. Two times now, he had been outsmarted by mere *children*. He would not let this slide; the damage to his reputation would be disastrous. Haven had hired him because their own goons proved futile in the simple task of capturing two young runaways from New Orleans. The fact that they were holding an artifact that could not fall into any other hands than those of the agency shouldn't make any difference.

Then how could this happen? There was something else about them, Kraal thought, something that the agency didn't know. What else were they hiding?

He gazed at the moon, now risen high above the desert. The moon cast its light off the grand mesa standing tall ahead of him, bathing the abandoned camp in an eerie shadow and catching on the silver trapdoor sticking out of the sand.

Kraal stared down the stairwell into the deep, dark abyss

below.

Paw and the twins never thought the solution to their malaise would be this easy. By simply taking the pathway that led downwards in some shape or form each time they encountered a fork in the road, the difference in their surroundings started to be noticeable pretty quickly. The tunnels turned into hallways, and the dreary, shadowy corners filled with cobwebs turned into well-lit passageways. Even though they still had no real clue as to why they were heading the way they were going, there was a distinct change in the general temperament of the group. The destination might be unclear, but at least they felt they were on the right track.

After about an hour's walk, the group encountered something that they hadn't seen before after entering the pyramid. It was a very wide and open space, a grand room supported by six great pillars engraved with miraculous Navajo symbols. Torches hung on the walls every few feet, and the air seemed clearer here, less dense. The big room was entirely empty, however, and it did not prove very useful to linger about.

However, about halfway in crossing the wide area, there seemed to be another change in the atmosphere. First, the lighter air became very humid and thick. Then a whistling started from somewhere on the far side of the room, sounding like wind blowing through cracks in an old building. That was preposterous, of course; there couldn't possibly be any wind down here. But when the torches on the walls flickered with no clear cause, casting irregular shadows on the ground, walls, and pillars, the oddity couldn't be ignored any longer.

"Did you see it?" Quincy whispered to Paw and Lilly while still looking straight ahead.

"See what?" Paw rubbed his eyes; for some reason, the heavy air made them water.

"I thought I saw a... There it is again, to the right!"

Quincy pointed.

There were unusual shadows playing off the pillars, but they didn't seem to move in accordance with the flickering torchlight.

Lilly tightened her hand around Tim's lamp. While not in the mood to talk or be helpful in any way, Tim still gave off a faint glow, and it somehow comforted her. "The shadows, they're moving."

The trio huddled closer together. From the back-left side of the hall came high-pitched laughter, like that of a little child, but as the giggling reverberated through the big room, it sounded like it came from everywhere at once.

Quincy swung the torch around, looking for the source of the creepy noise. He could've sworn that every time he pressed the light in a certain direction, he could hear a very soft hiss, like an animal fleeing from the painful heat of the fire.

Paw jumped up and yelled. His shoulder had fallen just an inch into a spot of darkness, and he was instantly grabbed by something invisible.

"Surround yourself with light!" he called out. "Whatever it is, it's afraid of it… I hope…"

The group inched forward bit by bit, but every time even so much as a single bit of shadow befell them, they were poked and pushed from all directions. The things were taunting them, laughing and shrieking every time one of them jumped.

Living Shadows were amongst the very worst of entities one could encounter, Quincy reminded himself. Why? Simply because there was no way of fighting them, at least no known way, and they wouldn't stop harassing you until you were either dead by "accident" or lucky enough to stumble out of their domain. The stories about them terrified Quincy and gave him nightmares, and now he was living them.

He looked over to his sister, seeing that she was deathly afraid also. Paw looked sterner, like a protective ward, but there was no denying the fear in his eyes.

One of the torches went dark, and Quincy instantaneously felt a great force smacking him between the ribs.

This is it, he thought. *What a way to go.*

He flew away from Lilly and Paw and landed hard on the stone floor. He hit his knee and cursed aloud as he rubbed it.

Another blow came, making him roll a couple of feet further away. He moaned in pain.

"Quince!" Lilly swung her torch in Quincy's direction, giving the Living Shadows another opportunity for chaos as they pulled Lilly's feet from the patch of darkness below her and caused her to smack to the ground, busting her head in the process.

"Lilly! Don't move!" her brother yelled at her even as she got back to her feet.

Paw ran towards them both, holding on to his torch for dear life. He tried to grab hold of Lilly as she suffered a new blow to her back but was just short by a couple of inches as

Lilly fell down again. This time, she tried to soften the blow by outstretching her hands and letting her arms suffer most of the impact. She didn't account for any possible pressure plates that might've hidden themselves in the room, and she felt a pang of adrenaline upon feeling the floor move beneath her.

The laughter from the shadow monsters was deafening now, and Lilly tried to yell but quickly noticed no words were coming out.

It pains me to speak of these events, but to tell a story is to tell the entire series of events, however daunting or terrible they might be.

The laughter died down as the room filled with an alarming green gas that took all visibility away. Coughing and choking sounds started to fill in the void left by the laughter, and Lilly was both terrified and relieved to hear both Paw and Quincy were still alive.

Once again, she tried to call out to her brother, to call out to Paw; she even tried to call out to Tim, his lamp lying closely nearby. But no words came out, and no more sounds were heard… well, except for the little voice in her head reminding her that she was about to lose consciousness.

"Ooh, seventy-six." Karl looked up from his game master screen. "That's definitely a failed roll for that poison trap save. That's… let's see, a minus three HP—your character lost consciousness, Lilly. Somebody's gonna have to get you out of there fast, else you'll probably die."

"That's *bullshit!*" Lilly yelled and slammed her hands on the table, causing her little plastic investigator to fall over.

"That's just the way the dice roll sometimes, Lilly. Calm down. You win some, you lose some, right?" Tim sat in the corner and gave a sly smirk.

"That's unfair as well!" Lilly pointed at Tim and glared. "It doesn't say anywhere in the rules you can play as one of the creatures from the monster add-on, so why isn't Tim playing an investigator like us?"

"It's a home brew," Karl said, smiling. "I got the idea off the official game forums; I thought it would give a nice twist to the game. Plus, Tim's character helped you out a lot; you should be thankful for it."

"Is my character still conscious?" Quincy asked shyly while hiding behind his handbook. "How about Paul's?"

"Barely." Karl started sifting through his notes. "But you gotta start rolling for your fortitude saves now, else you'll start to hallucinate and end up like Lilly's character."

"Hallucinate?" Quincy blinked. "I thought you said it was poison gas?"

"Yeah, whatever." Karl waved Quincy away. "Paul, roll for a save."

Paul grabbed the set of polyhedral dice and started sifting through them. "Which ones was it again?"

"The D10 and the percentile die," Karl pointed out.

"Can I make an idea roll later to maybe snap out of it?"

Lilly interjected.

"Snap out of it…" Quincy murmured to himself.

Karl let out a heavy sigh. "Lilly, just wait your turn, okay?" He turned to Paul, prompting, "So, what is it?"

Paul revealed the die results cheerfully. "Seventeen!"

"That's a save roll, for now!" Karl grinned. "What would you like to have Paw do?"

"Can I try to get Lilly to wake up?"

"Hmm, you'll have to spend most of your turn to scramble up from the floor. But if you manage to dodge the Living Shadows, you might stand a chance next turn. That is, if you succeed in your save roll."

"Worth a shot!" Paul cheered. "Don't worry, Lilly, I'll get you stable. After that, I'll check up on Quincy, and we'll solve the mystery of this inverted pyramid together!"

"I… uh…" Quincy looked confused, unable to find the right words to say as he fumbled with his handbook.

"Anyone want a beer? I'm heading to the bathroom, but I can stop by the kitchen on the way back." Tim stood up and walked off towards the hall. "Anyone? Lil? Paul? How about you, Kraal? Uh, Karl, I mean."

"What? I…" Quincy stammered on.

"No thanks!" Karl quickly intervened. "I gotta stay sharp and make sure these three don't cheat." He smiled wickedly.

"That'll end my turn. It's up to you now, Quincy."

Quincy was in cold sweat, his breathing quickening. He didn't think the game could have such an effect on him; it felt so real. But why?

"Quincy? Are you all right? If you don't act quick, I'm going to have to put your investigator up for dead," Karl said coldly.

"Wait, what?" Lilly protested. "It's a turn-based game; give him all the time he wants!"

"House rules."

Quincy felt the chance of vomit becoming a very real possibility as his stomach churned. Something was wrong, something was very wrong. It was all real: the silver key, the lamp, the pyramid. He swallowed hard; how was he going to get out of this? "I…"

"Tick tock, Mr. Swansong… If the shadows won't get you, *I will*." Karl laughed, and for a mere moment, Quincy saw the image of an older, terrifying, bearded man take Karl's place.

"I'm seeing through the illusion. I'm snapping out of it," Quincy finally managed to say.

"Roll."

"I don't have to. It's all a hallucination." Quincy hoped to whatever God was left that he was right.

"*Roll!*"

"Fine, here." Quincy took the required dice and casually rolled. It was a perfect roll, a critical success.

"Impossible!" Karl cried.

Quincy turned towards his friends gathered around the table. "Paw, Lilly!" He waved his hands. "I'm going to need you with me. This is a shared illusion; none of this is real, do you understand? We're currently on the floor of a giant underground pyramid in New Mexico, an inverted one at that. Got it?"

"Stop that! Stop it!" Karl angrily interjected. "You're ruining the game."

Lilly looked around in confusion. "I, I don't understand…"

"Roll your saves, go ahead, and think hard about that critical success. We can win this because we can take control of this. It's *not* real."

Lilly rolled. Another perfect roll, and all the memories of what had transpired flooded back to her.

Tim came back into room, only it wasn't the human player Tim that had just left for the bathroom; it was a floating oil lamp surrounded in a pink glow.

"By the light of Celaeno's leftmost sun, what is going on

here? I leave for a few stupid human hours, and all hell is breaking loose? Wake up! The lot of you!"

Paul rolled the dice. Perfect.

"No!" Karl cried, and for an instant, he changed into the image of the dangerous black mage Kraal. "It's not fair! *Not fair!*" Karl's face warped and twisted into an amalgamation of human tissue and deep shadows. The creature leapt up onto the table and hissed. Now completely made out of pure black void, it screeched again and jumped onto the ceiling, where it disappeared.

Then all went dark.

Lilly wheezed as she felt a sharp pain in her forehead, which in turn was throbbing like mad. She glanced around nervously. The braziers in the room were alight, and the Living Shadows were nowhere to be seen. Lilly sighed in relief as she heard her companions waking up in a similar fashion. Tim's lamp rested at the bottom end of one of the pillars.

"So, you finally find your way in this sinkhole, and the first thing you do once you reach something other than a cold, rigid corridor is take a nap? I cannot *believe* how your species survived this long. I—" Tim continued ranting, but Lilly tuned him out.

"Shut up." Lilly rubbed her head, moaning in pain. "Just shut up."

Quincy walked up to her with a slight limp and a pained look on his face as he clutched his side. Blood was seeping through his shirt near his ribs. "That was… something," he said in between labored pants.

Paw ran up behind Quincy. "You two. We need to get out of here. You're both significantly hurt."

"We'll be fine," Quincy protested.

Lilly's vision was spinning, but she wasn't about to give up. Not after everything that happened. They were so close; she could practically taste all of the enlightenment.

Paw shook his head. "Quincy, you're clearly dealing with a very nasty bruise there, possibly a fracture." He turned to Lilly. "And you. You can barely stand up straight. You busted your head so hard you'd be lucky if it turns out to be *just* a concussion. And—"

"We're pressing on, and that's that," Lilly interjected.

Paw had no choice but to follow. There was something about these two that he admired so much, even though they were putting their lives in danger again and again. They were brave, some of the bravest souls he ever encountered.

And so he followed the twins into the little alcove at the other end of the wide room and couldn't help but smile. "Quincy, I don't know exactly *how* you figured out how to break free of the Living Shadows' illusion, but I'm sure you're the first one to do so. Very *cunning*." He winked.

Quincy smiled weakly at Paw. It was the first time someone called *him* cunning. First times for a lot of things today, he thought and sighed.

Chapter 12

SEAN WAS GRABBED by his shoulders and ankles and was forcefully removed from his cell—his personal hellhole, the room of madness. The Haven goons tried to carry him across the dimly lit hall, but Sean nimbly freed himself from their grip.

"I can walk fine by myself, assholes!" he spat at them, realizing that there was nothing he could do; he was their prisoner, and there was no escape. The agents must've realized this too and didn't rebuke him. Still, being able to move around of his own free will gave Sean a sliver of hope.

From the corridor, just across from Sean's cell, the fat man emerged from the shadows.

"Mr. Cooper, happy to see you're joining us on our little expedition today. How are you feeling? Eating well, I hope?" The smile that appeared on the fat man's lips was nothing less than gross.

"Expedition, huh?" Sean managed. He felt and must've looked extremely weak; his eyes were deeply sunk in and bloodshot, and he was pale. "Please tell me we're going fishing, because I just can't wait to jam a hook in between those fat lips of yours." His laugh was quickly interrupted by a coughing fit.

The fat man simply grinned. "Laugh away, Mr. Cooper. It's all part of the process."

The group, consisting of Sean, two Haven agents, and the fat man, progressed slowly through the maze of identical hallways.

Sean still had no idea where he was; he only knew the cold outside was ridiculous. There was a small window very high up in his cell which automatically opened several times throughout the day. The biting cold froze up the already frigid space.

"So what do they call you?" Sean asked, shaking his head at the obvious advantage of the situation this guy had. Sean knew he was completely stuck in this man's hold, but he might as well try to get as much information as possible—just in case.

"You can call me Mr. Marsh," the man replied, licking his lips in an extremely unappetizing manner.

"So… Mr. Marsh." Sean had to stop to avoid asking him why he looked like a giant fish on legs. "Where are we going today?"

"You'll find out soon enough." Marsh blinked twice in rapid succession.

One of the agents jabbed Sean in the back with the butt of his handgun. "Pick up the pace, Cooper," he growled. "You wanna walk on your own, you step it up."

"Such military obedience," Sean snapped at him. "Do you like working for the Anti-Christ?"

Marsh burst out laughing. "Oh, Mr. Cooper, you truly are a funny fellow and closer to the truth than you may think. Such a shame things had to end this way."

Sean turned his head around and tilted it towards his nemesis. "End? How?"

"You really are a nosy little nuisance." Marsh snorted.

"Now do as the man says and move along, or would you rather us continue this conversation with you being unconscious?"

Licking his dry lips, Sean thought of a witty reply, but he was smarter than he'd led these guys to believe and instead stayed silent, gathering all his strength to march on like a good little prisoner of war.

Only a few seconds passed before Sean said, "So, Marsh—"

"*Mister* Marsh."

"*Mister Marsh.*" Sean rolled his eyes so hard he could see the inside of his skull. "What's your game plan in all of this?"

"Hmm?"

"Your purpose? What's your end goal? Why are we here, you doing what you're doing and me here trying to count which of my teeth aren't loose or rotting yet?" Sean huffed. "Spoiler, not many left."

"*You* are here for aiding wanted criminals and breaking into one of our secure databanks."

"Not *that* secure."

"You're right," Marsh acknowledged. "Those responsible for that mess have been dealt with accordingly."

"I asked you a question," Sean reminded, knowing he was pushing his luck at this point.

Marsh turned around and grabbed Sean by the neck. With apparent superhuman-like strength, the fat man lifted him up towards the ceiling.

Sean sputtered and gargled; he felt Marsh's gross green-tinged fingernails slicing his skin like tiny razor blades. "And *I* gave you an answer, fool."

Marsh then lowered his arm and let Sean collapse to the floor. His vision was spinning, and he couldn't for the life of him form a proper sentence.

"But if you must know," Marsh continued, "our agency is all about... science, Mr. Cooper."

Sean coughed hard and spat on the ground. It was blood, mixed with bile.

"Discovery! Research!" Marsh grabbed Sean by the hair and pulled him up towards him so their eyes met. "Experimentation."

"W… why?"

"Because *why* not?" Marsh shook his head and let go; Sean just managed to catch himself from slipping back onto the floor. "These events, these phenomena. It's the best thing that could've happened for us, for humanity—countless, *infinite* worlds; possibilities; and power. It all lies right at our feet. We need but to reach out." Marsh formed his gross fingers into fists. "Reach out and grab the opportunity."

They moved on, albeit slower than at first. Somehow, Marsh allowed for it—for now at least.

"What about Lilly and Quincy?" Sean asked, grunting now with pained and labored breaths. "They're innocent in all of this."

"Innocent?" Marsh howled. "They possess something that was taken from us a very, *very* long time ago. If they had been obedient little devils and handed it over the first time we made contact with them, they could've gone on to lead their useless lives to the fullest of their capabilities." Marsh narrowed his green, frog-like eyes. "But they didn't. They decided to run, killing one of our agents in the process. So, the consequences suddenly became a lot direr."

Sean thought back on what little Quincy and Lilly had said about their so-called mission back in Lafayette and the few strands of information he gathered from his text conversations with Lilly. They had said little, yet Sean was utterly convinced that whatever the twins had set out to achieve would be world-changing. He had no idea why he thought this; perhaps it came to him in a dream, or rather, during one of the rare moments that his cell allowed him to think rationally and clearly.

He narrowed his eyes and thought long and hard about what he wanted to ask next. He saw Marsh reaching for a huge iron door with one of the agents punching in some eight-digit code on a digital pad hanging next to it. He knew he had to ask fast. He had to know.

Sean swallowed and tried to ignore the copper taste of blood seeping down his throat.

"So, what will you do when God comes back to protect us?"

Marsh burst into uncontrollable laughter, obnoxious as it was loud. He swung the heavy iron door open and let an eerie green light fill the hallway. Sean heard first strange buzzing and beeping noises that likely belonged to unknown machinery. There was a distinct, unearthly smell in the air too.

Marsh swallowed before grinning at Sean. "God is dead, Mr. Cooper. Heh... We killed him."

The grand chamber that sprawled out ahead of them truly was, as Lilly once said, the end of the road. After the room with the Living Shadows, the path ahead of them was straightforward with a few twists and turns and some downwards slopes. They now arrived in an antechamber that looked like the most illustrious of halls in the whole structure. There were no other exits anywhere, so the conclusion was made that they had indeed reached the bottom of the pyramid, or top, depending on one's point of view.

In contrast to the rest of the rooms they had already visited, this giant chamber felt welcoming and warm. It was lined with candles and braziers, the light being soft and gentle —not in the least bit harsh. The walls seemed to have been hewn from the purest marble with dozens of sparkling gems hanging from the high, somewhat curved, dome-like ceiling. In the middle of the chamber were a couple of steps leading up to a heightened plateau. On it, there were two primitive-looking chairs that appeared to have been hewed from the same glassy stone as the walls.

After glancing around for a good while and determining no imminent danger was afoot, the twins were eager to press on, making their first steps into the majestic room.

Lilly took only a few steps before she turned around and glanced at Paw. He seemed disoriented and lost, hesitant to set foot in the place, a place that had not seen a living soul for who knows how many years.

"Are you coming, Paw?" she asked.

Paw appeared taken aback by her inquiry. He glanced back and forth for a bit, then smiled. "No." He shook his head. "No, I think this is it for me."

"Why?" Quincy walked up to stand in front of him. "Are you feeling okay? What's wrong?"

"Nothing, boy." Paw patted him on the shoulder. "I'm a simple soul, Quincy. I live by the motto that some things are better left unknown, and I enjoyed blissful ignorance for most of my life. While I have no idea what this chamber might reveal about my people, I'd like some of my beliefs to stay as they are."

"I…" Lilly looked at her brother. "*We* understand."

Paw chuckled. "Besides, there are only two chairs. Gods know you deserve a seat for a bit, what with all you've been through." He started to turn but hesitated for a moment. "Remember that alcove we passed a little while back? The one with the crucifix artifacts that you dimwits thought looked a lot like the ones the Hopi tribe carved?"

"Yes," Quincy replied, a bit embarrassed.

Paw motioned to Lilly. "I shall await you in the alcove. After all of this is said and done, I hope we can all enjoy another good steak dinner at my place soon. We deserve it." Paw laughed, then pressed a firearm into Lilly's hands. He gave her a stern look and a nod before wandering back into the dark corridor. Lilly said nothing; she swallowed hard and went after her brother.

Moving further into the room, Lilly let her hands glide over the smooth surface of the chairs. They were cold to the touch, yet when her fingers moved across the glassy stone, a miniscule shiver shot through her body. It was like the smallest spark of electricity, nearly imperceptible, but peculiar nonetheless. Magical?

"Did you feel that?" Quincy sounded distant, like he was unknowingly confirming her suspicions before she could ask.

"Should we sit?" Lilly looked hesitant. They hadn't had the best luck traversing the pyramid, and she hated to see it all go to waste if they'd get eaten by a pair of sentient chairs.

"I haven't traversed this far to turn back now." Quincy playfully pushed her. "We're here because of your perseverance, and I'll be damned if we don't see this through to the end. But if we get eaten by something, I'll also blame you..."

"Can't play the blame game if your face is eaten off." She smirked.

Quincy shuddered at the thought and tried to concentrate on less dire things. "When we leave, we should try and gather some samples of these rocks. I've never seen specimens like this before. Could be interesting!" he added.

He took a deep breath, leaning an arm against one of the marble armrests. "Okay, sis. Are you ready for this?"

Lilly felt a pang of excitement. This was it. Whatever secret their great uncle wanted them to protect, or find at least, it was here and now. She was sure of it. And she was right. Exceeding all of my expectations, here they were, about to unravel the most intricately woven secrets of the universe.

She nodded at Quincy, smiled, and shoved her butt against the seat.

"Three."

"Two."

"One!" they exclaimed in unison and pushed themselves up fully onto the huge stone-hewn chairs.

The room immediately went dark.

Slowly, the gemstones in the ceiling started lighting up, and the twins gasped in awe as they saw the ancient star map appear above them.

They basked in the soft glow of the universe sprawling out all around them.

Kraal smashed the ball of light hovering around his head and picked up the empty trail ration packaging.

"Hmm. Nuts and honey. So quaint."

Behind him, a skeleton came clacking out of the shadows. It was holding a primitive spear, and if it had a face, one could say it looked a tad confused.

Kraal flicked his wrist, and from the corner of the small, dimly lit room, another one of the dead arose. Its jaw snapped open and shut in excitement as it plucked away the spiderwebs from in between its ribs.

Kraal turned to the first skeleton behind him. "Go ahead, then!" he grunted. "Ask if he saw them come by."

The skeletons moved towards each other. After rattling on for a few minutes, the newly risen skeleton bobbed its head up and down in acknowledgement. Its bony finger pointed towards the western corridor before it scraped its hand along the floor until it located the spear that had rested beside it for centuries; once found, it clicked its jaw in approval.

"About time," Kraal muttered. "Both of you, follow me."

The huge chamber was alight with the colors of a million and one stars. The twins could see the splendor of the entire cosmos coming into view, piece by piece. Distant galaxies and nebulas shone bright and strong together with terrific quasars and a host of other, unidentifiable celestial bodies. The room was completely void of any sound—not even the wisps of wind scattering the tiniest grains of sand could be heard.

Quincy and Lilly didn't dare breathe, the absence of sound fitting for the cold and unhospitable dark universe before them.

Lilly tried to grab for her brother's hand; with the other, she held Tim in her lap. Both scared and in total awe, she felt she needed the guidance of her brother; she needed him close. Yet she could not find him. The atmosphere felt different now. She could feel Quincy's presence, but somehow it felt as if they were both living the same moment at the exact same time only in two entirely separate realities.

"Quince?" she tried calling out, but no sound escaped her lips.

On the other side of her, as little as a few feet away, Quincy felt the same thing. Lilly, his twin sister and the most important person in his life, seemed to have vanished, and yet it felt as if they were closer now than ever. Did she just call out his name? He didn't hear a thing, but he felt... something.

Magnificent beams of green and yellow light now connected dots across the entire planetarium. The few streaks faded into one another, and a picture started to form between the stars. It was a lonesome figure, some unknown biological entity.

Quincy looked closely at its cone-shaped underbody, its elongated head, and its claw-like appendages. It seemed familiar.

The lonesome figure soon multiplied: two at first, then four, then eight. Soon, countless figures emerged. Next to the legion of entities, the beams started to form a perfect circle. Sprawled throughout, they began to form the shapes of five-pointed stars.

Lilly thought long and hard, trying to reach Quincy. "Are those…?" she started, only to stop and squeeze her eyes shut.

"The ones from Celeste, the Great Race."

A voice suddenly boomed across the chamber. It was loud and distinct, but it made no sound at all. The twins both heard a metallic rasping, not with their ears, but with their minds.

It was scary, just not in a menacing way. It was scary because it sounded ancient, older than time itself. It was from a time beyond time, from a place that existed far before the first atom particle started to shape the ever-expanding universe that sprawled across the domed ceiling.

The first seeds were planted over one hundred million standard Earth-years ago. We came to this peculiar world to learn and to grow.

The light beams changed shapes, now showing the entities across a vast plain. Mountains could be seen in the distance. The figures appeared to be erecting massive, uniquely shaped obelisks from the ground up into the sky. The shaping of the diorama ended with several triangular-formed objects appearing in the sky above the obelisks.

Others soon came. Some, not unlike ourselves, eager to learn, eager to uncover the mysteries of this new world.

The image faded, and a new one started to form. Weird creatures with starfish-shaped heads joined the conical entities. Other lifeforms started to appear too: little humanoids with bulbous eyes, reptilian humanoids, and majestic winged beings similar to the mighty griffin known from Greek mythology. The griffin-like entities flew high above the rest and rained fire down from the sky.

Others came to conquer. They came to break the peaceful evolution of the beautiful celestial body we had grown to appreciate and lovingly named Terra.

The image changed again. At the bottom appeared the curved shape of the horizon at high altitude. In the middle, two of the conical-shaped entities, two *Celestians*, stood facing each other. In between them, there was a cradle-shaped object lined with dozens of recognizable symbolisms found in religion all across the world. A halo surrounded the cradle.

Above the tableaux, there was a spiked pattern of lines leaning against the starry expanse.

To protect Terra, our brethren came and brought the one we named Deus. Deus was deemed the protector of the world, and under the guidance of this protector, it was sworn that no harm would come to the planet nor to its newest and most advanced life-form to date—humanity.

The next scene showed the Celestians lifting themselves up into the sky, with the immediately recognizable, yet primitive form of the first humans standing to look in awe at the horizon.

The time came to let life take its course: Birth. Growth. Death. A lifetime for humanity but a mere blink in the eye for us. We had to leave. We would keep learning, but from a distance.

The diorama changed shape one last time, revealing a continent. Quincy wasn't entirely sure, but he thought he recognized the shape of the place we call Antarctica, albeit a couple of million years ago.

If you are here now, it means Deus has failed. Look for the last bastions we've left behind or patiently await our return. Lay your eyes on Arctica and let the kin of the cosmos guide your way.

Lilly jumped up from her seat as the light unexpectedly turned back on. Quincy still sat in the seat right beside her, looking just as bewildered.

"Wha..." Lilly started.

"I, I have n-no..." Quincy stammered.

"By the obnoxious light of the great horsehead, what happened to you two?" Tim flickered wildly. The lamp was entirely bright again as it lay on its side in the chair. "You merely sat down like a couple of morons, and gone you were, zoned out for a good while! Are you humans really that useless? Oh! To be like me, a being of pure celestial light, born from the ashes of a living star! I—"

"Kin of the cosmos?" Quincy asked, puckering his lips in anticipation.

"An adequate, yet primitive title, I'd much rather prefer *overlord of the pitiful*, but all right."

"What *was* that?" Lilly's eyes widened as she reached for Quincy. "Did we just witness what I think we did?"

"That God is an ancient alien sent by an even older race of extraterrestrials in order to protect our planet from malign forces? That God is gone? That we need to find the Celestians in order to get him back? That in all probability *Tim* is the one that will lead us to find them?" Quincy rattled. "Oh, I'm getting a headache just thinking about it."

Lilly swerved around and dropped to her knees beside the lamp. "I'm so in for, like, a three-year vacation right now."

"What's this about me serving as a compass? *Again?*" Tim complained.

"We'll get to that as soon as we figure out where we're off to next," Lilly said, poking the lamp. "Meh, I had hoped all of this would've resolved by now. Then again, what did I expect? That reaching the bottom of this pyramid would magically make Haven lose interest in us?"

Quincy knelt beside her. "At least we made it this far. We solved all of W.A. Swansong's riddles, used the key, and found enlightenment. Mom and Dad would be proud." He smiled, which Lilly kindly returned.

"I think they would've preferred us never knowing at all though," Lilly added.

I agree. If I could take back this wealth of knowledge that comes with having the origins of our species laid bare, I would. It is a burden I do not wish upon anyone, and even though I am proud of Lilly and Quincy for having come this far, I feel the enlightenment is a curse. Sadly for the twins, getting enlightened was inevitable for the sake of our world.

"So sorry to have to break up this little quality time you two are having, but I believe this is as far as I'll allow you to go." A dark voice broke the silence.

Out of the corridor, the ghastly apparition of Kraal entered the grand chamber. Behind him, Paw stammered on his feet; he was being held in place by a pair of animated skeletons that held their spears at the sides of the old Navajo's throat.

"Let's skip all of the formalities, motivational speeches, and evil master plans. Point is, you have a price on your heads, and I aim to collect that prize—by turning in your heads…" He snickered. "Oh! But first!"

Kraal snapped his fingers, and the two skeletons reacted by jamming their spears through Paw's back. Paw's mouth spat blood; gurgling in pain, he stared at the two spearheads sticking out from his chest.

Lilly screamed.

Somewhere in time, on the other side of the world, Sean screamed too. It was so loud it could be heard from miles away.

The fat man, Mr. Marsh, stood next to him, grinning. He grabbed Sean by his cheeks and pulled him close, staring deep into Sean's bleeding eyes. "What's it like, Mr. Cooper? Staring into oblivion?"

Sean retched, slinking down as vomit and bile splattered between his knees. "You won't win," he whispered in pain and anger. "You can kill me, but you won't win."

"Your friends burn. A fate worse than death has befallen them."

"No. I don't believe you."

"*You* are the lucky one, Mr. Cooper. We might still spare you, in the interest of science. But the twins? They probably wished they'd never been born."

"You bastard!" Quincy yelled. He was bright red with anger and hurt. "He was innocent in all of this! He had no part in any of it." Quincy trembled from adrenaline as Lilly looked at him with tear-filled eyes.

She had seen her brother angry before but never like this.

"Your friend was *dead* the moment he laid eyes on you two," Kraal snarled. He watched in delight as Paw's body sank to the floor. "Guilty by association," he spat before raising his hands. "But enough now!" Kraal glanced at his two skeletal minions. "Get 'em, boys!"

The two skeletons lunged forward towards the twins. But Lilly, though full of guilt for her friend's death, was ready for it. With her right arm outstretched, she shielded Quincy and pushed him back up onto the plateau with the chairs. Then, to Quincy's surprise, she pulled a .357 Smith & Wesson Magnum out from behind her back and took four shots in quick succession.

The skeletons fell to the floor, dazed and confused, their legs blown out from underneath them.

"Lilly! W-where did y-you…?" Quincy stuttered.

"A last gift from Paw before we parted," she said, determined, fixing the gun on Kraal's surprised face.

Tim's lamp bobbed up and down. "That's my Mistress! Muahahahaa." The orange and pink light swirled around behind the glass.

Lilly's finger was itching around the trigger. "Last chance to tell us what you really want with us, what Haven wants with us." Her hands were shaking.

"It's simple. They only wanted to prevent you, prevent anyone, from figuring out their secret." Kraal chuckled. "Their puny little secret, bah. If you'd only just given up your inheritance like the good little boy and girl you should be, you'd be happily oblivious to all of this."

"We made a promise," Quincy said, struggling to breathe as the adrenaline faded and the pain from his earlier chest wound started to burn.

"And we won't let those people down," Lilly added. Her head was pounding. She squeezed her eyes tight, one after the other, not daring to close them both at once since she had no idea what the black mage was capable of.

Kraal shook his head. "I'm getting a bit tired of this charade," he admitted and rubbed his fingers together. "I have a new proposition for you"—he stretched his hands outwards, fluently, almost as if it was part of a dance—"and I'd like to name it…" He stopped, his eyes narrowing. "*Why* won't you *die?*"

The black mage slammed his hands hard against the pillar beside him. The ancient stone structure rumbled and cracked loudly in complaint of the sudden force striking against its foundations.

Lilly and Quincy could see the cracks shooting upwards towards the ceiling of the chamber and felt dust and sand begin to fall down into their collars and hair.

A work of destruction was now in motion. The die was cast, the first domino tipped over.

The whole building was ready to come crashing down on them.

Lilly yelped and fired three bullets straight at Kraal, but unfortunately the rounds hit the ground a few inches from the mage's face—a red ripple, like cascading water, appeared where the bullets hit; Kraal had protected himself with an energy shield.

"A valiant effort!" the black mage cackled. "But ultimately a futile one!" He waved his arm straight down.

Quincy looked up to see a giant piece of ceiling debris tumbling down towards his sister. It was as if the world had gone into slow motion, either that, or his reaction time was simply heightened by the sense of impending doom.

He slammed into Lilly, knocking her a few feet back towards the stairs at the opposite end of the plateau. He sighed in relief, seeing that she was safe, but a sharp sting called him back to reality. He looked back, prone on the ground, and saw his mangled leg disappear beneath a chunk of ceiling rock. Quincy's face fell to the floor, and he bumped his forehead on the hard stone.

He looked back at the ceiling crushing his foot. "I refuse to make that pun, *refuse*," he jabbered to himself.

Growing delusional from the shock that was setting in, Quincy looked up and saw Lilly rolling and dancing around on the plateau, avoiding rocks, braziers, and other big objects the now mad-cackling wizard was throwing at her.

"Lilly!" Quincy felt as if his lungs would burst. He hoped his ribs hadn't punctured them... then again, it would be the least of their troubles.

"I can't reach you!" Lilly looked at her brother, her eyes red rimmed. "He's toying with me! But if I come near you, he'll squash me!"

"Get..." Quincy swallowed back the blood that came bubbling up. "Get... the damn..." He threw up a vile crimson liquid that splattered the floor beside him. "Get the *lamp*!" he yelled.

"Yes!" Tim suddenly yelped, his promise to his Lilly voided. "Get the lamp before it's buried forever!"

Lilly took two quick hops back and snatched the lamp from its resting place in the smooth stone chair. *Not yet though,* she thought.

"Action! Actiooooon!" Tim cackled.

"Hush," Lilly hissed at the lamp, "*almost*, okay?"

"Time to *end* this!" Kraal screamed and brought the ceiling down. Literally. The entire roof of the chamber started to crack.

Not yet, Quincy thought.

"DIE! HA-HA-HAAA!" Kraal danced around, waving his hands in the air.

Here we go. Lilly counted backwards from three in her head as huge pieces of rock came crashing down towards them.

"Tim! Second performance!" Lilly yelled.

"Finally, yaaaaas! Muahahahaha!" The voice from the lamp boomed with the strength of a thousand bulldozers.

A blast of pink energy shot across the chamber. The falling pieces of ceiling debris were caught right at the rippling borders of the body of energy. The pieces drifted in the air, buzzing from the pressure. But the pink and purple energy dome started to sink, and Lilly watched the huge rocks lower towards her.

"Tim?!" she pleaded. "You can do this, right?"

"What's this now?" she heard Kraal yell in outrage.

Tim twirled around in a soothing velvet sea of orange and indigo. "Just adding some dramatic effect, hehehe."

The energy field expanded again.

"No! Not like this!" Kraal let out a bloodcurdling scream.

Lilly looked up just in time to the sec the black mage's head being lopped clean off by one of the bigger, triangularly shaped pieces that flew towards him like a projectile.

"Ho! Did we... Did we get him?" Quincy laughed, borderline hysterical at this point. His laughter transitioned into a coughing fit. "We got him, didn't we?"

"Tim!" Lilly's eyes fluttered around, unsure of what to do. "Get Paw out of there; I don't want him to be buried like this."

Smoothly and without sound, Paw's body floated towards the twins, the boulder that was crushing Quincy's foot drifting up and off in the opposite direction.

"Dammit, Paw." Quincy seethed with rage in a moment of clarity. "You didn't deserve this. It's all our fault."

Paw's eyes opened, and for a moment, there was a flicker of hope between the twins.

He managed to curl his lips into a smile as he looked up at Lilly and Quincy. "Strength," he said with great effort, "like the mighty buffalo."

The light faded from his eyes; Paw was gone, and the twins felt as if all was lost. Quincy tried but couldn't stand up. Lilly stared up towards the broken ceiling and saw torchlight flickering high up from the upper floors that were now laid bare.

The pyramid shook and grunted. More sand, stone, and dust started to fall down. Lilly knelt beside Paw and her brother; she held Quincy's hand tight and squeezed it.

"Until the end," she sobbed.

"Until the end," Quincy repeated.

A brazier fell from a higher level and crashed down between them, the hot coals scattering around them. Lilly and Quincy closed their eyes.

More debris started to fall.

PART III

Orphans of the Universe

Chapter 13

A MOMENT OF REFLECTION, if you will. For this came to me in a vision just now, as emotions always tend to run rampant when the stakes are highest.

Many years ago, I was walking up and down the cobbled harbor street of a tiny island just off the coast of New England. The rain was pouring down hard, and the ocean had pulled a thick blanket of fog over the little town and its close-knit community. The entire island seemed obscured by the mist, save for the tiny red light of the radio tower blinking in and out of existence high up in the dunes and island hills.

W.A. Swansong was my name. I was a writer, and I loved to meander around in a thick storm as much as the next man.

It was at this very distinct moment, just when I was about to step inside the cozy little bistro, the one next to the bronze war memorial statue looking over the sea, when I was approached by a beady-eyed little man sporting a tiny moustache.

"You look like you are in the market for a companion," the man proclaimed, looking smug.

"I beg your pardon?" I replied.

The shifty little character pulled out a cardboard box with

something obviously shuffling inside of it.

"A dog," the man said. "You look like you are interested in a dog." He opened the little latch, and the face of a gorgeous and curious corgi emerged from the box.

I chuckled. "Not now, my friend. I am currently on my way to visit my grandniece, of whom I hear is expecting twins." I eyed the cute little animal thoroughly and reached out to pat the dog gently before giving it a quick scratch behind the ears. "Someday in the future, a dog might find a place with my family. In fact, I'm sure of it. But today is not that day."

I walked on as the cold drops of wintery rain dripped from my umbrella onto the silted welcoming mat of the bistro. This would become one of my fondest memories. It was also one of the first, and one of the only, memories I have involving my dear twins.

Flashes… buzzing… strange machinery…

Quincy couldn't remember much of what had happened after the pyramid came crashing down on them. He pretty much had made peace with what, by all means, should've been the end for him and his sister, but apparently *someone* had other plans.

But who?

He thought long and hard, trying to recall the images that sometimes popped up in his head, only for them to disappear again in the span of a nanosecond. He remembered waking up and finding himself lying on a slab of unidentified metal. It was cool to the touch, but somehow, he got the idea it was brimming with life, *actual life*.

He remembered looking to his left and seeing Lilly lying next to him, still unconscious. Near her, he had seen the silhouettes of the unnerving beings of which their uncle had wrote about so long ago. Most details were obscured by the absence of direct light, but he knew for a fact it was them:

Broad conical underbodies morphing into an abnormally elongated neck, bulging eyes, and claw-like appendages. Were they real? Was it… *them?*

The beings then had bent over his sister and, with utmost care, started removing scraps of her clothing and carefully dressing the nasty wounds and gashes across her head. They were helping her, *healing* her. He recalled it as if it were a dream, but he knew it to be real; it had to be.

Quincy looked away after they proceeded to check for wounds below her neck.

He tried looking around the room, tried to ignore his own pain that was tugging at him from the inside. The room was dark, save only for a soothing green light originating from nooks and crannies in the odd angled walls. He remembered wanting to speak, but not a single syllable managed to escape his lips.

Quincy then remembered looking down at his own body, feeling his belly and ribcage, remembering the red-soaked clothing and the terrible gnashing pain of bruised, broken bones and the sharp sting of a punctured lower intestine.

It was gone, all of it.

He recalled feeling absolutely fantastic, in fact, where he had been ready to take the world by storm, even though a gut feeling was telling him without their help, whoever these beings were, that the world wouldn't be there for much longer.

Now he didn't know what to think—about anything. Was it a gut feeling? Or something else? Where the hell was he anyway?

Did they try to communicate something?

"Oi!"

Quincy blinked, staring right into the eyes of his sister crouching in front of him. The entire scene with the dark room, the green lights, and the curious beings faded from his mind. He returned to the present, the entirely wrong, out-of-this-world present he was now actually living. Lilly was chewing bubblegum obnoxiously loud, wearing a thick coat with a fur-lined cap, strong gloves, and a pair of heavy-duty all-purpose boots.

His hands brushed against the fabric of his pants—*yup, I'm wearing the same kind of thing*, he thought. The material was a light, science fiction-like kind of synthetic, but it was miraculously warm and super agile. A parting gift from those who'd helped them on their way, Quincy guessed.

"You were staring again, mumbling." Lilly moved to sit nearby, resting her chin on her hands as she looked out towards the cold sea. "Remember anything new?"

"Eh… No. Unfortunately, I didn't." Quincy pulled his hands away from the sides of the small boat; the water was freezing as it sprayed his fingers. *We are on a boat in the middle of the Antarctic Sea*, he reminded himself, looking over at the front of the little boat.

Tim's lamp was hanging off the bow and was rocking back and forth, whimsically glowing his favorite palette of colors as they approached a fog. Behind Quincy, the soft whirring of the boat's motor reminded him of the room with the Celestians.

Did it?

"*Hello!*" Lilly snapped her fingers and waved at him again. "I asked if you were okay?"

"I'm fine, just tired," Quincy answered, but in truth, he felt as if he was losing his mind.

Lilly remembered a lot more than Quincy had about their half-awake adventures after the collapse. She had told him about the creepy robed figures that had transported them from one room to another. She told him about the conversations they had with each other, of which Quincy couldn't remember a single thing and Lilly couldn't either and deemed it to not be important. But Quincy thought it *was*.

Lilly finally told him about the waiting room: The barren little closet the twins had to spend more than a day in without knowing what was coming next. The room only had two chairs and a table with a voice recorder on it. The rest was blank for them both. Even Tim hadn't a clue of what happened. And *that* was really worrisome.

"Really?" Lilly snapped.

"What?"

"You just *did it again!*"

"Did what?"

Lilly slammed her fist on the boat's edge. "Really?" Before she could say more, a translucent ghost-fish shot up and chomped down on her hand—hard. Luckily, she didn't feel anything because it was literally a *ghost* fish, and she shooed it away. "Man, if they ended up putting a brain parasite in us, I'd be so pissed off."

"What makes you say that?" Quincy shook his head. "Amnesia or not, Lilly some*thing* helped us. We would've never made it out of there, not even in a million years."

"Hmpf."

"Play the tape again."

Lilly grunted and reluctantly reached into her coat pocket. "How many times can you hear the same thing and expect to find something different?"

"Just press the button!" Quincy groaned.

Lilly pressed rewind. "At least you're back in the *here and now* with me for longer than a minute." The tape clicked, she pressed play, and the recording began to play aloud.

"My dearest, dearest twins." The voice of Aleister Crowley was so recognizable, Quincy told Lilly that he was convinced he'd be able to find Crowley even if he hid in a group of over fifty thousand people that all yelled "Cuckoo!" at once.

"First of all. Let me tell you how dreadfully sorry I am for what happened to your Navajo friend. Believe me when I say that there was absolutely not a single scenario in existence where that little tidbit didn't not happen, and, believe me, I searched."

"Still don't know what that means," Quincy whispered.

His sister nodded.

"Secondly. I'd like to congratulate you on officially becoming a member of our little elite group. The world's oldest and most powerful

secret is now known to you, and now you know what you are fighting for." There was a pause, a shuffling sound. "Why us? I can hear you ask. Well, my dear Swansongs, you are simply the only two people still alive that know the secret and want to reverse what has transpired. You do want to help, don't you? Such a terrible shame if the Great Ones had helped you escape and nursed you back to health without at least getting the favor returned.

"Simply put. We need your help. God lives, children, and he is being held in one of the Great Cities beneath a Haven base in Antarctica. Those few among the Great Race that haven't been destroyed or captured cannot be put at risk. But Haven would never suspect a couple of mortal humans to go in and do some cleanup." Another pause, followed by a laugh. "Now up and at 'em, tigers. Go get them."

Quincy scoffed. They were the last hope for humanity? Meant to save God? Crowley couldn't be serious; it all sounded way too ridiculous. Then again, it was a voicemail left by a bloke that had been dead for about a hundred years now. And they *did* also have a trapped Fire Vampire that proved to be a useful, yet a tad annoying, sidekick.

"Are we really going to go through with this?"

"Considering we're already on a boat in the middle of an ocean, I'd consider the negotiating phase to be over." Lilly grinned. "Besides, until the end, right?"

"I just hope for the end of our journey… Not the end of the world."

She shrugged. "So, did you gather anything new after hearing Crowley's scratchy, annoying voice for the billionth time?"

"No."

"Great." Lilly gave the fakest of smiles. "I'm sure that was all worth it then." She then tapped her brother on the knee and gave him a concerned look. "Quince?"

Quincy looked up at her with tired eyes. "Yeah?"

"Remember that time when you were just starting out in college and I wanted to borrow your music player to listen to some tunes while I jogged?"

"I think so; why are you bring that up?"

"Remember how I thought it was funny that there were a bunch of hip-hop tracks on there and you got all defensive trying to come up with excuses? I didn't do anything to make you feel bad about that; it was all *you* that was embarrassed to listen to them."

"I really don't see your point here…"

"The point I'm trying to make is that you're so *hell-bent* on being this doomed, lonely, smart guy with the weight of a notorious last name dragging you down. You were trying to be the misunderstood loner on purpose.

"The thing is I don't know *why* you would want that. Why be embarrassed with listening to some admittedly kick-ass tunes? Well, that's neither here nor there, but why drag yourself down now? There's more to the world, even with being a Swansong. I've always looked up to you. I've always been equally proud and jealous of how smart you are. But it breaks my heart time and time again to see you not being able to just go out and get some ice cream and shoot the breeze in the park like people our age should be doing."

Quincy held back tears as he gazed into the antarctic mist. "I hate that I make you feel that way," he answered after some time. "Rest assured, I'm not doing it on purpose, but I've always had trouble finding my way in the world, and this whole"—he waved his arms around—"this whole situation isn't really helping.

"I get jealous too. Sometimes I think I get jealous of you— the most important person in my world—for being able to think happy thoughts in times like these. But mostly I'm jealous of them, the people *not* in the know. The people that think all these supernatural things, these things that go bump in the night, are just a few ghouls and ghosts. The people have already forgotten things like Egypt and the Carpathian Mountains. Incidents like Lafayette will be forgotten soon enough too.

"We've seen the power of suggestion through Haven's

enforcement. And right now, it sounds great to know as little as possible. It makes me sad that we both know, and we've both seen how terribly hostile and unforgiving all of this can get. I shudder to think the entire world can be erased in the blink of an eye without so much as a warning."

"I'm so scared," Lilly admitted. "I've never been so scared in my life ever since the wars broke out."

"I know." Quincy nodded. "And yet, you can keep up this happy persona, even though I know there's a woman in there that lives with a darkness always hovering over her shoulder, following her wherever she goes."

"I, I—"

"It's okay, Lilly. Just like you told me that it's okay to enjoy the little things that matter, I'm telling you now that it's okay to say you're scared, to say you're uncertain about things."

"We've got a lot to teach each other if we ever make it out of this place," Lilly whispered.

"Let me start right now then by saying that *when* we get out—'cause I'm trying to look at this positively—first thing we'll do is go out for ice cream and chill in the park, okay?"

Lilly looked around at the myriad slabs of ice, water, and snow surrounding them. "Eh, let's not decide on *what* we're getting just yet, okay?" A smile managed to form on her face, and even Quincy chuckled.

"Lilly, Master," Tim's voice fluttered up from behind the front of the boat, "look up; there's land ahead."

The fog bank slowly dissipated, leaving Lilly and Quincy in awe of the spectacle that unfolded before them. A great sheet of ice stretched out towards the snowed land ahead with huge mountains, their peaks disappearing high into the clouds, forming up ahead. Between the mountains, the twins could see towers of smooth stone rising in the distance: a marvelous sight to behold.

"Is that it?"

Quincy nodded. "I think it is, Lil." His eyes feasted on the grandeur of the extraterrestrial architecture. They saw tall obelisks, multi-angled walls of deep emerald, and broad, highly advanced bridges and aqueducts. Further away but still between the mountains, Quincy could even swear he saw something that looked like a giant upside down pyramid. "The city of the Great Race." His heart was racing.

"One of their last bastions." Lilly couldn't look away from the beauty of it all.

"Guided there by our very own kin of the cosmos." Quincy chuckled and reached forward to pet Tim's lamp.

The boat slowly ran aground, and the twins carefully lowered themselves onto the thick sheet of ice. The city was breathtakingly huge but still some ways away.

Lilly grabbed the oil lamp and got the go-ahead from Quincy to lead. First she pushed the boat around in the water and turned on its engine. They both watched it disappear back into the fog before turning to head for the city. They didn't want any evidence indicating some strangers were poking about. How they would get back home was anyone's guess at this point.

"Ever get the feeling we might end up dead very soon?" Lilly asked to break the silence. "Because I'm totally getting those vibes right now."

"Only now, huh?"

A mind flayer.

Sean laughed uncontrollably.

The walls in his cells laughed with him.

The surprise Marsh had for Sean was to have half of his brain scooped out by a freaking mind flayer.

"Genius!" Sean cried out before banging on the door of

his cell to try and get the attention of the Haven personnel on guard duty.

"Tell your boss, he's an absolute madman but a genius!"

When the thing's fleshy tendrils had first wrapped around his membrane, Sean had realized quickly enough that he'd spend the rest of his life terribly insane.

The mind flayer had shown him thousands of images: Worlds being destroyed by some unknown malevolent force. Children and animals being tortured; thousands of people being killed in the streets. It even showed him the gruesome death of his friends Quincy and Lilly—it had been one of the only scenes it showed him that subdued him.

And still the thing slurped and chuckled, waggling its gross, squid-like head in delight as it fed him more and more and watched the will to live drain from Sean's face. It would then stop, and the elite Haven enforcers handling the flayer would maneuver the thing back into its containment cell, taking the utmost caution not to let it pull anything funny.

This had happened around four to five times now. Each time, Sean felt his rationality slip away a little bit more as the terrible creature fed him awful truths. Sean noticed he was getting more and more desensitized and didn't even flinch the time a breach in protocol had taken place and the mind flayer had caused the heads of two Haven agents to explode in a fountain of blood and gore before it could be subdued. Sean simply stood there, smiling and wondering why the mind flayer didn't go for his head first.

The truth of the matter was that the creature was a particularly deviant one. Not only did it delight in showing Sean the terrible things that happened around this world and many others, but it was also a creature fond of toying with whatever and whomever was close to it. It was not only scrambling Sean's psyche, but it was also showing him loads of information he could use to his advantage. It was simultaneously breaking him and helping him, or so it seemed.

Why are you showing me this? Sean had once thought to the

thing as it fed information about the whole base's structure, floor plans, armory locations, and guard shifts into his head. It had not answered, but the implication seemed to be clear. Sean was now an insane and unguided projectile. Appearing harmless, the mind flayer had transformed him into an unpredictable force to be reckoned with.

A madman yes, but a madman that was just a few minutes away from breaking out of this place.

Sean giggled and looked at the walls. "Yes, I know," he told them. "It has indeed been a pleasure, but, you know, gotta do whatcha gotta do!" He slurped the drop of snot descending from his nose into his mouth. "Also…" He stopped, his eyes narrowing.

The mind flayer had shown him something else too. "Some fools will arrive soon in a boat, and I'm gonna get on that thing no matter what."

"Hurry!" Quincy shouted from his spot on the slippery shore rocks.

Traversing the giant sheet of ice had proven to be a lot harder than they thought, and the whole process was dangerous and slow. The closer the twins got to solid land, the thinner the ice seemed to be. Quincy wondered if it wasn't the other way around usually, but he couldn't remember.

"Watch it! Please… Look out!" Quincy saw Lilly dance across the thin streaks of ice that were now breaking apart at a pretty rapid pace.

"Don't you think I know that?" Lilly shouted. "I'm doing my best here!" She hopped from plateau to plateau as carefully as she could, hoping each time the little jump she made wouldn't be her last.

Quincy saw a fish swim under one of the sheets. It was clear as day; the ice was way too thin. He watched in horror as Lilly made the short hop to it. "No! Not *that* one!"

Too late.

Lilly's foot disappeared, and she screamed as the sheet of ice started to vertically rise in front of her; she was close to slipping away into the cold depths of the antarctic. Lilly tried to hold fast to the slippery surface, but it seemed to be of no use.

"Quincy!" Her voice trembled with fear. "I can't do it!"

Her brother started rooting around with the few bits of equipment they had brought with them and laid eyes on the long rifle that had been among the salvaged goods. The pyramid felt like a million years ago already, a whole other lifetime. But Quincy remembered how Paw always had tidbits of wisdom to share, among them the fact that a rifle was also pretty handy at getting someone out of a sticky situation.

Quincy pointed the rifle butt towards Lilly. "Hold on!" His own foot nearly slipped from a loose rock, and he cursed. "Stop thrashing around, too! If you can."

"I got it!" Lilly held on for dear life. "I…"

"What?"

"Something's wrong!" Lilly's hand slid across her belt. "Wait!"

Quincy didn't wait and pulled his sister to the shore—she landed right in his arms. He looked at the rifle and smiled, thinking, *Thanks, old bastard.*

"Quince!" Lilly looked around in shock.

"What is it? Did you say something was wrong?"

The twins set their eyes on the melting sheet of ice. The old oil lamp, Tim's lamp, had slipped off of Lilly's belt and was now rolling steadily towards the antarctic waters.

Lilly jumped forward to get it, but her brother held her back.

"It's too dangerous! Lilly!"

"No! We need him!" Lilly reached out with her hand.

It was no use.

The lamp casually rolled from the tilting sheet into the water. Tim briefly flashed an angry red. "What!" His voice sounded like a mixture of astonishment and tiredness. "What's this? No! FOOLISH MORTA-BLBLBRBLBLR…"

The twins watched the orange and purple light sink deeper into the bottomless sea.

Lilly shivered, either from panic or the relentless cold. "What do we do now, Quince? We needed him. Crowley said so. We can't do this on our own."

"We'll figure it out!" Quincy sounded harsh, determined. "The most important thing is that we need to get inside somewhere as soon as possible. Your leg is in bad shape; it's been in the freezing water for too long, and I don't think our miracle healers are available at the moment."

Lilly let herself be pulled away from the freezing shore. "We'll find a way to get you back," she whispered. "I promise."

Sean leaned against the little trap window of his cell door. He licked the screws that held it in place and wondered how it could possibly taste so salty when he expected a rustier kind of flavor considering the humidity.

His ears pricked up at the sound of footsteps. Ah, yes, there they were, just as the mind flayer had so graciously informed him of—the 32nd Haven division guard shift: some geezer named Al, who had a bad leg, and his partner Benny, who had asthma.

This was the shot Sean had been waiting for. He had no clue how these two morons managed to rise through the ranks of Haven, but, to be frank, he couldn't give less of a damn. He just had to figure out a way to get them into his cell.

"Did you see what they got locked up in Cellblock Xeta-1?" Sean heard Al bragging to his partner through the door.

"See?" Benny remarked. "I heard looking at it is enough to make it go haywire and snap your neck. I'm not gonna *see* shit when they put me up for Xeta-duty."

Sean heard the mind flayer whisper sweet words of

carnage in his head. It wouldn't leave his head anymore. "Yes," he answered softy. "I know. Positively membranous!"

Footsteps came closer and closer towards Sean's cell.

"Can you believe this Cooper guy?" Al grunted. "Manages to escape the whole Dimensional Shambler fiasco in Lafayette but gets caught while trying to hack into *our* servers?"

"Hmm. Guy has a death wish for sure," Benny wheezed.

"Hey! What are you doing here?! I'm only to be escorted by Marsh! Help!" Sean shouted from his cell. This was it; his timing had to be unequivocally on point.

"What the hell?" Al muttered. "Benny, get the padlock."

Sean crept into the corner behind the door. "Don't do this! Marsh will have your head; it's not worth it!" He smiled at hearing the *beep-beep-beep* of the digital code being entered.

His cell door clicked open…

"Inside! Quick!" Al yelled.

The two agents leapt into the cell and frantically looked around. Sean emerged around the corner of the room, slithering from behind the door like a snake. The door slammed closed with a loud bang.

"Hi!" He waved right before kicking Al in the right knee so hard he crumpled immediately to the floor. Benny gasped and started coughing, which Sean took advantage of by pushing him down towards the floor, hard. He finished his attack off by delivering a roundhouse kick to Al's face. The feeling of his boot slamming into the broad man's jaw and hearing his teeth shatter from the impact was invigorating, Sean decided. Al dropped to the floor like a wrecking ball, right on top of his comrade Benny.

"While you boys enjoy your little love embrace…" Sean started to go through their equipment. "…let me decide which one of you is more my size."

The two men grunted in pain; they had no idea what the hell just transpired. From an outsider perspective, it looked rather comical.

Sean held up a standard issue 9mm pistol, and his eyes gleamed a bit. He picked up the newly found silencer as well. "*Man*, you guys are resourceful!" He giggled and fired two shots—one carefully placed bullet per cranium.

Okay, that is a lot less funny.

Sean decided Benny's uniform would prove to be the most fitting and started to remove each article while trying to keep the bloodstains to an absolute minimum.

Meanwhile, the mind flayer was whispering its congratulations, along with the passcode belonging to the door's lock.

Sean cackled.

A ventilation shaft was hardly the ideal spot to be in, but it was the only entrance into the Haven base that wasn't crawling with agents. The twins were slowly but steadily making their way into the heart of evil. Evil, that's how it felt to deal with Haven. It didn't matter how many monsters were prowling around on Earth, most of them acted out of survival instinct. But Haven was different; they were malicious.

"How's your leg?" Quincy whispered, looking back at his sister. The vent was large enough to crouch in but not big enough to fully stand up.

"It's okay. It wasn't in the water for that long. It's tingly, but I'll manage."

"Good. Because I'm not really in the mood to drag your butt all around," Quincy joked before wiping a bead of sweat from his brow. "Warm here, huh?"

"It's a welcome change," Lilly mumbled.

"We're going to find Tim, Lilly. I promise."

"Yeah, yeah..." Lilly sounded distant. "Hey, find an exit yet? My hair is getting all cobwebby. I didn't even know spiders could live in temperatures like this."

"Spiders are probably the least of our worries." Though Quincy imagined a giant, terrifying ice-spider lurking around in the dark corners of the Great City and shuddered. "You know… Let's just not think about spiders, okay?"

A hard bang came from just up ahead.

"Tell me now! Where'd you put the keycard to Sector Gamma? Why isn't it in its place, huh?" A harsh voice echoed through the ventilation shafts.

"I'm telling you again. I can't say, y-you're not authorized for Gamma, you'd need to report to your superior," a meek voice answered.

Quincy looked back at Lilly and nodded towards the light coming from the roster up ahead. They slowly made their way up a small slope and positioned themselves in such a way that they could both see downwards into a small security room.

It had a small desk chair and a console, but most of the room seemed to consist of stacks of boxes. Just in the left-hand corner they could see an agent standing with his hands up. Another unknown pair of hands could be seen to the right— they were holding a gun, but the rest of the figure was obscured by the cascading shadow created by the heavy industrial lighting on the other side of the room.

"Last chance," the assailant warned the unarmed agent. "Where's the keycard?"

"You've got some n-nerve, agent. You won't get, get away with this!"

The twins saw the agent trying to reach for a red button hanging off the way slightly to his right, but he was too late. The other man shot twice, the loud bangs muffled by the silencer protruding from the gun's barrel.

Quincy gasped as brain matter splattered against the far wall. He didn't feel very good at all now and tried backing up into the shaft, pushing Lilly to the side.

"Hey, what the hell?" she whispered and pushed him back towards the roster.

Quincy's eyes widened as he managed to swallow the vomit making its way up his throat but lost his footage instead. He tried grabbing onto his sister. Eyes pleading and skin a tad greenish, Quincy fell hard against the roster, and, pulling his sister down with him, their weight combined was just enough for the weak metal to give way.

The twins tumbled down into the security chamber together with a load of dust and some chunks of concrete.

The unidentified assailant turned around; it was another Haven agent. He was a bit of a sloppy dresser and wearing a heavy-duty gas mask.

"What?" The agent sounded startled by the unexpected noise. "Freeze!" he yelled, holding up the gun.

Dizzy but fully aware of what was happening, the twins held up their hands high in the air.

"Any chance we could bribe you with the location of a really cool oil lamp?" Lilly whimpered. She was already closing one eye and bracing for impact.

"Wait. This can't be real…" the garbled voice muttered from behind the mask.

"Huh?" Quincy's eyes narrowed.

"Quincy? Lil?" The agent removed his mask—
it was Sean. The look on his face was a mixture of confusion, happiness, and dread.

The twins mimicked his expression before Lilly cried out,

"Sean! How? What?" She paused and shook her head. "HOW?"

Sean welcomed Lilly's embrace when she stepped forward to hug him. In the back of his mind, he could hear the whispers of the mind flayer trying to convince him to do terrible things, but something was different now. A wind of change breezed through Sean's consciousness as he realized that the images the mind flayer showed him were not always the truth. He had seen the twins die, but here they were right in front of him. *Alive.*

A piece of Sean's sanity seemed to have been restored upon laying his eyes on his friends, and it gave him a sliver of something wonderful.

For the first time in ages, Sean felt hope.

Chapter 14

"GIANT WORMS BURROWING through the desert, an inverted pyramid deep underground…" Sean whistled. "Sounds like one hell of an adventure. I wish I had joined you guys."

"I don't think you do." Quincy shook his head. "It was terrible, most of it at least."

He and Lilly had purposely left out anything they had learned in the ancient planetarium.

"Besides…" Lilly interjected, taking a long look at the corpse of the Haven agent lying on the floor. "You might want to fill us in on what's been happening to you. We don't *really* condone the killing of innocent people…"

"He wasn't innocent."

"He wasn't exactly threatening to kill you either!" Lilly pointed at the dead man. "We both heard it; what happened to you, Sean? This doesn't look like something you'd do."

Sean sat down and told his story, at least the parts he remembered and was conscious for. He started from the moment he had sent Lilly his final text and explained everything he had witnessed since coming here. He went into explicit detail about the mind flayer and the power it still seemed to hold over him, telling them how it drove him mad and full of bloodlust, how it wanted him to kill and maim for its own sick pleasure.

Finally, he explained that upon seeing them after thinking they had died a horrible death, it changed something in his mind, and he had felt the powers of the mind flayer weaken somewhat.

"I've read about mind flayers," Quincy said after Sean fell quiet. "They dwell in between dimensions and worlds. Some researchers believe they have the powers to show you alternate realities of yourself and the world around you and make you believe it's real."

"Let me assure you, Sean, that *we* are definitely real," Lilly was quick to say. "It'll probably make you doubt that fact real soon if I'm to believe the stories I heard. It'll try to make you think it's toying with you by making you think we aren't dead."

"Perhaps you're saying that on purpose to double-cross me…" Sean chuckled, but the twins could see the gleam of doubt in his eyes.

"Oh boy, this is going to take a while." Lilly expression could be described as a mixture of a smile and contempt.

"So, you can actually hear it? Whispering to you?" Quincy asked, scratching his head.

"Yeah, but not all the time," Sean admitted. He glanced over the security cam monitors another time to make sure the next guards on duty weren't heading their way just yet. "It's been reasonably quiet ever since I found you two." Sean shuffled his feet. "Are you… afraid of me?"

"Uh…" Lilly was caught off guard. "No, not really. I'm sure deep down you're still the same guy we met a couple of weeks ago and totally not a horrible psycho murderer." She laughed a little nervously.

"What Lilly is trying to say, Sean," Quincy intervened, waving his arm, "is that if you *do* feel something coming up, please let us know. Okay?"

Sean leaned down to the body at his feet, then handed Quincy a pair of titanium handcuffs.

To Quincy they felt really heavy as if they weren't merely for restraining humans.

"Here, I doubt this guy will miss 'em." Sean looked at the body at his feet in disgust, disgust not necessarily stemming from the corpse itself, but rather due to the fact that it was right there by his hands. "If anything goes haywire, I'll give a shout and you can put these on me, okay?" Sean held his arms behind his back. "Like this. *Not* in the front. Even though they're heavy duty, I can do a lot less if you tie me up 'round back."

Lilly snorted a laugh. "Gross."

"Yeah, I heard it once I said it." Sean smiled. "Anyway, what's the game plan here?"

"Nothing major." Quincy huffed. "Just finding *God*."

"We need to get into the Great City, and something tells me this isn't it." Lilly pointed at a monitor overlooking one of the containment zones. "This looks more like a prison to me, and I'll be damned if I want to be here when *that* humongous alien turd hits the proverbial giant industrial fan."

Quincy raised an eyebrow. "Since when did you become so… creative with words?"

"Maybe the alternate reality version of me that was killed was *super* creative, and I somehow got worst-timeline Lilly's powers?"

"That's a scary thought."

"The fact that somehow in an alternative version of the universe we died a horrible death?"

"No." Quincy laughed. "More versions of you."

Lilly raised her fist in jest. "Really?"

"Yo! Stick with the program!" Sean intervened. "Listen, I vaguely remember some weird green room with an elevator that looked totally different than the others. You know, back when Marsh was trying to show me all of the messed-up stuff Haven is holding down here to," he ran his hands through his greasy hair, "prepare me for the mind flayer."

"You think it'll lead us down into the city?" Quincy looked cautiously optimistic.

"It's the best shot we've got." Sean started looking around the room, digging through several of the boxes. "Ah, great, let's see. Yes. This'll do. Uh-huh."

The twins stared at each other; Lilly raised up her shoulders to give a sly "*I have no freaking clue,*" and Quincy mirrored her.

"There!" Sean revealed a couple of synthetic bags. "They use these to keep people in the dark, literally and figuratively." He threw them towards the twins. "Put those on, *loosely,* then let me see."

He continued his little experiment by grabbing hold of Lilly's arms then Quincy's. He even found some measuring tape and a… drafting triangle?

"Presto!" Sean exclaimed. "Hold these cuffs like this… don't worry, they're a lot less heavy. It should make it look as if they're fastened tight, but I jammed them with bobbin pins. I'll put the gas mask back on, and you'll be my fake prisoners."

"You can't be serious." Quincy sounded doubtful.

"Oh, I'm dead serious." Sean sneered. "Believe it or not, but I survived here as long as I did mostly due to the fact that the majority of the agents, at least the lower-security ones, are absolute idiots."

"*IDIOTS!*" Marsh stomped around his office. The agents in front of his desk hadn't seen him this mad since… well, ever. "Are you telling me that Cooper is loose *right now?*" he snarled at the men, each looking positively terrified.

"He can't get far, sir!" a remarkably brave, or very stupid, agent exclaimed. "The base is too well-guarded, and he'd never find a way back to the civilized world."

Marsh stared long and hard at the man. Slowly he crept closer and closer towards the agent's face, almost drooling at the mouth. "And...?"

"Besides, the mind flayer has got him, sir. The guy is positively insane. The chicken has *flown the coop*, if you will..." The agent chuckled while wiping the sweat from his brow.

"Oh, bad move," one of the other agents in the room whispered to the agent beside him.

Marsh responded swiftly by jamming a knife right into the "funny" guy's chin. The man, gurgling and choking on his own blood, collapsed on the desk, and immediately Marsh shoved him onto the floor in disgust.

The three remaining agents took a collective step back.

"Find him," Marsh murmured, "or you all will end up on Containment Block Zeta duty."

The agents knew that *containment* was just a word in the Zeta block, it didn't actually mean anything. No agent had ever returned from Zeta duty before, and they knew that getting a knife jammed in your lower jaw was a lot more merciful than having to head down there.

Sean led the twins across an array of endless, identical, and badly lit hallways—at least that's what he told them, considering their vision was pretty much fully obscured most of the time. At certain times, the trio could hear some terrifying sounds coming from nearby containment or experimentation chambers: growls, furtive whispers, howling, and screeching— it was enough for them to keep on walking as fast as they could because if something *sounded* like it could rip your face in half, it was probably a good bet to not linger around for too long.

Patrolling agents were few and far between, and Sean proved correct when he said that most of them were very dumb, considering they had breezed through a couple of security checks already without much more than a nod or a wave of the hand.

"Heads up," Sean whispered. "Here comes another one." He tried to avoid eye contact with the broad man walking up towards them, but the badge he wore might actually predict trouble. This was no Haven meat shield; this was a higher-up.

"Halt," the agent demanded. "Pull off that mask, agent. Identify yourself." He looked at the twins trailing behind Sean, bound and hooded, "and your prisoners too, I guess."

Sean pulled out a card. "I've got level-six clearance, and I need to be on this floor. You don't need to see my identification." He waved his hand in an odd manner.

"A level-six clearance pass?" Lilly whispered to Quincy. "That sounds like a big deal."

"I don't want to know just how many agents died before we found him," Quincy whispered back.

"What's that?" The agent looked over Sean's shoulders at the twins. "You need to keep your prisoners in order." He grimaced. "And I *do* need to see some ID. We've got an escapee on the loose, last seen near Sector Gamma."

"Oh really?" Sean said playfully, but he felt like a man gambling for his life. "Sector Gamma is near emergency exit red-dash-X-5; he's probably long gone by now, huh?"

The agent took a step forward. "Why won't you pull off that mask of yours… agent…?"

Second door to the right. They'll rip him to shreds! the mind flayer whispered in Sean's head.

"I need it… to… survive. Yeah. My lung got punctured by a… festering… Hell… Kite…" Sean lied through his teeth. He tried not to pay so much attention to the voice now in his mind telling him to wreak havoc.

"Really?" The agent's eyes lit up. "A Hell Kite? Code-name: Fallen Angels?"

Did that really *work?* Lilly thought. *What kind of paint have these guys been huffing?*

Sean was surprised by the man's genuine reaction but

managed to keep composed. "Yeah, really!" he lied again. In the meantime, he was trying to figure out if he was coming up with this himself or was he merely listening to what the mind flayer was putting in his mind. "Do you… want to see one?" he asked carefully.

"We have one here? Where?"

"This guy is *insane!*" Lilly hissed just a bit too loud. Quincy quickly jabbed her in the side.

"What was that, prisoner?" the agent demanded. "Hmm?"

"It's nothing," Sean reassured. "Follow me." He walked over towards the second door to the right… after he took a good hard step on Lilly's toes—at which she yelped a minuscule, barely audible apology.

"In here?" the agent stood in front of the titanium door.

Sean scanned his pass, and the door leading to the initial decontamination chamber opened. Sean followed him, taking the twins with him and sealing the huge door shut again.

"Can't see anything through this glass," the agent grumbled.

"Yeah, nocturnal and stuff like that, but you can go in if you want; their containment protocol is S-level."

The agent scanned his pass, and the second door, the one leading into the containment cell, opened slowly. "Oh, okay, great."

Sean moved up behind him, his hand hovering on his security pass like a bandit's finger would be on the trigger of his gun at high noon. The agent stepped inside, and Sean immediately scanned his pass, closing the containment cell door and overriding the agent's personal code.

"Wait? What are you doing?" the agent yelled from within the holding cell.

Then, a dozen or so gray figures started running through the cell, screeching a terrifying high-pitched noise.

"No!" the agent screamed. "These are *plague monkeys!*"

Oh dear. I once saw *one* of these on an expedition in Peru; let me be there first to tell you that, *ugh,* indescribable.

The noises became unbearable; the agent's screams nearly rose to the same level as those of the horrible gray monsters jumping up and down in the cell.

"Well, at least I got the *festering* part right!" Sean yelled back.

"Aaaaaah! Help me! Heeeee—" The agent was instantly silenced, his bloodcurdling pleas replaced by the gory sounds of tearing flesh and gushing blood.

And then a big red stain splashed against the tiny window looking into the cell with a piece of entrails, which unceremoniously splattered to the floor a couple of seconds later.

"Guess we're done here," Sean said without real emotion and shrugged. He turned and tapped both twins on the shoulder. "Come on."

Lilly and Quincy had peeked from under their hoods out of morbid curiosity long enough to watch the terrible scene still playing out in front of them; Quincy shook his head. They had to do something to help Sean. If they couldn't, they'd have to abandon him.

Marsh took the beautifully crafted porcelain duck sitting idly on his desk and crushed it between his hands into a mess of tiny splinters and blood. Furious, he rewinded the security tapes to have the video of the rogue agent played again. He meticulously examined the picture of the two prisoners lifting their hoods for a moment and froze the frame.

"This can't be happening," he wheezed. The realization finally struck. The black mage Kraal had failed him. He had probably been transferring money to a corpse's private account for weeks now.

"They LIVE? And they're HERE?" Marsh flipped his desk over in a rage, spilling all of the electronics onto the floor where they crackled and popped.

A monitor hanging in the corner of the office flashed white for a second before turning on and revealing a bald figure sitting behind a desk, fully obscured in shadow.

"Status report on the escapee, Marsh?" the man asked. His voice was garbled with anti-speech recognition software.

Marsh licked his swollen lips and tried to compose himself. "A minor inconvenience, sir." He kicked the broken computer away from his feet. "Tell the high council I will take care of this problem personally."

"Hey, hey, hey! Can you hear me?" Lilly was mumbling to herself as she stared off into space, looking towards the ceiling with her eyes somewhat slanted to the right. She could just make out the shape of the tube-lights hanging above them through the fiber of the sacks over their heads.

"What are you doing?" Quincy asked, tilting his head.

"I'm trying to reach out to Tim," she answered distantly. "I figured if the mind flayer can speak to Sean telepathically, maybe we can contact our own pet as well."

Quincy wanted to answer but swallowed the words back. It wasn't a bad idea, actually. If only Tim had proven to work like that in the past, then he'd be a bit more optimistic about the plan. "So, is it working?"

"Not really." Lilly sounded disappointed. "Not yet, anyway. But there is something. I feel *something* listening to me, but I can't make out who or what it is."

Sean turned around and forced the twins to a halt. "You need to be very careful here, Lilly." His tone was serious. "There are things all around us that are way worse than whatever your Fire Vampire friend can do. We cannot take the risks. I'm already tainted with a monster living in my head and feeding my thoughts. I'd like for the two of you to stay clean until all of this is over and dealt with, you understand?"

"Only until then?" Lilly asked skeptically.

"Bah, you know what I mean," he retorted. "We're nearing the green room and the elevator, by the way. Until we do, we need to stay sharp. I have a plan."

"A plan?" Quincy asked. "What plan? When were you going to let us in on this?"

"It isn't really a good time to keep stuff like this from us, Sean!" Lilly agreed.

Sean threw up his hands. "I'll tell you once I make sure that I'm not being tricked, okay?" He shook his head. "Besides, I get the feeling there are a lot of holes in what you've told me so far. But hey, that's your business, I guess. I just think that anything any of us know that could help us should be out in the open, don't you agree?"

He took a step forward and lifted both the twins' hoods for a second in order to look them in the eyes. "Get this. I have a plan, yeah. But it might just backfire so hard that we're going to have a real problem on our hands—a problem that your little bits of secretive knowledge may end up solving. If that could be the case, then yeah, I'd like to be in on it, agree?"

Lilly and Quincy nodded nervously. Sean looked battle-worn, both from the actual torturous experiences he had while being a prisoner in the base but also on a mental level. It was clear the mind flayer still had a hold of him, and the life seemed to be literally draining from him.

The twins felt helpless. They wanted to help Sean, but they had no clue if it was even possible to return from the state he was in now.

For a second, Lilly caught a glimpse of Sean's expression when he pulled her hood back down. It was an expression she'd seen a lot in her time in the military. It was the look of a person who had nothing more to lose. The look that said, "I'm going to win this thing for you, even if it means I'll have to die myself."

Lilly thought about discussing it with Quincy, but there was no time and it wasn't the place to do so. *He has enough on his plate as it is*, she thought. Discussing the fact that their friend might be planning to bring the base down on top of them in a suicidal last stand just wasn't a very clever move.

"There it is," Sean whispered.

Ahead of the group was a glass door emitting a very peculiar green glow. Sean swiped his card, and the trio went inside. The room was obscured in strangely placed shadows, but the soft glow of the green light contrasted against the heavy darkness of its forgotten corners.

By all intents and purposes, the room was very similar to the one Quincy and Lilly could remember snippets of right after they had nearly died in the pyramid collapse. There was no mistaking it. The room wasn't a modern, man-made structure. It wasn't even man-made at all.

It was Celestian.

In the middle of the room was a broad set of doors leading into a tube made from a dark green, unclear sort of material. It *looked* like an elevator. Here's hoping the fact that it actually was one. Sean had said it was an elevator but then confessed it was just a hunch, considering it looked so much like one. Nevertheless, he was right; it really did. It was also simultaneously the best and only shot they had at getting somewhere without getting caught sooner or later.

Probably sooner, considering the moment the trio stepped into the room an alarm went off. It was the kind of alarm that was only used in the absolute worst of crises, the kind that'd disturb and upset all the animals in a zoo and make them go mad.

The ambient noises of screeching, yelling, screaming, and yelping coming from all manner of terrible monsters Haven held, sounds that the twins had been getting used to, now seemed to have increased tenfold.

There was a horrible feeling of dread hanging in the air—a bomb under the table, ready to go off at any moment. It was the moment right before thunder strikes, where the air is laden with electricity and the poor folk stuck outside wonder who's going to be the unlucky ones next. It was as if… okay, you get the point.

Sean, Lilly, and Quincy all felt it.

"We need to get out of here right now!" Quincy yelled, holding his hands over his ears. He dropped one of his hands to grab ahold of one of Lilly's before inching backwards towards the maybe elevator doors.

"Freeze. Don't move! *Don't you move!*" a harsh voice rang through the green room, amplified by a megaphone.

The room started to flood with agents holding all manner of weapons… and they were all pointed at Sean and the twins.

"End of the road, assholes!" the megaphone agent screeched. "Boss said shooting you was too forgiving. So you're coming with us right now. No hassle, no funny business. Nice and easy, got it?"

Sean slammed his back against the elevator wall and pushed the single slimy green button in the wall, then took a hold of Quincy. The look in his eyes was *off*; he seemed distant, distant but determined. "Get yourself and Lilly into this thing *now!*"

"Stop talking!" the agent yelled into the megaphone. He pointed at some of his subordinates, who started breathing some ghastly vapor through their facemasks into the air. "You two!" he wheezed. "Get them!"

Lilly grabbed Sean by the shoulder and tried pulling him into the elevator with her. "We won't let you stay here; you'll be killed!" She pulled harder, but he wouldn't budge. "*Come on!*"

Sean pushed the twins fully into the elevator and grinned. "Don't worry!" he yelled. "I have a plan, remember?" He slammed the button again, and the doors closed before they could argue.

As the elevator groaned behind him, he turned towards

the horde of Haven agents. "Oh, you guys just made a big, *big* mistake."

Oh, this isn't going to be pretty.

The elevator cracked and groaned as it made its descent deep into the bowels of the Earth. Above them, the twins heard dozens of men screaming in anguish and the rattling and banging of guns being fired wildly.

Lilly and Quincy stood in the middle of the tiny green cube falling down into the primordial ruins of an ancient city and huddled closer together.

"Once again, digging deeper and deeper," Quincy whispered.

Lilly listened as the noise of violence above them slowly faded. "I wonder what's happening up there." She swallowed hard. "Sean…"

"Let's try not to think about it," Quincy told her. "He was up to something. This whole deal with the mind flayer, I…"

A voice emanating from one of the dark corners of the elevator popped up without warning. "A worthy foe! A mind flayer, almost matching myself in cosmic brilliance, muaha-ha!" It sounded familiar.

"Tim!?" Lilly lit up. "Wha—? Where are you?"

"Still on the bottom of the Antarctic Sea, you dimwit! I tried to find a chance to speak to you earlier, but something was isolating me."

"How'd you get on the speaker?" Quincy asked, looking around him to see exactly which corner the sound came from.

"There is no speaker, stupid human! I'm in your *mind,* muahahahaha!"

This had to be the real thing, the twins agreed. The voice sounded too much like Tim's both phonetically and personality-wise to be a trick. This opened up a whole new array of possibilities, Quincy thought. But most importantly, it gave them hope—hope that Tim would fulfill his destiny, as would they, if only they'd get him to do the right thing.

"Tim, do you know what's happening out there?" Lilly carefully asked.

"That idiot Sean isn't the best at making friends. Offence entirely intended." Tim's voice echoed through the small chamber. "He encountered a mind flayer, and it marked him."

"What does that mean?" Quincy scratched his head.

"They share a bond now; just like you and me, they have made a pact. A pact your friend Sean wasn't aware of until very recently."

"A pact to do what?" Lilly was biting her nails and spitting the chewed bits out onto the cold elevator floor.

"To tear down this base from within," Tim said with great admiration. "The mind flayer got the go-ahead from your friend and pulled the kill switch on the whole establishment. It's absolutely beautiful, really, muahaha! Every single cell, research lab, and containment chamber has opened, and the absolute worst horrors you could ever imagine are now freely slithering around slightly above your heads."

"Good Lord, that's… that's like opening every cage in the pet store at once," Lilly realized in shock.

"Only twenty times worse and without the GDF on stand-by," Quincy agreed. "Insanity. Absolute insanity.

"I know!" Tim sounded like an excited child. "If only *I* had come up with this brilliant idea! Ack, I probably would have if I was there with you instead of down here avoiding eye contact with the zombie killer whales. Foolish mortals, *ugh!*"

"I wouldn't want that on my conscience!" Lilly snapped, turning up her nose in disgust. "We'd never allow it!"

"Oh yes," Tim agreed. "Anything for my masters… speaking of. When are you going to come and get me? It's colder than the vast nothingness of space down here, nimrods."

"We're working on it, okay?" Quincy shouted towards the ceiling. "We haven't forgotten about—"

Quincy broke off as the elevator halted and a small bell jingled.

The doors slid open, and on the other side there was a hallway lit with a familiar green glow now cascading off of crooked, abnormally angled walls made of what looked like solid mercury.

Tim's voice faded from the room, and a new voice popped up, one clearly coming from a speaker in the right corner just outside of the elevator.

"We have… waiting a long time… for you. The heirs…" The voice sounded electric and buzzed like the whirring of ancient machinery.

"Follow the lights… Find us… Help us…" another voice chimed in; it was more metallic, as if someone spoke through a row of tin cans.

"Find us… and help… God…" the first voice said.

Chapter 15

FOR A WHILE I just stood there, taking in the beautiful ferocity of the primal ocean crashing down onto the cliffs just a short distance away from our ancestral home located off the coast of Maine.

W.A. Swansong was my name, for that was the man I was back then, an ancient, silly git of a writer bent on engaging readers with colorful stories about worlds beyond their own plain one. A man who aged so severely in his twilight years on Earth that everyone always assumed it was a horrible disease or some other sort of malignant affliction preceding my well-being. *Oh, if only it was*, I would've thought back then.

It was already long after the first dark dreams came and after I had first laid my eyes on forbidden texts and lost knowledge that my own grandfather had shown me so long ago. Only now did it start to catch up with me, as it would eventually overtake everyone.

But, alas. I remember little of those omens now, at least on how they affected me when I was still who I was then and not what I am now.

A feeling I *do* remember, and which I shall never forget, is the feeling I got from seeing my grand-niece's cheeks blush and her eyes light up every time anyone mentioned those little ones she was carrying, so close now to finally seeing the poor, old, doomed planet Earth.

Currently Emily had quietly crept up to me while I stood on the porch lost in my thoughts, moving to hold an umbrella over my head to catch the downpour but for a moment.

"You're going to catch a cold, Uncle," she scolded, shaking her head. "Do be careful; you're not the man you used to be."

"Believe me, Emily. If there's one person that knows how I feel, it will be myself." I looked down at her protruding belly. "Get them a dog."

"What?" Emily shot back. "Where did that come from?"

"A dog," I repeated. "A Corgi. They'll need some companionship in the future, especially growing up here, all secluded."

"I—"

"Name it *Hewie*; it has a nice ring to it."

And with that, I went back inside, knowing my last few hours were approaching. It was my *second* fondest memory, and the second ever I had pertaining to the twins.

It was also one of the last things I can remember at all; for the black hand of death overtook me that very night.

I wondered if dogs had a similar afterlife as human's might've. I wondered if I would meet some.

I was not disappointed.

The twins silently moved through the breathtaking underground city. They didn't have a lot of time to sit around and admire the scenery as much as they would've liked, but they certainly appreciated the grandiose vistas that lay in front of them as they walked.

Tall spires of smooth black rock high up into the grotto shot right through the cavern's ceiling while green and yellow lights danced all around the dark cave, every last one of them lighting up at the right time for the twins to never lose their way.

The lights shot upwards into the cave now and twirled around some of the amazing megastructures that loomed in front of them. It was as if the lights were alive and felt the twins' desire to see and take in as much of the scenery as they could.

They saw bridges rising over channels of antarctic water, chiseled in the strangest of shapes, nonsensible to the human mind but nonetheless created with thought and precision backing every cut of glossy stone that had once taken place.

Even *I* had never seen the splendor of the Celestians' awe-inspiring cities on Earth firsthand, not when I was *alive* anyway. Perhaps I felt a pang of jealousy, just a little bit.

Quincy and Lilly realized they must have been some of the first human beings to have ever stepped inside of the dead city. If the elevator hadn't been there, they'd argue they *were* the first. A distinct crackling a few feet ahead of them dispelled that theory, however, as a soft voice rang through the hallway of black marble, silt, and seawater. Neither of the twins could make out what it was saying, but it sounded vaguely electronic and jumbled.

"What *is* that?" Lilly's voice echoed in the dark. "It's coming from up ahead by that… I guess a dock?"

"Look! One of the wisps is twirling around it." Quincy pointed.

"Wisps?"

"Well, what else should we call them? They look and act exactly like will-o'-the-wisps."

"Yeah, so in the event that they might actually be will-o'-the-wisps, I'd advise we proceed with caution."

The twins got closer to the source of the noise and realized they were staring at the body of a dead Haven agent propped up against a waist-high obelisk. He couldn't have been there very long, considering the smell hadn't set in yet. Either that or the underground cavern was icy cold enough for preservation. Neither of the twins wanted to dwell on the thoughts of what might've killed him. The agent held a walkie-talkie unit in his hands, grasping it tightly between stiff fingers. A never-ending stream of sound was emitting from the radio unit.

"...Overrun! B section is entirely gone. I...AAH!" A short transmission lit up the small indicator on the side of the unit.

"Squad Tetra! Report back in right…. *Kzzzzzzgggrr.*"

The deafening sounds of gunfire and explosions burst from the speaker and echoed towards the ceiling above them, dropping some dirt and loose sheets of ice into the frigid canals surrounding the city.

It was a reminder that whatever the twins' plans were after they found what they came for, getting out through the base was not an option.

"*Kkrrrzzzz…* blood everywhere! Hel….oming from… walls!"

More gunfire, more explosions, and most of all, more screaming.

"Quincy, I…" Lilly looked away from the device, and Quincy saw the tears rolling from her cheeks. "Sean?"

Quincy looked disheartened. "I don't think there is anything left we can do for him, Lil." He glanced at the huge gateway rising in front of them. "All we can do for him is make the same promise as we did Mom and Dad: Finish this mess."

After heading through the enormous gateway, the twins figured they would've arrived inside the proper city interior by now. Yet they were in what appeared to be living quarters stacked upon each other, rising high into the ceiling and beyond. Ice had formed around thin tubes of metal standing in rows along a broad, beaten path of irregular rock.

Lilly watched the little balls of light dancing from one tube to another. Their green glow plonking down on top of them and emitting yellow, green, and orange sparks until they rose up and flew to another.

"Quincy, do you see what I see?"

"They're following a set path; I see it." Quincy watched the wisps twist then turn. "They're rounding up around that… marketplace? Hmm, city square, most likely, do you see the doorway?"

"Yes!" Lilly's eyes widened. "That's where we need to go. I can feel it."

"I can too. The final end of our journey, the real one this time."

The twins froze as a peculiar tingling sensation shot through their bodies and looked at each other for confirmation. Yes, they both felt it.

Lilly looked up as if expecting something, and like a piece of refined clockwork, something met that expectation.

"The… lights…" The raspy metallic voice they had heard earlier returned. "You are… so close."

"Not much… time… left." The second voice chimed in.

As if a cloak of smog had risen up, the sensation disappeared as quickly as it came.

Sean pressed the code into the control pad as quickly as he could. "Come on… Come on!"

The door slid open in silence, and Sean threw himself in. Still lying on the ground, he took out his gun and aimed. He fired two quick shots in rapid succession, and the titanium door fell to the floor, closing off the hallway from one side. Jumping to his feet, he briskly turned around and pointed the gun towards the door at the other end and stopped, his finger twitching on the trigger.

"This wasn't part of the deal!" He stared at the ceiling; his eyes widened and shot around rampantly—whenever the mind flayer started to speak to him, this happened.

"I don't *know* where Marsh is!" Sean twirled around and sank to his knees. He placed his hands on his temples and screamed, "You said you'd get me out of this! I can't take any of this much longer; I'm just waiting to be hunted down by whatever you throw at me now!"

Sharp pangs of pain shot through Sean's skull; the mind flayer was cackling.

"Argh! Don't get smart with me, you son of a bitch!"

The pain intensified, and Sean could hear the screaming of agents and their horrifying predators beyond the door he just locked.

"Aah! *Fuck!* The city beneath the surface... But..." Sean squealed in horror and pain. "Don't... hurt *them. I beg you!*"

"Wait. I want to try something before we go in." Lilly stopped right before the threshold of the green-illuminated chamber.

"Hmm? What's up?" Quincy looked around in apprehension before focusing on her.

Lilly glanced up to the high ceiling of the cavern, closed her eyes, and took a deep breath. "Tim? Are you there?"

"I am always with you... my masters..." Tim's voice echoed with regret throughout the abandoned streets of the primordial city.

Lilly took a deep breath and looked at her brother with pleading eyes. "It's the only way..." she whispered to Quincy. "Tim?"

"Yes."

"Break free of your chains. We release you from your prison... It's over."

"What are you *doing?*" Quincy asked in disbelief. "We need him!"

Lilly ignored him. "Go, Tim. If there is any mercy in your

cold, dead heart… do you have a heart, I wonder? Eh, never mind. If you do, Tim, you will know where to find us."

Everything got really quiet after Lilly finished speaking. Even the muted violence above their heads seemed to fade.

"Heh. Hehehehe. Muahuhuahahahahaaaaa!" Tim's voice boomed louder than ever, bringing stalactites of ice down with it. "You *fools*! You have no idea how long I've been trapped in that lamp and what it really felt! I thank you humbly, you terrified little apes of a race, for setting me free forever. Goodbye! Muahahahahahahahaaaaaaa!"

And with those parting words, the usual noises from the cavern and the base above returned, and Tim was gone.

"*Well*, that worked like an *absolute charm*, Lilly!" Quincy squeezed his eyes shut and tried to dispel the headache he felt coming.

"I, I…" Lilly stammered.

"Did you really think that would work? Did you?" Quincy felt defeated. "Man… like, I get what you were trying to do, but you didn't even think to give me a heads-up or something? He could've been the only thing that would get us out of here!"

"We'd probably *die* anyway. Don't you get it? This is a one-way journey, Quincy! Our chances of seeing this through to the end are slim to none." She glared. "You said that once in a while everyone gets a bit melancholic, so here's me laying down the fact right now, okay? I had an idea that might, just *might* give us a fighting chance to escape and what?"

Lilly eyed her brother up and down. "What's that look on your face? You want to call me stupid, don't you?"

"No! It's just that… we should discuss these things before-hand and—"

"Bah. Don't say anything." She shook her head, waving him inside. "After you, *genius*."

The twins made their way underneath the archway leading into the green room.

"Sorry," Quincy mumbled after a while.

"What's that?" Lilly turned around with fire in her eyes; she was still furious.

"I said I was sorry, okay? It was a good idea, and I should've trusted you to act on your gut instincts because I know that's what you do best in situations like this. Perhaps I'm too much of a control freak but—"

"Shut up!" She averted her eyes and lifted her hand up towards Quincy.

"Geez, you don't have to be—"

"Ssshh!" Lilly's eyes nearly bulged out of her sockets when she looked at him. "Quincy, check this out."

The room was dark except for the unnatural green glow. There was a constant humming in the air that sprawled around the room were giant computerized devices beeped and cracked in harmony. Strange tubes of perplexing bio-engineered material hung from the ceiling and linked every last bit of machinery together.

More weird noises came from somewhere in the darkest nooks of the chamber; they were almost like whispers but totally unintelligible. Once in a while, one of the devices hissed as if it was processing some kind of data. At other times, puffs of smoke rose up from seemingly damaged parts. And a big screen hung from the smooth obsidian ceiling right in the middle of the chamber—it displayed nothing.

However, none of the strange machinery or the peculiar sounds could prepare the twins for what they saw in the right-hand corner of the chamber.

Quincy and Lilly laid their eyes on two real extraterrestrial biological entities that appeared to be trapped in some sort of vise and dripping slime, blood, or some other kind of mucus-like substance around them.

The twins knew in their hearts that they were standing face-to-face with two members of the ancient race of the Celeste—the large lower bodies, the unusual clawed hands, elongated necks, and small heads, it all checked out.

One of the entities lifted his long arm and his claw-like appendage and tried to reach for Lilly in desperation. Halfway there, the arm fell back against the entrapment, and the entity moaned.

"They're in pain…" Lilly held back tears. "Quincy, look at them. They are beautiful, but… they're dying!"

Quincy's breath had been taken away, and for a little while he couldn't say anything, but then he rested his hand on his sister's shoulder. "We've seen them before," he assured her. "I can only remember flashes and quick images. The memories from after the pyramid are fading, but I'm sure of it. These beings helped us; they rescued us."

"Not us…" the left entity spoke. Its voice was like hearing the orchestra of the cold, dark cosmos or, rather, a metallic rasping that was smoothly shifting its pitch in intervals, like a classic rock synthesizer or one of those old computer sound programs. "Friends…"

"They talk! *Talk!*" Lilly jumped in excitement, the possibility of having a conversation with the eldest beings of the world nearly made her lose it.

"I hear you! I hear it!" Quincy couldn't look away. "What can we… what can we do for you?"

The right entity's head slumped lower as it pointed its appendage to one of the unremarkable cables lying on the floor next to the twins. "Life…" its voice grated, like a robot's. "Give us…"

The twins saw a triangular-shaped hole oozing fluid coming out of the entities' underbodies, like a gushing wound. The spell of awe that held Quincy in place faded, and he was quick to act.

"This one?" he tried.

The left entity nodded.

"Lilly, there's another one; can you…?"

"On it."

The twins pulled the cables closer to the enormous beings and, with some hesitation, stuck them into the gashes in their lower bodies. The wound flashed with light for a second, then instantly healed and fused together with the cable like an organic power socket.

"Life," the right entity whispered and nodded; it looked invigorated. "A fighting chance, perhaps."

The left entity merged its short facial tentacles together in what could be considered a smile if one would look long and hard enough.

"Who… who *are* you?" Lilly was shaking from anticipation.

The left entity lifted its appendage and pointed at the right one. "This… is Caine. I am Abel. We are guardians of the One."

Quincy gasped. "No way. *The* Caine and Abel? As in the biblical Caine and Abel?"

"A funny tale…" The right entity groaned. "But nothing more than that."

"We have been waiting for the heirs for a long time…" Abel's many eyes glanced over the twins and inspected them, bit by bit. "Ever since…" His voice cracked.

"Ever since we failed," Caine finished.

"Failed in what?" Lilly asked, cautiously looking around the room. "And by heirs, do you mean me and Quincy?" Lilly glanced over to see Quincy was shuffling around uncomfortably. The room was too much to take in at once; it was something he seemed to have trouble with.

"Failed in protecting Him," Abel mourned. "Your family was chosen long ago, yes… to be the keepers of the secret… until… the time came to act."

"And… help…" Caine's voice became a high-pitched sting.

Lilly glanced over at her brother again before her eyes met

those of Abel's, whose long neck had bended in an irregular way to look at her.

"How can we help?" Lilly straightened, Abel's face following her movements; it was awkward communicating with a face hovering somewhere between your knees. "We're just humans… we have no power."

"And yet here you are…" Caine reassured her. "You have helped already…"

"This place, what is this place?" Quincy shuddered. "We were under the impression we'd find God here."

"God… Deus… all around you…" Abel nodded.

"We've heard that one before. That is, until He isn't, right?" Lilly remarked with cautious sarcasm.

Caine waved a claw-like hand around the chamber, and the buzzing and humming of the machinery grew louder for an instant.

"We don't understand." Quincy felt his heart pounding in his chest. He had a hunch, but it was a very heavy one. You could say that hunch carried the weight of the world and all of humanity's known history with it.

Forgive me, my dear twins, for ignorance is bliss, and I should have known better than to place this burden of knowledge on our family.

"You humans…" Abel retched; Quincy could swear the noises he made could only be described as an alien life-form chuckling. "Ancient humans… you learned one… of our more common languages… *butchered* it, as you say…"

"I beg your pardon?" Lilly was lost and wondered when exactly she stopped following the conversation.

"*Not* Deus ex machina…" Caine buzzed, the pitch of his voice lowering so much there was a blast of sonic energy emanating from him.

"*Deus* est *machina.*" Abel confirmed.

Quincy felt the world around him crumple. That was that, then. Humanity, like prophesied by their great uncle nearly a hundred years ago, was nothing more than a speck of dust waiting to be wiped away from the grand and infinite history of the ever-expanding universe.

"Deus est machina," he whispered. "Not *God in the machine*, but *God* is *the machine*."

Lilly took in all of the beeping devices and the mess of machinery parts humming and buzzing in the quiet obsidian room. Her eyes met her brother's, and she shared his state of absolute shock. "*WHAT?*"

Sean looked up at the flickering ceiling lamp as the base rumbled all around him. At least most of the screams from Haven agents meeting gruesome deaths right outside his little self-made prison had, by lack of a better term, died out.

The tiny hallway was now shaking wildly, and he knew something had found him. He had come to terms with the fact that the mind flayer had ultimately left him to die, unlike the promises it made to him.

Sean accepted this fate.

From the moment he was brought into the base only half-conscious, beaten half to death, and with a bullet hole in his hand, he knew he'd never make it out alive. But it was at that time, when the agents had first stuck him in his peculiar cell, that Sean swore that he would raise hell against everyone that did him wrong. He was satisfied with the fact that he made good on that promise.

Above Sean, the ceiling was ripped open, and a blinding light filled the tiny hallway he had locked himself inside; Sean shielded his eyes. *Yup, this is it*, he thought.

"You humans… really. Truly peculiar specimens, all of you," a voice boomed.

Sean wanted to reply. He wanted one last jab, a last satirical or sarcastic remark at whatever had found him and was now going to, hopefully, eat him quick and without too much pain.

But Sean couldn't respond—the velvety orange and indigo light swept him away too fast.

Quincy was hyperventilating as Lilly sat on her knees next to him, shaking in her boots.

After a moment, Caine and Abel stirred. "Is something… wrong?" Abel asked carefully.

Lilly looked up at the magnificent entity. "It's kind of hard to explain to, eh, non-humans? I suppose." Lilly helped her brother up before trying to explain. "It's a pretty big chunk of new information to drop, what you just did," she told them, not taking her eyes off Quincy.

"We… do not understand." Caine shook his small head, his facial tendrils curling inwards.

"Everyone has their own image of God," Lilly began. "Humans do, at least. They imagine an old man with a big gray beard sitting on a cloud somewhere, or to some, God can be an entity that takes many different forms and shapes. But in the end, from a human perspective, He's always…"

"Living? Breathing? Tangible?" a new voice said dryly, interrupting Lilly.

In the entranceway of the chamber stood the big fat form of Mr. Marsh in all of his repulsive glory. A faint shadow fell on his face, but the twins would have been able to see his terrifying grin from a mile away. He was holding some kind of contraption in his right hand, his thumb eager to press a big red button on top of it.

The appearance of Marsh startled Quincy out of his trance. "Who are you?"

Marsh cackled. "I'm the one who'd rather see a dead god than a living one, in whatever shape or form that entails…" He sneered. "You may call me Agent Marsh."

The room then burst into sound; heavy alarms started

going off, and the green light was whisked away and replaced by a bright, flickering red light. The twins instinctively reached to cover their ears as Marsh slithered further inside of the room. Lilly sneered at the disgusting façade of a man.

"What is this? What's happening?" Quincy yelled at Caine and Abel.

The twins heard one of their voices, now unclear whose it was, slightly above the ringing of alarms. "Danger! Something… Something is heading for Terra… A dark, malevolent force… an eater of worlds… it will cast the planet into an everlasting era of pain and suffering. Ah… the continents will be entire graveyards… a cadaver world…"

"We… must… restore… the balance…" the other entity chirped in with a weirdly high-pitched raspy voice.

"You will do absolutely nothing of the sort!" Marsh intervened. "God is dead, and so are *you*!" He

pressed the big red button on the device he held in his hands.

A bright spark of energy flew from somewhere up on the ceiling down towards Caine and Abel, and a surge of electricity zapped right through the vises the two entities were trapped in. Smoke and the smell of cooked meat penetrated the area. The strong electric current was enough to make anyone's head spin; the twins wouldn't want to find out what it did if it had hit someone with its full force.

But unfortunately, they would figure out soon enough, for as the smoke dissipated, Caine and Abel's bodies, burnt to a crisp and beyond recognition, crumpled from the vise-traps to the floor.

"No!" Quincy hurried towards the bodies but bounced back as he felt the surge of energy still flowing though the sleek metal of the vises.

"This can't be happening!" Lilly stammered.

"Oh, but it is!" Marsh cackled like a madman over the sound of the alarms. "Endgame, my dear twins! *Endgame!*"

"Why are you doing this?" Lilly had her hands wrapped in

her hair. "Wasn't interfering with GDF operations enough? Wasn't the researching and containing of all of *this* enough?" Lilly felt like she was caving under the pressure of it all, and it proved to be a task too difficult for anyone to undertake at this stage.

"Do you expect me to make my grandiose villain speech now? I don't believe I owe you any explanation!" Marsh shook his head, laughing.

"But you do!" Quincy moved away from the smoldering remains of the once majestic beings of Celeste. "You're the agent Sean spoke of; he called you kind of a wimp who's too afraid to fight his own battles. The agent in our apartment, he was sent by you, right?" Quincy took a step closer. "Lafayette, that was on you too. And I bet that even that black mage was on your payroll. You're a coward."

"What are you doing?" Lilly pulled Quincy back closer to her, looking perplexed. "Why are you taunting him?" She hissed, "He's crazy!"

"I know," Quincy replied in a low tone.

"Afraid to fight my own battles?" Marsh repeated the words in a mocking way. "I just killed your two friends without batting an eye"—He pulled out a gun from his back pocket and pointed it straight at the twins—"and I'm not afraid to do it again!"

Quincy squeezed his hands tight. "You're just a lackey following orders. There's no master plan involved… at least, not one of your own making. You're just a foot soldier, a grunt. A nobody."

Beads of sweat were stinging Quincy's eyes and rolling off his nose. It was the gamble of a lifetime, but Lilly had reminded him they had nothing left to lose at this point.

Marsh made a horrible half-laughing and half-retching sound. He narrowed his eyes. Slowly, he moved forward, still pointing the gun at the both of them. "Cooper has been telling you *lies*! I can hear it! He knows nothing about the grand scheme of things, about how *we* found God and how *we* destroyed the machine and unleashed terror upon the Earth, how *we* plan to harvest the power of interdimensional travel and aim to reach a new pinnacle in human life."

Marsh paused to catch his breath. "A *new world order*. Not on Earth, a planet stripped of its resources and purely a playground for us to test what all of this is capable of, but somewhere far beyond in endless space, between the living quasars of the infinite universe."

Standing at attention and careful not to let the barrel of the gun out of their sights, Quincy still managed to discreetly poke his sister in the side. His nod was almost invisible. Lilly followed the gaze; behind Marsh, they could see a shadow figure silently getting closer.

Just a tad more, Quincy thought. *Marsh just needs to ramble on a little bit more.*

Marsh laughed then. "Okay. You got me, you've had your speech. We *will* establish the new order. But, for us to do so, *lesser* humans will need to go…" He took a look at some of the flashing screens and grinned. "Heh. So soon… It'll all be over Swansongs; three minutes and thirty-eight seconds before something *very bad* enters our atmosphere. The Earth will go down in history as a mere blip on the radar, a couple of eons of sweet nothings that ultimately did nothing to stop our grand design. I'd love to watch you two go down with the flames, but I'm afraid I have errands to run, places to go, other dimensions to see…"

Marsh pointed the gun at Quincy, then Lilly, then back to Quincy. "You first… Goodbye, Swansongs…"

He took the shot.

The bullet bounced off a small, round energy concentration that materialized right before Quincy's eyes. The twins both sucked in their breath, and for a moment, they heard and felt nothing more save for the intense beating of their own hearts.

"I've invested too much time in these foolish humans! If they are ever to die, it will be on *my* terms! Muahahaha!" The familiar voice of Tim the Fire Vampire echoed above the blasting sirens. A huge cloud of pink, purple, and orange vapor sparkling with the light of a thousand stars swerved through the chamber.

"Tim!" Lilly yelled; she didn't know how to feel seeing the formless cloud of gas flash by, but she felt relief wash over her when the familiar voice shot through the air. "You came back!"

Marsh was visually taken aback but didn't falter in his determination. He shot again, twice, this time aiming at Lilly. Both times, the bullets fell neatly in front of her feet. "A minor setback!" he snarled as he started to back away from the twins. "*We* shall prevail!" Marsh took another step backwards.

Quincy saw the shadowy figure inching closer—it was almost right behind Marsh. He cupped his hands around his mouth and yelled, "Hey, Marsh!" as loud as he could. "Whenever you say *we*, do you mean you and your friend back there?"

"What?"

And that was all Marsh could say before the squid-like head of the terrible mind flayer appeared behind him and wrapped its tentacles around Marsh's mouth and throat. Marsh's screams would have been legendary were they not stifled by the loud alarms, the slimy appendages covering his face, or the fact that his trachea was slowly dissolving from within.

In a matter of seconds, all that was left of the terrible man known only as Agent Marsh was a puddle of red and green slime on the floor with a single eyeball floating on top.

The mind flayer looked down at his creation before taking a moment to stare at the twins. It was a nightmarish experience to stand face-to-face with a being of such immense power, and both Lilly and Quincy dared not move a muscle. The mind flayer then looked up at Tim floating past before its gaze went back to the twins for a brief second.

It nodded before turning, then backed through the doorway from which it came.

"Did a mind flayer just *nod* at us?" Lilly asked her equally mesmerized brother.

Quincy ran his hand through his hair, gaping. "I don't know... I... Lilly!"

"What?" Lilly jumped up from the panic in Quincy's voice.

"The screen! There's only fifty seconds left before some "not very well explained but probably very bad" thing will happen to the entire planet!"

"Oh no, I totally forgot that was a thing for a second. What do we do?" Lilly yelped. The alarms and sirens were screeching so loud now it was hard for the twins to hear each other anymore. The red flickering light was blinding.

"Tim!" Lilly screamed.

"Lilly?" Tim answered calmly and collectedly right next to her right ear.

"I know we set you free and all. But can you do us a favor and perform your third and final act of selfless kindness now?"

"Thirty seconds!" Quincy yelled, shivering in front of the monitor. High above them, the ceiling shook, and strands of dirt and rock fell down all around them.

"I suppose I owe you and that old coot Crowley a favor..." Tim sighed. "Don't know how I could terrify every little corner of the known universe knowing I left a job hanging..."

"Twenty! Ah, I don't know what—" Quincy's voice fell away with the noise.

The alarms blared over everything now.

Lilly concentrated and sent her thoughts directly to Tim —*Get the hell in that giant God machine and* fix *this!*

Tim twirled, leaving spots of purple and orange vapor traces in the air. He flashed in and out of the loud machinery. Lilly could see the dials being switched, circuit boards sparking, and screens turning off left and right. The humming and groaning of the great cluster of devices rose and rose, stifling even the sharp pangs of the sirens.

Then the noises stopped entirely, and the low humming of electronics working as intended were all that was left.

"THREE!!" Quincy screamed.

Everything fell silent. The twins had their eyes closed, their hands clutched tight around each other. They couldn't hear anything anymore except for their own labored breaths. Even I held my breath, and I've stopped breathing for years!

"What happened? Did we die? Is this heaven?" Quincy fought the urge to black out as he opened his eyes and squinted at Lilly.

"Tim performed his last task admirably." Lilly smiled and followed the streaks of gold and velvety blue vapor left hanging in the air by the Fire Vampire.

"You… you came back." Quincy mumbled; he couldn't believe it. Everything that had transpired in the past hour was a blur; the realization was just now setting in.

"It's a good thing for you I know fluent Sumerian, Navajo, Latin, and even Celestian," Tim boasted, his full vaporous form now hovering above the twins, showing off streaks of every single color in the known spectrum visible to humans.

"So did you reprogram the entire machine? I mean… God? Eh, screw it, it's a machine." Quincy shook the dust from his hair.

"I tried to. But I couldn't get some things to stick. Earth has its protection back, yes, I think. But I'm afraid that some damage was… irreversible," Tim admitted.

"We did what we could; I doubt there was anything that *we* actually could've done to prevent more." Lilly nodded, then smiled at Quincy. "Still, fat chance Haven will come back soon after what's been going down upstairs, right?"

Tim flashed a satisfied orange. "Oh yeah, hehe. It's a bloodbath up there." The Fire Vampire rose up into the air and started to expand. He ended up as wide and as long as the entire room. "Well, that was fun and all, but now that I'm free, I'll be setting off for good."

"Tim, why'd you do it?" Lilly asked, her voice a mere whisper.

"I like you," Tim answered gleefully. "Those who have the courage to stand up to something that's way over their heads with all of the cards stacked against them... those beings are... admirable."

The Fire Vampire flew close to Lilly and Quincy, and what looked like a pair of glowing yellow eyes stared straight at them from the brightly colored mist. "Farewell, Lilly and Quincy."

"Hey, wait a minute!" Quincy sprung forward. "Can we get a ri—"

Quincy opened his eyes, the soft, fresh breeze of the waterfront hitting his nose and rejuvenating him. He watched the small waves carefully splash against the shores of the river, then looked behind him and saw Lilly already sitting there in the grass, just staring.

"Huh, what, where..." Quincy jolted towards her. "Is this...?"

"Yup," she answered. "The end of the world. The good one, the one that isn't an actual apocalypse. The one in—"

"New Orleans." Quincy smiled and plopped down in the grass next to her. "I'd call it a dream, but I doubt either of us could ever come up with it after everything that happened just now—not even subconsciously." He paused. "We did it."

"Whatever it was, yes, we did," she answered a tad mournfully, a tear gleaming in her eye. "Mom and Dad would be so proud."

"I'm sure they are." Quincy moved to hold his sister tight. "The secret was kind of out of the bag; there was nothing we could do about that. But damn if we didn't protect the hell out of it. The Earth itself may still be afflicted, but we know now that's something's watching our again." He yawned and shifted away, letting his hands flow through the freshly cut grass. "So, what are we going to do now?"

Lilly wanted to make a remark about ice cream, but she fell silent after she saw two suspicious-looking men in black exiting a car across the other side of the Mississippi.

And so, the twins had learned our family's greatest secret, and with it they had stumbled upon a conspiracy to destroy the world, and they stopped it from happening. But true evil is never done, and many more trials are waiting for the Swansongs.

EPILOGUE

Weeks later

Sean emerged from the dank subway tunnels and slowly made his way up the steps into the busy streets of New York City. A shrill breeze swept through the masses, and Sean saw people huddle closer together. Winter had arrived, and with it the days grew shorter and the nights longer. In recent years, the cold period at the end of the year was less a time of celebration and more a time of fear and dismay. Usually associated with holidays and cozy times in front of a fire, the end of the year was now in a time when the most dangerous of predators moved out from the wilderness and into the city border for protection and hunting.

Sean took out his smartphone and double-checked the information that was given to him. He nodded before pulling up his navigation app and starting to walk. His destination was close, and he was *very* interested in what he might encounter.

After a brief walk, Sean took a left into an alleyway. The alley was dark, the smell terrible, and it looked like nobody had dared set foot in it for years. His eyes fell on the graffiti adorning the dirty walls and the message at the drawing's center—the one just above waist-height and just a bit higher than the piles of trash heaping up.

It read: Stay away, only death below!

Yes indeed. Sean thought of the stories about the ghouls prowling about the oldest and mostly forgotten sewer systems and subway tunnels beneath the city. The problem was solved ages ago, Sean reminded himself, but seeing the warnings displayed on the walls still sent shivers down his spine. He then smiled and shook his head. It was the perfect hiding place.

Near the back of the alley, in the right-hand corner, a small stairway led down to a narrow passageway obstructed by a decrepit wooden door. Sean thought it looked kind of like a sinister entryway into the bowels of the old city. He was a little reluctant to head back underground, having actually enjoyed the cold, fresh air after just traversing a good stretch of subway to get here.

Nevertheless, he cautiously maneuvered down the steps and for a moment quizzically stared at the rather modern-looking intercom device next to the door. He shrugged and pressed the button. For a moment, there was no indication that anyone behind the door was ready to answer—or able to. The occupants might even have left some time ago, leaving Sean to wait in the filthy alley for absolutely no reason.

Then, after a good twenty seconds of nothing, a shrill, robotic voice answered with

"What's the password?"

Sean scratched his chin for a moment while reciting the awkward phrase in his head. "Cold is the dew that hangs off the trees' dead leaves while we wait for the Silver Spring," he answered, confirming once more his total lack of poetry prowess.

"Incorrect," the lifeless computer voice answered. "What have you to say for yourself?"

"Protocol states that before announcing the correct password, one must state the previous week's password as a test," Sean replied.

"An acceptable explanation," the voice murmured. "Now, what is this week's password?"

"Sausage," Sean said with much more confidence.

"Access granted," the voice chirped.

Sean could hear the clanking of the door mechanism unlocking, and after a few seconds, the door creaked open, standing slightly ajar. However, his puzzled look turned into a broad smile as he saw the familiar face of his friend Lilly Swansong appear before him. Her hair was significantly shorter and mostly covered by the hood of a stained brown sweater, but Sean instantly recognized the look of mischief in her eyes.

"Do you like my voice this way?" Lilly's voice crackled through the speaker next to the door as well as the tiny speaker of the voice synthesizer modulator she held in front of her face. Behind the device, Sean saw Lilly's teeth shining in her trademark grin.

"I'm more of a baritone man, myself," he said, "but I guess it has its charms." Sean smiled. "It's good to see you, Lilly."

The flashlight illuminated most of the stairwell on the way down, but the humid, slippery stairs made the trek more adventurous than necessary.

"So…" Sean started, careful not to grab hold of the railing too much, considering its many slimy spots. "New York City, that's a change of scenery if I ever saw one. How are you liking the city?"

"I guess it's pretty nice," Lilly said slowly as she moved down the steps, keeping an eye out in front of her. "The city has many interesting spots and all these different cultures coming together, so much history. I guess I kinda see what Billy Joel was on about."

He laughed. "And how about Quincy? What is his thought about all of this?"

"Well, you can ask him yourself soon enough." Lilly

stepped down onto even ground before turning around and shining the light towards the last steps to guide Sean towards her. "The new temporary *casa de Swansong* is right around the corner."

She laughed before knocking

on the door at the end of the tunnel. The knocking was a peculiar pattern, reminding Sean of an old song from the 1980s.

"Secret password," Lilly whispered with a wink.

"Lilly, I know it's you out there, just come in, will you?" Sean heard the familiar voice of Quincy call from behind the door.

Lilly rolled her eyes, but Sean and herself soon entered the small, cellar-like storage space that the twins now called home.

Considering how everything looked on the outside—the dank alley, the filthy staircase, the general reeking of the entire place—the little room was actually quite tidy. There was a table with some chairs, two bedrolls, and enough candles to last a lifetime. Scattered about were papers containing all sorts of writing, but even those seemed to have some sort of system to them, albeit one that Sean didn't quite grasp. The only unfortunate thing seemed to be that there were no windows at all and, thus, an absolute absence of daylight.

At the far side of the table, Quincy Swansong was eagerly typing on an old laptop. But upon Sean's arrival, he looked up and grinned.

"Sean! How good to see you're safe." Quincy shoved the laptop aside and pulled out a chair.

Sean slid behind the table and took another good look around. "So, New York, huh?" He grinned at Quincy. "Something tells me that wasn't your idea."

"Not in the slightest." Quincy looked at his sister, who sat down on a chair beside Sean. "But Lilly made an excellent point. Rather than hide out in the middle of nowhere, it is often far less expected for refugees to hide in plain sight."

"Plain sight?" Sean retorted. "You're holed up in a dark

storage room of an old subway station!" He laughed. "How is that possibly *in plain sight?*"

"Apparently you haven't seen the throng of Haven agents sprawled all across New York yet." Lilly picked up a nearby lighter and started flicking it. "This city is a time bomb; one wrong move and the entire thing will blow up."

The lighter clicked, and the light of its flame danced eerily across the walls.

"So, you're still on the run?"

"You can cut off the head of evil, but somehow something way worse will always grow back." Quincy tapped the lid of his laptop. "We don't know if we're still being sought after by Haven; we don't even know if they know if we're still alive, but we'd rather not take the chance. There are still very powerful people running that organization, and we feel we've only seen the tip of the iceberg of what they might be capable of."

Both Quincy and his sister shared a look of sadness; Sean felt for them. He knew how desperately they wanted to settle down and lead semi-normal lives, but after all that had happened, it just wasn't possible anymore.

"We've come to terms with it," Lilly said, suddenly sounding invigorated. "We both agree that chilling around New Orleans won't be in the cards for us for a very long time. So, we decided on another plan of action."

"Oh?" This certainly piqued Sean's interest. He had thought the twins had both seen enough adventure for one lifetime.

"This stuff is in our blood," Quincy added. "It's in our DNA… so to speak. We're Swansongs, and this is what we do."

"Do what?" Sean replied, visibly confused. "You two are talking in riddles."

"There's still a lot of misery out there," Lilly chimed in. "Scary stuff happening all over. Consider this, the GDF officials only respond to threats big enough to severely damage or influence a large chunk of the population most of the time, right?"

"Right."

"Meanwhile, Haven is studying, containing, or who knows what else they'd like to do with these things. Absolute bad stuff," she said. "I… *We* want to *help* people. Everyone and anyone. People are afraid everywhere, not only in big cities being attacked by enormous monsters."

"I don't know what to say." Sean was struck with awe. "You are both absolutely crazy."

"Well, that seems to be almost a requirement in this field," Quincy joked.

"We have stared the possible end of the universe right in the face," Lilly said and made grand gestures with her hands. "But, for real though, we actually did." She smirked.

The trio was silent for a while until Lilly looked up at Sean and grabbed his wrist. "Listen, we'll never forget what you did for us, Sean. You risked your neck more than once getting us out of trouble. But I won't allow that to happen again. We'll be leaving New York soon, and… well, we invited you out here to basically say goodbye."

Sean looked up at Lilly's teary eyes and chuckled. "It's okay. I had a feeling you two were planning on getting off the grid entirely, at least for a while. I just hope we'll see each other again sometime in the future."

"We can never be sure. But I have a feeling we will." Lilly nodded.

Sean looked over at Quincy. "So, when are you leaving?"

"Not sure yet. We got a deal lined up tomorrow to possibly buy a new car. So pretty soon, I guess."

"Better have good heating, considering the weather that's coming up."

"We've actually felt the shrill cold of the cosmos at our backs," Quincy answered. "I think we'll be fine."

"Oh boy." Sean's eyes flew from Quincy to Lilly. "Save the world once, and you both start talking in true *eldritch* fashion."

He laughed but suddenly grew serious. "Say, about that whole cosmos thing. One thing's been bothering me endlessly."

"Shoot," Lilly replied.

"That whole base, wherever it was we were at, was overrun with all kinds of monsters. Even when I felt the influence of the mind flayer finally leaving me, I knew there was absolutely no escape possible. But then I remember feeling light as air at one point, everything went black, and suddenly I was back in my old apartment with the door still kicked in and everything." Sean looked at the twins. "How in the hell did I get out of that?"

Lilly and Quincy exchanged glances and laughed. Lilly looked Sean straight in the eyes. "Call it... divine intervention."

First Look at The Nearly Departed, Book Two of The Eldritch Twins!

TRANSMISSION

SEAN WATCHED the small bulb of red light blink in and out of existence. The sun had set on the Chihuahuan, and the hyacinth sky was fading off into the dark blue hue of twilight. Several streaks of cloud vapor, left by whatever sort of experimental shadow government or black ops flying vehicle, were slowly dissolving overhead.

He flicked the extinguished butt of the cigarette out into the desert night and headed back inside. There, he performed the elaborate scheme of tilting antennas, hitting switches, and tuning dials to get his ancient radio equipment functioning.

"Hmm, this oughta do it."

Following his words, the speakers crackled and came alive; Sean looked up as the distinct voice of his good friend, and radio host for the freethinking people, Harold Summer drifted into the small confinements of his motorhome.

"*...absolute mayhem, oh, how I wish there was something the* GDF *could've done for those poor people.*

"*In other news, I have gathered trustworthy intelligence that* Haven *might, in fact, have planted spy equipment into all of our homes. It apparently involves a pocket dimension created by a* Tuba, *which is a small, lesser daemon that many of us have had the displeasure of encountering. Usually they like to hole up in our attics for the winter, nevertheless..."*

Loud static burst forth from the big speakers. Sean, used to faulty equipment, cursed under his breath and slammed a hand down hard on the top.

The voice that returned on the radio wasn't Harold's; he held his hand aloft and listened closely.

"...*stop what you are doing.*" The voice was deep and full of authority. "*Everything you know is wrong. There are no monsters. There have never been any monsters.*"

Sean slid the chair towards the desk and sat down, eyebrows raised. "What the hell."

"*Supernatural and paranormal phenomena do not exist. Everything is an illusion. We expect better of you.*

"*You believe in lies.*

"*You have seen no truth.*

"*We expect better;* Haven *expects better.*"

Sean forced himself away from the speakers and turned a couple of dials on the tuners. The voice shifted in pitch slightly, and a faint rumble could be heard over the strange broadcast.

"Let's see," he murmured and turned another dial, flicking some more switches. "Aha! I knew it." Sean laughed and pulled a switch slightly to the right of the mess of cables running from the elaborate setup to the speakers and the wall. One of the sound channels fell away from the broadcast, and the voice returned, sounding more hollow and sinister than before.

"*There are no monsters. You have been told lies.*"

"Subliminal hypnosis," Sean groaned. "They're actually doing it. They're covering up."

He ignored the light rumble beneath his feet, turned the dial off, and started pacing around the room impatiently. After a minute, he grabbed his smartphone and sifted through his usual channels of communication to check if he had any new messages.

Annoyed then at the empty inboxes and lack of notifications, he spent a good ten minutes trying to put into words whatever it was he was trying to relay to whomever he wanted to contact when a text message from Harold Summer sent shivers up his spine.

Got pulled off the air. They're f#^@$(g onto me, man. Pulling the rug underneath all of us. Popped the Swansong twins a while back too, I heard. That right? You gotta help me out here, man. H.*

Sean felt a wave of panic. He tried hard to keep a steady hand while he nervously typed out a reply to Harold, asking him what the hell he was on about.

Did Harold just casually mention that the twins got killed by Haven? He couldn't believe that. Sean knew the twins long enough now to know that they're about as hard to kill as a rock is to shave. Haven couldn't possibly have gotten them, especially not them.

Sean was running all kinds of disastrous scenarios through his head when the radio suddenly burst alive with static again.

"H... He... Hello?" called the voice of a young woman. There was a distinct distance and echo—a delay like when someone calls you from the other side of the world. "A-Anybody t-th-there-here?"

Sean dropped the phone onto the floor in awe and relief, then snatched the microphone up and checked if it was plugged in. He couldn't help but smile.

"Hey! Lilly! Can you hear me?"

"Sssssean, g-g-good to hear y-your…you…your voice, b-buddy!" a male voice rang out from the void between the desert and wherever the place was the transmission originated from.

"Quince!" Sean fist-pumped the air awkwardly. "Wait one second while I fix this." He pulled at some wires, turned a dial all the way off, and then gave the setup a good kick. "How's the connection now?" He didn't wait for them to respond and continued talking. "Glad to hear you guys are okay! There were rumors going around you guys died. Gave me quite a scare."

"Yeah, it seems a lot better." Quincy still sounded robotic and hollow but less far-off at least.

"Funny you'd mention that last titbit, Sean!" Lilly interjected with her trademark sarcasm. "You still believe in an afterlife?"

Sean's smile dropped. "What? Whatcha mean?"

"We don't know where you get your info from exactly, but you're going to want to sit down." Radio waves made Quincy's voice sound very analytical and droning, like a high school math teacher Sean had years ago. "You see, we are temporarily indisposed of—"

"We're dead, Sean." Lilly ripped the proverbial band-aid off as best as she could, which meant with no subtlety whatsoever.

"Well, okay, just tell him directly then," Quincy complained, his voice drifting further away in the background.

"He's seen and heard worse!" The radio static crackled and buzzed as Lilly hissed vaguely at her brother.

"Doesn't mean you can just drop this bomb on him without giving him proper warning."

"What else was I supposed to do then?"

"Guys," Sean interjected, "please tell me what the hell is going on. You tell me you're dead, but I'm talking to you right now. That doesn't seem right, does it?"

Lilly started laughing. "Have you been living under a rock? Is this the same guy that got his brains almost turned to soup by a mind flayer? This is perfectly normal stuff."

Sean felt a wave of embarrassment cascade over him. He knew she was right, but as far as dying goes, he thought that was at least something that'd stick. "So… how?"

"We're not quite sure—" Quincy was interrupted by a barking off in the distance.

Sean scratched his head. "Wait, is that a dog?" He heard

Lilly softly murmuring sweet nothings towards something too distorted to make out now.

"We'll get to that," Quincy replied. "Point is we're… half dead? Is that what you could call it?"

"Sounds about right," Lilly added.

"Half dead," Quincy repeated. "We're stuck in this void, this limbo that's apparently a plane between life and the after-life. It's a shadow-riddled place of emptiness and depression… Anyway, we're not sure how we got here, but we've got it on good authority that we can get back."

Sean couldn't believe his ears. Lilly and Quincy were the strongest people he knew; he'd never thought in a million years they would end up in a situation as sticky as this one. "So… How *are* you going to get back?"

"We don't know," Lilly answered.

"Figuring that out right now," Quincy added.

"WOOF!" the unseen dog piped in.

The glass of scotch nearby was already empty; somehow Sean was sure the bottle beside it wouldn't make another sunrise. "Okay… So how are we talking right now?"

There was some shuffling heard on the other side before Quincy answered, his voice trailing with a bit of embarrass-ment, "Y'know, we're not really sure."

"We found this old radio setup and kinda tuned into what-ever we tuned into. I don't know what to tell you, Sean." Lilly sighed. "But we ended up right where we had to be apparently!"

The floor beneath the motorhome rumbled again. Sean made a mental note that he really needed to get moving before the quakes turned out to be something worse, as he recalled Lilly's horror stories about the Primordial Wurms. He sighed. "Okay then. What's it like there?"

"The near-afterlife?"

"Yeah."

"Well, it's like…" Lilly fell silent for a moment and mumbled something which sounded too distorted to hear, then the barking started again. "Hewie, sit down!" She cleared her throat and restarted, "Uh, have you ever been inside a mall after all of the shops closed down for the day? Or a public bathroom when the cleaner's been by and all the lights are turned off and you're unsure whether or not you're supposed to be there?"

"Actually, yeah, I can quite vividly imagine that."

"That's how it is all the time here. Only with deeper and longer shadows, vague yet menacing figures always staring just off in the distance, and random screams during the night, which is all the time. It's always night here." Quincy supplied coolly.

"That's terrifying." Sean gulped and reached for the glass of scotch, downing it. "Anything else noteworthy?"

"Neon streaks that light up the sky, cloaked hermits knowing everything about our past and possible futures—an afterlife or near-afterlife mafia?" Lilly said. "Perhaps it's best to just start at the beginning?"

Sean lit up a cigarette and popped the cap off the bottle of scotch before taking a big swig. "All right. Have at it."

Acknowledgments

I never thought I'd be in the position of writing thanks and acknowledgements for a book that was being published worldwide, so consider me sitting here, kind of flabbergasted thinking about what I managed to do and the cool things still to come. So here goes, none of this would even been possible without the help and support of the following people: My parents, who apparently beam with pride every time they tell people of my accomplishments; My wonderful and supportive girlfriend Nathalie, who never once shut me down after telling her about all my weird story ideas; and my closest friends Ashley, Rik, Micky, Kelly, Jasmijn, Kaz and Stefanie, I love you all. A pat and a kiss for my three cats Lou Lou, Ollie and Marley, thanks for not making a habit out of sitting on my keyboard.

Further thanks goes to Chervàse, who inspired me profoundly; Raven, my awesome editor who has the best ideas and Rick, who's always there to ask to help with his fantastic creative projects. I also want to give a shout out to my old media-studies friends. We may not see much of each other anymore, but you made my initial shyness and loneliness melt away. Thanks for the awesome years in Utrecht. Another shout out to all the people working hard in the Dutch Indie film scene, let's all make creativity thrive together.

Of course, I can't thank everyone over at The Parliament House enough for giving me an opportunity to put my work out there and giving me a chance. Shayne, Chantal, Amanda, Erica and the summer 19 acquisitions group thank you so very much. Additional thanks to all other staff and every single author over at TPH, you are all truly wonderful.

Last, but certainly not least, I'd like to sincerely thank *you*, the reader. If you made it this far, it probably means you read my book from front to back, and I simply can't convey the joy that gives me. Whether you liked it or not, you saw my work and gave me a chance, and I cannot begin to tell you how much that means to me. Thank you.

About the Author

Nick Vossen was raised on blockbuster films from the 80s and 90s as well as fantasy and sci-fi novels, comics and games. No matter the medium, his love for storytelling grew ever larger. Having always had a fascination with the fantastical and weird, he quickly grew fond of authors such as Terry Pratchett, H.P. Lovecraft, Neil Gaiman and many more. During the winter of 2017 Nick released an anthology of short, weird fiction entitled The Fissures Between Worlds, which delves into the strange places on Earth where time does not flow as it should. It was received quite favourably, and so Nick's desire to tell more stories grew. He has since been privileged to appear in several other anthologies, magazines and short story compilations and has quite a few projects still in the works. His biggest fascinations and inspirations are old forgotten woodlands, the deepest depths of the oceans and the unsettling, uncanniness of retro futurism.

Nick graduated in Media- and Culture studies at Utrecht University in The Netherlands. He is currently working as a freelance creative writer and author. He also frequently works on projects in the Dutch indie-film industry, putting his talents to use in art-direction, set-dressing and of course screen-writing.

Nick has been working on and off on The Swansong Conspiracy since the tail-end of 2017. The idea first came when Nick wanted to give Lovecraftian Horror a much lighter and charming edge. But what started as a 'Monty Python-esque' parody eventually turned into a tale of equal suspense and horror but also humor and personality. Nick likes to write fluently and to the point, resulting in fast-paced action and quick & witty dialogue. It is also no secret that The Swansong Conspiracy is dripping in pop culture references and easter eggs, all done in loving tribute. Nick is extremely proud of the little strange world he created, and is ecstatic to be able to work on its two sequels for The Parliament House, as well.

www.nickcronomicon.wordpress.com